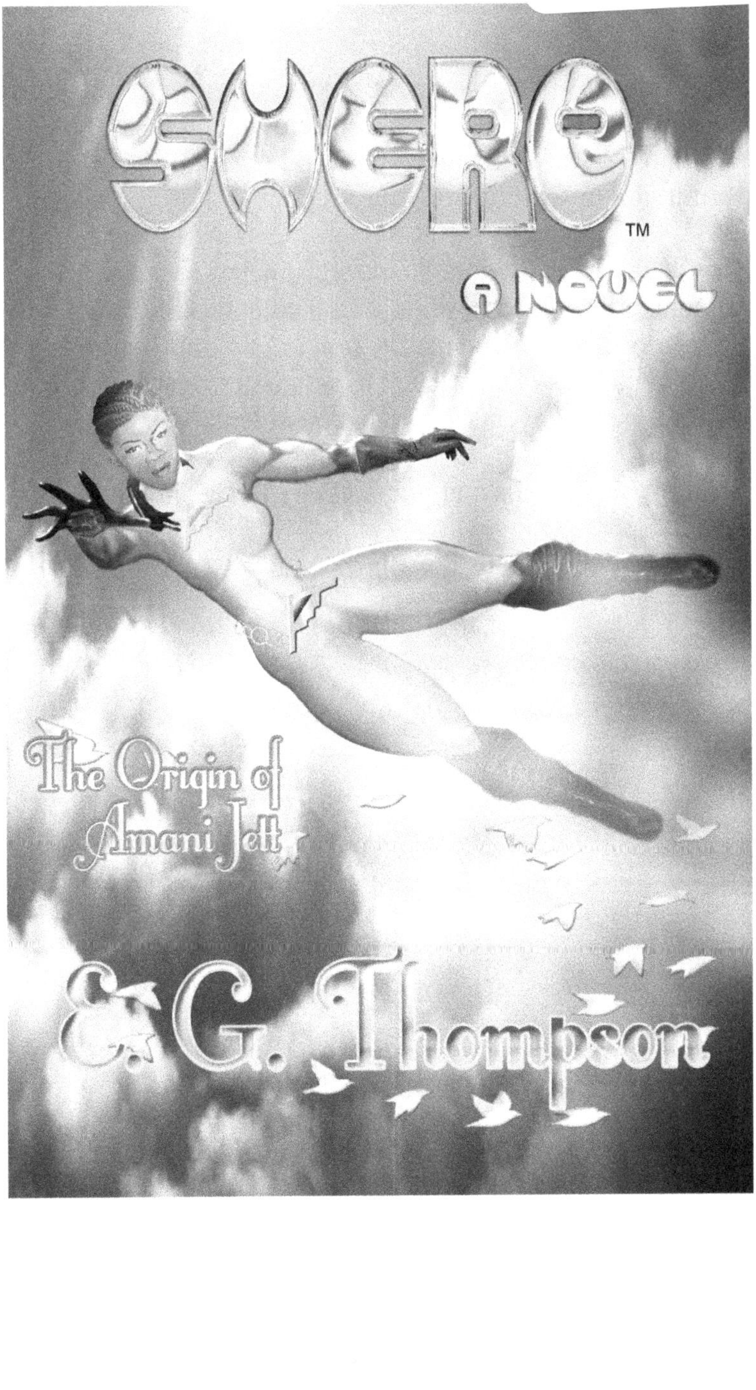
SHERO
TM
A NOVEL
The Origin of
Amani Jett
E.G. Thompson

Illustrations (pencils and graphics) by E. G. Thompson

Editor: Rev. Claudette T. Callaway

ISBN-10: 0615942628
ISBN-13: 978-0-615-94262-9

Special Thanks to...

Claude Thompson III
CAM Florist- www.camflorist.com

Law Offices of Paul M. Hughes
www.attorneyhughes.com

Rob Whittaker
Affordable Auto Repair & Wash
16100 Puritan Detroit, MI (313)-468-4614

Rev. Claudette T. Callaway
Universal Christ Temple
20222 Albany St. Detroit, MI

Support Your Local Small Businesses!

Other Writings of E. G. Thompson...

Flip the Script (2012)

Stalemate (2014)

Born-Again Virgins (2014)

AMANI'S DIARY

A NEW DISCOVERY

October 15, 1999

Dear Diary,

I'm so glad the weekend is here! No more stupid boys and fake girls for two whole days! Yes!

But, I do like the high school environment. They have a lot going on. They got sports, marching bands, the glee club. I still rather keep to myself, though.

Dad always told me to focus on my books and avoid distractions. Everything I put my time into is going to help me get to where I'm going. I haven't changed my mind about wanting to be a defense lawyer when I grow up.

Oh yeah, that girl, Yolanda, tried to talk me into joining the cheerleader squad. That is so not me! What makes her think I would want to kick up in the air and do cartwheels for some weak football team? Not me!

Cheering for the team is not going to get me that far. I won't bother. But, I just might try out for the girls' basketball team.

Amani

October 16, 1999

Dear Diary,

I really thought I was prepared for my teenage years. I expected my body to change one day and that day came. Auntie Eva told me about it. So did Dad, but what does he know about being a girl? It was funny to hear him explain it.

I was warned of being cranky. And I am! I get irritated over every little thing! I hate having to deal with this! But, my dad and auntie explained to me the process of the cycle and why it's so important.

I just want to know, why did it have to happen during my school years? Why couldn't the period come after I graduated? It's not like I'm trying to have kids anytime soon! I don't even think I want kids! Yuck!

Amani

October 18, 1999

Dear Diary,

How was school, how was school, how was school? Ugh! I hate it when my dad asks me that! What does he want from me? Then, he asks me what I learned. I just want to throw my books at him! Turn to page blah, blah, blah!

I learned that girls gossip, boys are always trying to get some, and high school is nothing but a popularity contest! And from the looks of it, not much changes when you get older!

Cheerleaders become groupies, jocks remain jocks or wannabe jocks, nerds stay nerds, toys become sports cars and shoes and jewelry, and everyone still wants to be a celebrity! I hate high school!

Then, Coach Sanders tells me that in order for me to play basketball, I have to run track! What for? I already know how to run!

And who wants to run in a circle over and over again? There's no strategy in running in circles! That's only for dogs and horses! I hate high school!

Amani

October 19, 1999

Dear Diary,

I love high school! I ran faster than any girl on the track team **and** any boy on the boys' team! A new school record! I don't remember being that fast!

The girls were so happy for me! They weren't even jealous like I expected. Instead, they cheered me on! They teased the boys for losing to a freshman girl. It was so funny!

But, I just finished talking to Dad. He's not so excited about my skills. He's happy that I can earn a scholarship by playing sports, but doesn't want me to slack up on my studying.

He was a star football player back in high school, but he was injured in college. I guess that has him bitter when it comes to sports. Anyways, I won't be as clumsy as he was.

I'll still study hard, but I like this track thing. Didn't know I would be this good. I bet my mom would've been very proud of me. I miss her so much!

Amani

October 20, 1999

Dear Diary,

Yes, I'm a star! It's like that and that's the way it is! Now, the boys are asking me out and stuff. I ain't got time for that, and they just don't know my dad.

I made a big fool out of David Davis. It felt good! He had the nerve to challenge me on the track, one-on-one. Big mistake! I left him so far in the dust that, halfway, I ran backwards on his silly self!

Something weird is happening. I guess that's what you call puberty. But, my dad and Auntie Eva never told me it would be like this! I feel stronger. I mean **way** stronger!

Everything is lighter, like paper. My books are like feathers. That heavy door to the gym is extremely light now. I thought Mr. Bob fixed the hinges at first, but other girls were still having a hard time opening it, like I used to.

I guess running strengthens you overall, but that makes no sense. I never lifted weights in my life! Maybe I'll do that tomorrow...

Amani

October 22, 1999

Dear Diary,

I want to kill my little sister! I have so much I want to write about and she stole my diary! Good thing I got it back. Now, I can catch up on the crazy stuff that's been going on. But first...

TOUCH THIS BOOK AGAIN, IVY, AND I SWEAR I'LL KILL YOU!!!!

Okay, I'm better. Dad grounded me, because I got mad and told Ivy she was adopted. It's not true, but she believed it. So, anyway, this is going to be a longer diary.

Something is happening to me and I'm afraid to tell anyone. I don't know how they would react. I'm starting to freak out, myself!

Thursday, in the weight room, I exercised with the weight that I was allowed to, being a girl. That wasn't enough. I couldn't wait until that room was empty!

I went back in there, then I took the heaviest weights I could find and lifted them with no problem! I am only 5' 5" and 125 pounds, got a little junk in my trunk, getting heavier in the chest, but I shouldn't be this strong! Now, I'm scared of myself.

Not only am I running faster, I'm jumping higher. There is no doubt that I can dunk a basketball, but I sure ain't about to show people. Nope!

I haven't told anyone about this. Not my best friend, Joanie, not Auntie Eva, and not my dad. I probably shouldn't compete in any sports. Not unless I find a way to hide my strength.

So, here I am in my room. I hear kids playing outdoors, having fun. I was supposed to go hang out with Joanie, but oh well. I'm stuck inside.

Dad wants me to study. I will, but I got all weekend to do that. I'd rather see just how high I can jump. I wonder if I can become even faster. More stronger.

I just benched 300 lbs! What if I could reach 500? I'd like to find out, but I do **not** want to wind up looking like those female bodybuilders. That ain't for me. No way!

I wonder if this is hereditary. If it is, it's probably from my mom's side, because my dad never showed this type of strength. Or maybe he's hiding it...

Amani

CHECKLIST FOR DAD

How fast were you in high school? ✔

How much can you bench press? ✔

How did you injure your hip playing football? ✔

Could you dunk from the free-throw line with two hands? ✔

How many flips can you do with one leap? ✔

October 25, 1999

Dear Diary

My dad is a super dad. That is all, and nothing else. He can't do half the things that I can do. He's nowhere near as strong as I am. He never was the type of person who would tell a lie, either. I wish I could talk to mommy again. She would probably know.

Amani

October 26, 1999

Dear Diary,

Coach Sanders is upset with me. Or maybe she's disappointed in me. I left both of the track teams and I won't be joining the basketball team.

My excuse was lame, but I really want to discover who I am and why am I this freak of nature. That's how I will invest my time. I need to start off with mom's side of the family, then ask Auntie Eva some questions, along with the rest of my dad's side of the family.

I'm getting stronger. I'm scared. Some people would be glad to have this ability, but I don't know where this all leads. I don't want to be put away, because people are afraid of me.

I'm so afraid, because I just lifted a car off of its back wheels without breaking a nail. That is so not normal! But, I had to test my limits. It was heavy, but not heavy enough. It gave me a good workout.

Lord, is this a blessing or a curse? Or is it a result of something scientific? I am only a child. I need an answer.

Amani

November 1, 1999

Dear Diary,

My report card showed that I wasn't doing my best. My dad was not happy with it. I didn't care as much. I'm going through something special. I don't believe he can understand. I told him I'm changing. That's all I said.

I should do something with these abilities. I see them as powers, now. I've thought about this for almost a week. This is not something to brush off my shoulders.

I am fourteen years old now, and I must become more than just a kid. I am becoming a woman now. People around me are maturing. So am I, but in a unique way.

I have found nothing special about my mom's side of the family. No athletes, no police officers, no firefighters, or anyone whose physical abilities are above average.

If there were people in the family who could do the things I can do, then I won't hide like them. There must be a reason I can outrun a Doberman Pincher and jump up to rooftops. Yeah, I know. Freaky.

Amani

SCIENTIFIC EXPLANATION

November 4, 1999

Dear Diary,

Nothing intrigues me more than science, these days. Thanks to my new discoveries. But, science class is so lame! I've been spending more time at the library.

I am studying every part of the human anatomy. I want to understand the changes that our bodies go through. I wish I had an x-ray machine.

I'm looking at life totally different. There are a lot of things I want to look into, but I got to get my grades back up. I wish my teachers would give me work that can lead to answers for the questions I have, instead of this crap!

I need an assistant. Someone who can research with me. I need someone to calculate my attributes.

Amani

November 5, 1999

Dear Diary,

I must tell Joanie. She won't be afraid of me. She will understand. Well, she might not understand, but she'll be supportive. That is my best friend. She's a weirdo, anyway, which is why I like her.

I must plan this right. Can't be seen, but it can't be too late in the night, either. I don't want to be grounded again. I'll be home when the streetlights come on.

I got to show Joanie what I can do without scaring her to death. First, I'll tell her everything up 'til now. She will be my voice-box, or whatever they call it. I trust that she'll still treat me like a girl instead of a monster.

This will be my last Diary letter, I think. Ivy already stole this book once, and since then, I put some top secret information in here! From now on, I will share my thoughts with Joanie.

Joanie has always been into science, too. That girl is a lab head! If this doesn't work out, then I'll be right back to writing in this diary.

Amani

Amani closes the diary after the reminiscing of childhood days, as she lounges in the Honors Room of her modern-style mansion. She is a grown woman now, who is highly respected and feared.

This particular room is designated for her memorabilia. On the four walls are Guinness Books awards, many City of Detroit certifications, NAACP honors, Humanitarian awards, a signed picture of the President of the United States, and much more. She has accomplished a lot in her lifetime.

Surrounding her is both fan mail and hate mail. She already took time to read as many pieces as she could.

Amani leaves the room to enter her media room, where she turns on the television to see what is going on in the world. The very first thing on display is an advertisement.

"Today, at 8pm eastern time! The interview the world's been waiting for! Channel 5 brings you live coverage of Susan Dunn's one-on-one with the incomparable, Amani Jett!

"Don't miss this revealing interview with the most talked about woman in history!

"This is a one-of-a-kind interview with a one-of-a-kind super woman! No question is off limits! And it is all <u>live</u>!

"Tonight! Only on BSC! Keep your eye on the ball." (That is the channel's slogan.)

Amani shakes her head. "Oh my. I really did it this time." She walks to her window facing the front lawn and looks out to see news vans, reporters, and their camera men from a distance. She never gives these people the time of day, but they continue to hang around outside of her property.

Amani hasn't done any televised interviews, simply because she does not care for them. She gets enough attention as it is.

But now, Amani believes it is time to address the national public. There has been more said about her from strangers who speculate than people who know her personally.

Now is time for her to reflect on events of the past that have brought her to this day. Reading through her old diary brought back many good memories. She laughs at her younger self.

Back in November of 1999, when Amani and her closest friend, Joanie, were walking home from the bus stop, she listened quietly as Joanie went on and on about high school matters.

"I have a question," Amani said, once she had a chance to talk. "What have you noticed differently about yourself when you first had your period?"

Joanie was thrown off by the question. "Well, I... I found myself cramping. I had mood swings."

"Me too!"

"And, of course, I buy what I need for it."

"That goes without saying, Joanie. Have you discovered any physical enhancements?"

"I have boobs now, if that's what you're talking about. I have hips, too!"

"Girl, you ain't got hips."

"Yes I do! Just not like yours. You have hips like a grown woman, already, and a big butt like those rap video girls."

"No I don't."

"Uh, have you looked back there lately?"

Amani stopped and looked back. "Yeah, you're right."

"That's why seniors are starting to notice you. Well, that and you outrunning them."

"Yes! I started running faster soon after I hit puberty!"

"Amani, puberty doesn't make you into an Olympic-caliber athlete."

"Then, it's a coincidence?"

"Sure... I guess. But, why did you quit sports anyway?"

"I just don't want all of that attention anymore."

Joanie stopped in her tracks. "Amani, what's been going on with you? One minute, you're happy with being the talk of the school, the next minute, you're back to being anti-social. What's up?"

"I haven't been feeling so... normal."

"Every girl goes through that!" They started to walk again. "And you are passing up on scholarship money. You would be wanted by every university!"

Amani wasn't sure how to reveal her current physical state to Joanie. "I feel that it would be unfair if I competed in sports."

"Unfair?" Joanie asked. "Is it unfair that I'm better in my Biology class than my classmates? Should I drop out of my class because of that, the same way you are dropping out of sports?"

"But, you're good because you exercise your brain. You study hard and you're really into it. I'm not even sure how much of my physical talent is natural."

Joanie looked worried about what Amani just claimed. She said nothing else about it for the rest of the walk.

Amani arrived home from school after her walk with Joanie. Her father, Calvin H. Turner, was waiting there for her.

"Hi Dad!" Amani greeted her father. She dropped her book bag, took off her coat, and headed straight to the kitchen.

"Hey, hon," he said. "How was school?"

Amani filled a teapot with water to boil. "It was okay."

"Can't you give me a different answer sometimes? Every time I ask you, you say it was okay."

"You don't give me different questions. How do you expect different answers?"

"Don't you get smart with me, young lady."

"Sorry, Dad."

"So, what did you learn today?"

"Oh my goodness! Dad, I learned a lot!" She turned the stove range knob on "High" to speed up the boiling process.

Mr. Turner gasped. "Before you touch anything else in that kitchen, wash your hands."

"Yes, sir." Amani went into the bathroom to wash her hands. With the water running at full blast, she heard something. It was a voice of someone other than her father's. She turned the faucet off to listen closer. This voice belonged to a woman.

This woman's dialogue was erotic. A frown came upon Amani's face as she stormed back to the front room where her dad sat.

"Dad!" Amani shouted.

Mr. Turner lowered the newspaper that he was reading in his reclined chair, having no idea what Amani was so excited about. "What?" he asked.

Amani said nothing, then went upstairs to look around for the woman she was hearing. There was no one to be found, but the sound was still there!

She went back downstairs and checked all of the rooms. Still, there was no one. Mr. Turner watched on, as she searched with a puzzled look on her face.

"Girl, what's wrong with you?" Mr. Turner asked.

Amani played it off. "Uh... I'm looking for Ivy."

"It's only 2:45! You know your Aunt Eva doesn't pick her up 'til three! Goodness gracious!"

"Oh, that's right." The sound she heard in her head was interrupted by the whistling of the teapot.

In the kitchen, Amani stirred up a mug of steamy hot cocoa. She blew in the mug to cool off the beverage before sipping.

Mr. Turner called his daughter to the front room, removing his glasses before saying, "Amani, I ask you questions about school, because I care. You might get tired of me asking, but I will always inquire about what's going on with my girls."

Amani said, "Yes, Dad." She blew into her mug again.

"There are other parents who don't ask, because they don't care. They're just waiting for their sons and daughters to get old enough to move out. They don't care what their children grow up to be, they just want them to grow up and out of their houses, so they can be free of them."

"Yes, Dad." She tried to take a sip of her hot cocoa, but could barely get a drop out of it. The drink was almost completely frozen!

"I want you to be a strong Black woman with integrity. Proud, grounded, educated..." He paused. "What are you looking like that for? What's in your drink? It better not be a cockroach!"

"N-no, Dad! Something... I need to reheat this." She rushed back into the kitchen.

"Oh, I was about to say, 'cause we don't do roaches in **this** house. I'd get this place fumigated immediately!"

"No need for that, Daddy."

Hours later, Amani went to Joanie's place to meet with her. They agreed to go to the library and do homework together. This was Amani's idea, so she could reveal more to her friend.

Joanie's mother answered the door. "Hi there, Amani! Come on in and have a seat."

Amani wasn't expecting her hospitality, just a pick-up and a visit to the library. "Sure, Mrs. Hutton," she said.

Joanie and her father sat at the dining room table, eating sandwiches. Amani looked at this and thought it was odd, because it wasn't normal for her and her father, Mr. Turner. They would only eat at the table during dinnertime.

Mrs. Hutton sat down with them. "Would you like a sandwich, Amani?" she asked.

"No thank you, Mrs. Hutton," Amani answered. "I'm not that hungry."

"Okay, just know you're welcome to it."

"So, I hear you're quite the athlete," said Mr. Hutton.

Amani shrugged. "Yes, I'm athletic."

"That's good." He nodded. "That's good. You know, I had an older brother who was an amazing athlete. He was just awesome!"

"You <u>had</u> an older brother? So, what happened to him?"

"He died. It was heart-breaking, losing Jim the way we did. I really looked up to him." Mrs. Hutton held his hand.

"Sorry to hear that, Mr. Hutton," Amani said.

"Yeah, thanks. And this guy, he set records in college, playing defensive tackle. He would have done the same in the pros had he not been sick."

"What was his illness, Mr. Hutton?"

"Well, a big part of his athleticism was due to illegal substances they call steroids." Joanie ducked her head. "I'm sure you've heard of steroids."

"Oh, he was doping. That's such a shame."

"And there are people who are still doing it today. These pills and things are still in our colleges and even in our high schools." He waited for Amani to admit to using steroids. "Have you seen these drugs around, Amani?"

"Honestly, I can't tell you what they look like."

"Have you... Do you know anyone who is selling any type of pills or medicine in your school? Maybe passing them out for free, then later charging for them?"

"No. If it's illegal, then I doubt it would be out in the open." She looked over at Joanie, who would not make eye contact.

Amani started to realize what was going on. This arrangement was obviously set up. Clearly, Joanie suspected Amani of using steroids to enhance her physical abilities.

Mr. Hutton said, "Just let us or the police know if you see any strange activity going on in your school. We really need to keep it a drug-free zone."

"Sure, I'll do just that," Amani said. Mrs. Hutton smiled brightly at her.

～～

Later, Amani and Joanie sat at a table in the public library after finishing their homework.

"Alright, Joanie," Amani said, "what was with your parents?"

"Nothing," Joanie replied. "What's wrong?"

"Your parents were talking to me about steroids as if I knew something about them. People don't do that!" The librarian shushed her. "You wouldn't even look up at me," she said quietly. "What did you tell them?"

"I'm concerned about you, Amani."

"Girl, please."

"I really am. No girl can outrun guys like that."

"I did!" The librarian shushed her again. "Why do you think I need steroids to beat a guy running?"

"You said it yourself; you don't know how much of what you can do is natural."

"That doesn't mean I'm doping."

"What else could it mean?"

"Actually, that's what I want to find out, but now, I'm not sure I can trust you. Our conversations are supposed to be between just you and me."

"I'm sorry, but what else could I do when you're damaging your body like that?"

Amani leaned forward. "I... am not... using drugs. Is that clear to your brain?"

Joanie looked afraid. "Y-yes. Sorry."

"Please take that worried look off your face. It's irritating."

Joanie tried to straighten up, but she was having a hard time. Amani's tone made her more nervous than she already was. She knew of one side effect caused by the use of steroids; Rage.

Joanie said, "I'll do whatever you say, just please don't hurt me."

"What?" Amani responded. "What are you talking about? I'm your friend, right?"

"Yes, but I feel you are getting belligerent with me and it's making me nervous."

"How am I being belligerent with you? You don't even know what belligerent is. You've been in the 'burbs for too long."

"Aren't you angry with me?"

"Not to the point where I'd hurt you!" She looked to the librarian. "Excuse me." She turned back to face Joanie. "I just know from now on not to tell you any of my secrets. That bond is broken."

"But, what about our friendship?"

"We can be cool, but I won't tell you much. I can't trust you. That's that."

Joanie clang her hands together. "I'm so sorry! Now, I feel bad about this. Please forgive me."

"I do forgive you. I'm not holding grudges."

"Good! We're best buds again! So, what were you talking about when you said-"

"Did you miss that part? No secrets." The saddened look on Joanie's face was priceless. "Joanie, what I need from you is your knowledge in Biology."

"Biology? But, aren't you taking Introduction to Physical Science?"

"I know, but I'm doing extra research. I have a lot to learn and I could use some help."

"So, you're studying independently?"

"Yes. Will you help me?"

"I'd love to!"

PHYSICALITIES

When Amani made her return home after spending time with Joanie at the library, she found her dad sitting with Coach Sanders in the living room.

"Hello, sweetheart," Mr. Turner said.

Amani replied, "Hi Dad... uh, what is she doing here?"

"You address grownups by their names, young lady."

"I apologize, Coach Sanders."

"Mrs. Sanders told me you're more than an outstanding runner. She considers your talent extraordinary." Amani's heart skipped a beat. "She thinks that you could very likely earn yourself a **full** scholarship to the most acclaimed universities."

"Oh, um, you support it now, Dad?"

"You told me you were good, but not how good. You ran a 4.4?"

Coach Sanders added, "And I told him about our after school programs designed to aid students in maintaining their in-class performances while being involved in sports."

"It sounded reasonable to me, dear, but I want you to make the decision."

Amani had other things on her mind. She did not want to accidentally expose her supernatural abilities by competing. She was getting stronger and could hardly adjust to her strengths. Also, Amani knew that she could smash that 4.4 record with no problem.

"No thanks," Amani said. "I have too much on my mind right now. That's why I quit."

Coach Sanders said, "Amani, your father told me you were going through changes." Amani became nervous again. "That's what you told him, right?"

"Uh, yeah. I meant, yes ma'am."

"Being a woman, I understand what you're feeling. This is something I dealt with many times with our female athletes. It's a part of life."

Amani was relieved that Coach Sanders was only referring to her menstrual cycle. "That's good to hear, but I'm already doing well with it. I might do sports next year, after I... get some stuff together."

"Good! That's great news. I'd just hate for you to totally lose interest, being that you are such a talent. And you truly are a real talent, missy." She smiled.

Mr. Turner said, "Well, I guess that sums it up. Thank you for dropping by and sharing your time with us, Mrs. Sanders."

Coach Sanders shook his hand. "Thank you for having me. It was great meeting you." She said goodbye to Amani and made her exit.

Right after the door closed, Mr. Turner said, "Those White folks sure know how to talk us into some stuff."

Amani said, "Come on, Dad."

"Naw, I'm serious! They don't make phone calls and stop by people's houses when students drop their math class, do they?"

"But, Dad-"

"They want to see you run in circles, like a greyhound or a thoroughbred."

"Black schools do that, too, Daddy. Can't you just be happy that she was willing to work with me?"

"For what she can get out of you?"

"I thought it was a two-way street."

"Okay, honey. You made your decision, anyway."

Amani's eleven-year-old sister, Ivy, came down the staircase. "Ooo! Amani came in after the streetlights came on! I saw it! You're in trouble, Amani!"

"Nobody's in trouble, Ivy," Mr. Turner said.

Amani boasted at her little sister. "Nah! That's what you get for being nosy. All up in my business."

"Amani, you're becoming a woman, now. No more cat fights with your little sister. It's time to do away

26

with childish mess. I know it's an adjustment for you."

Mr. Turner was right. Time to do away with the bickering, the neck-rolling, and "sassy 'tude" that she displayed as a younger child. The preparation for womanhood was at hand. And no more diary.

☞ ☜

Amani awakened at 3am. Curiosity and her anxieties prevented her from sleeping. She was desperate to know what she was capable of.

Again, she heard the same woman's voice from the previous afternoon. She crept to her bedroom window and opened it to increase the sound.

She pulled her clothes tighter to reduce the chill of the Fall season's wind. By leaning out of the window, she was able to trace the sound coming from next door.

This time, the neighbor was cursing at someone on the phone. The content revealed that the person on the other end was her mate.

"Why aren't you here, Marcus?" the woman shouted. "Are you at that bitch's house again? You're with me, now! You have no business over there!"

Amani was glued to this half of the debacle and wanted all of the juicy details. The more amused Amani became, the more she leaned out the window.

Amani leaned too far and slipped out of her window headfirst from the second floor! She screamed on her way down until she hit the ground, sounding off a big thump. The noises were loud enough to wake up Mr. Turner in his first floor bedroom.

Amani sat up with her hair covered in dirt. She checked her face for broken bones and loose teeth, but found no damage was done to her at all. The bush beneath her window and the ground it stood in, however, was destroyed.

She arose and looked toward the window of the master bedroom, where her father slept. Once the window curtain whipped open, Amani zoomed away in a blur.

Mr. Turner looked through the window, but saw nothing. Amani moved too quickly! She positioned herself with her back to the house, away from his view.

Then, Mr. Turner opened the window and looked around from right to left, yet he still couldn't find the cause behind the ruckus. By this time, Amani was hanging above him from her window ledge, twenty feet in the air. She got up there by leaping.

Mr. Turner looked down and saw his bush thoroughly damaged. "What the hell?" Then, he looked up. Amani was no longer hanging from the ledge.

Mr. Turner grabbed his shotgun rifle, then went upstairs to check on his girls, starting with Amani's room, but her door was locked. "Amani!" He banged on the door. "Girl, we don't lock doors 'round here! Not in my house! Unlock this door!"

Amani yelled, "Dad! I'm trying to sleep! I got school in the morning!"

Mr. Turner said to himself, "No this girl ain't yellin' back with this door locked." He yelled out, "Open this door!" Once he heard the door unlock, he hastily opened it.

When he swung the door open, he saw that Amani was fully covered under her comforter. "How did you get back in bed so quick? And why is it so cold in here?"

"Come on, Dad!" Amani shouted from beneath the covers.

Mr. Turner looked and saw the window slightly cracked open. Amani didn't fully close it, to avoid any alerting sounds once she got back inside of the bedroom.

"You got the window cracked!" Mr. Turner said. "That's why it's so drafty in here! Look at you, freezing all under the cover, running up my heat bill." He shut the window completely and locked it. "You better not had no boy up in here, I know that much."

"Dad, please!" Amani shouted.

Ivy crept in, rubbing her eyes. "Daddy, why are you so loud? I can't get any sleep." She paused and observed. "Is that a gun?"

"Everything is okay, Sweets," Mr. Turner said. "You can go back to bed. Get rested up for school in the morning." He walked Ivy back to her room.

Amani flipped the covers from over her head. The pillow was covered in dirt and her night clothes were filthy. She couldn't wait to hit the shower later that morning.

VIGILANTE

Amani and Joanie rode together on the bus which was heading to the high school where they both attended.

Joanie said, "Even though you scared me a bit, I still feel safer with you around."

"Why is that?" Amani asked. "It's not like we're really in the city. This is the suburbs. Most of the crazy stuff happens south of 8 Mile."

"I know, but there is still crime out here. Just not as much of it."

"How do I make you feel so safe?"

"Well, because you are from the streets. And you have street smarts. You are more likely to handle situations better than I can."

"You can dial 9-1-1 quicker than I can."

Joanie laughed. "Sure, I got it on speed dial. You never know. This cellular technology is way cool!"

"But, I do know one thing. If someone messes with me, they're in for the fight of their life."

After a few minutes have passed, the bus arrived at its stop. The two girls were dropped off in front of their school.

Joanie asked, "Did you hear about the girl who was raped on her way to school?"

"No I haven't," Amani answered. "My head was in the books."

"You know, Amani, you should take time to see what's going on. Don't you watch the news?"

"Not much. It's too depressing. Every day it is someone getting shot, murdered, robbed, or raped. I can't deal with it."

"Yeah, it's sad. Wouldn't it be great if we could do something about it?" This question made Amani think about her new abilities. "They have the guy's description on the website."

"I don't have that internet thing, yet. My dad is late on everything. We just got our PC last year."

"Bummer... I can print it out and we can make copies! And then, we can pass it around for the neighbors to see!"

Amani heard Joanie's rapid heartbeat. "Wow, you're very excited about this stuff, Joanie."

"I just want to help change the world. In my heart, I believe it can be done. We have to just try, and not wait for everyone else."

Amani admired Joanie's passion and was moved by her caring words. Joanie is from a tranquil environment, making her more sensitive to bad news. Amani, on the other hand, is calloused to such occurrences by being from the streets.

After getting back home from school, Amani took a look at her father's newspaper. In one of the sections was the sketching of the rape suspect.

"What's that you're looking at?" her dad asked.

Amani said, "I was wondering why do you buy the Detroit newspapers instead of the Eastpointe news. You still care about the city, don't you?"

"Of course I do. And it will always have my memories of better days. You just don't know how wonderful that city was!"

"Yeah, Dad, you told me a million times already."

"12th Street, Linwood, Dexter... It's nothing like it was before!"

"And they all got burnt to the ground. The end."

"So you say, Amani. It'll be back!"

"Anyways, I would like to go to the library again."

"Sweetheart, you know I am proud of my little girl getting as much knowledge as she can, but why the library? Doesn't your school supply you with the books you need?"

"No."

"They better!" He huffed. "I pay taxes, so they better have every book for each class." Amani began to walk away. "And, miss lady, don't think you're going to finish this day without talking about last night. Your door was locked and your window was unlocked. Those two things don't mix in this house."

"Yes, sir."

"Okay, then. You get back here by six, this time. Not 6:05, 6:15, or 6:01. You hear me?"

"Yes, sir."

Amani lied to her father. She was not going to the library this time. She took the folded piece of newspaper out of her pocket and took another good look at the sketch of the rapist. Because she moved so quickly, her dad didn't notice her taking the sheet of newspaper.

Amani walked the streets of Detroit, lurking in the area where the sexual assault reportedly took place. She wished that she could speak with the victim herself.

Ninety minutes had passed and Amani was getting impatient. She wanted to run into the suspect, but more than likely, he was in hiding. The only interactions she had were a few flirts and an older lady chastising her for being out there by herself.

Amani had enough of waiting around, so then she decided to catch the bus back to her home. She didn't know the bus schedule, but anticipated an arrival within the hour.

Minutes passed by before Amani took notice of a shady-looking man approaching the bus stop where she sat and waited. This bus stop is closed in, shielded by glass.

When the man got closer, he spoke to her. "Hey, little lady. You're out here by yourself?"

Amani said. "No, I'm waiting on someone. He will be here soon."

The man looked over his shoulder. "Looks to me like that someone is the bus driver."

Amani looked closer at the man. There were similarities between him and the rape suspect. She stared at his torso area, then suddenly, his gun appeared.

Amani stood up and began to walk away from the booth. She felt the man's hand on her left shoulder.

"Hold on," the man ordered.

Amani turned around with a punch right to his chest, sending him straight through the glass, ten yards away from where they stood. She was shocked by what she just did! When Amani hit him, she felt his bones shatter around her fist.

As the man lied helplessly on the ground, Amani could hear his abnormal breathing, along with his fluctuating heartbeat. She rushed to him, then reached under his puffy jacket and spotted his gun in holster. Then, she noticed something else. The man carried a badge.

Amani put her hands over her mouth in total shock! She had no idea this man was an officer! He was just trying to help her and possibly warn her of the dangers in that area.

She called Emergency on a pay phone and reported an officer down, then hung up after giving their location. Her plan was to not stick around, though she felt too responsible to take off running.

Amani knelt down, crying, "Sir, I didn't mean it! I'm so sorry!" The man became stiff and cold. Amani did not know CPR, and if she did, she still would have been too afraid to perform it with her abnormal strength and freezing whist.

"Help me, somebody!" she shouted. No one came to aid. She could hear the man's heart fluttering. It slowed down. Then, it stopped.

Amani was terrified! She decided not to depend on the ambulance to show up in good time, so she chose to take matters into her own hands.

She picked the off-duty officer up with ease, then took off running with him in her arms. She ran in miles of 50 to 60 per hour, but unfortunately, she was not used to traveling at this speed.

En route to the hospital, she accidentally collided with a van at an intersection. This sent her flying through a brick wall, losing the off-duty officer in the process.

After the collision, Amani rose to her feet. She felt physical pain for the first time in over a month, as she staggered to the main street where the accident originated. She spotted the slain officer and had to accept the fact that it was too late for him.

"No!" Amani screamed out loud, falling to her knees crying.

Most of the people in the area saw only a portion of the accident, but there was one bystander who witnessed the whole collision. This witness walked up to Amani and asked her, "What are you?"

Amani got up and distanced herself from him, looking away so he couldn't see her face. She noticed that people were rushing to the other side of the street, which was where she located the totaled minivan. Amani proceeded to this vehicle surrounded by witnesses.

"I see her breathing," one bystander said. This lady was on her cellphone with a 9-1-1 emergency operator. "The car is messed up! They need to get here quick! Naw, I don't see the other vehicle! They must've took off!"

Another bystander said, "Something hit that building over there. You see the hole in the wall?"

"What was it?"

"I ain't sure what it was. It happened so fast."

Amani stepped closer to the van and saw the driver with her head against the airbag. This lady reminded Amani of her late mother, which caused her to tear up even more.

In the backseat was a little girl whose face was covered in blood. Amani heard her shortness of breath and rapid heartbeat. This horrified Amani!

She backed away and bumped into the witness, again. He startled her, but she didn't swing when she turned around this time.

Again, the strange man asked her, "What are you?"

Amani screamed at the man, "Back off!" The man was petrified.

Amani walked away from the scene. The time was 6:32pm. She was not willing to face her father. Her jacket and jeans were badly damaged from the accident. Her thoughts were haunted by trauma.

The question echoed in her head, "What are you?" She can't handle the pressure, her faults, or her failures. She came to the hard conclusion that she was too much of a danger to society and was convinced that the world would be safer without her.

Amani felt worse about herself than she did the rapist. Her guilt ate away at her. She walked and walked with no destination in mind. She was too afraid to run. In her travels, an ambulance passed by her in pursuit to the scene of the accident that she was involved in.

From a far distance, she heard a train arriving, then she decided to wait for it. After a twenty minute wait, the railroad crossing gate let down as the signal rang. Soon after, the train rode toward the street with its extremely loud horn. A tear dropped from Amani's eye.

Once the train got close enough, Amani jumped in front of it in an attempt to end her life. The huge impact sent her a far distance.

Hours later, Amani awakened in a field. She was in excruciating pain, possibly from a bruised rib. She couldn't believe she was still alive! Amani had to deal with her mistakes, after all. Death could not help her. Or maybe not. ❦ ❦

Amani sat on the edge of the Ambassador Bridge, between Detroit City and Windsor, Ontario, CA. She stared down at the cold, flowing waves. She didn't fear the fall, but she was terrified of the cold and hoped this would end quickly.

Amani dove into the Detroit River. No bad luck. All she did was get soaked with cold water. She swam to the nearest shore as fast as she could.

Once Amani made it to the dock, she pulled herself up to surface. She shivered like an old-fashioned alarm clock once she made it to her feet.

Amani ran to the nearest building for heat. She found herself in a bar that she was too young to be allowed into.

A customer asked Amani, "Aren't you kind of young to be in here?" He looked at her ruined clothes. "Where did you just come from? A hurricane?"

"Where am I?" Amani asked.

"You're in Windsor!" Amani was amazed by this! Everyone turned and looked at her.

A waitress asked, "Who are you here with?"

"Nobody," Amani said. "I don't even know how I got here."

"Your clothes are all ruined, dear! And you look so cold! Let me get something to cover you up with."

"May I use the ladies' room?"

"Of course you can, hon."

People stared as Amani walked to the restroom. On her way there, she spotted a food tray which contained a steak knife. When she entered the lavatory, everyone turned their heads, back to minding their own business. Then quickly, Amani zoomed out to grab the knife and went right back inside the ladies' room unnoticed.

Amani was no longer determined to end her uncanny life. She was, however, vexed by her survival. While using the toilet, Amani inspected the steak knife and its sharpness. It was very sharp.

She ran the fine edge across her index finger. It did absolutely no damage to her finger, but instead, the edge of the knife was bent inward.

"Am I invincible?" Amani thought to herself out loud. "I just swam through the river, like it was a swimming pool!"

She blew onto the metal point of the knife like she did the hot cup of cocoa, but only with more force. The knife's edge turned frosty and frigid. Then, she took the frozen end of the knife and broke it in two. It was like snapping a pencil.

UNCONDITIONAL LOVE

J oanie was passing out fliers with pictures of her missing friend, Amani Turner. Some of the residents showed their concern and some didn't.

This was a chilly Saturday afternoon on a busy street. Joanie rested her legs, weary of constant walking, by sitting on a bench with her head down.

A sheet of paper flew in the wind, traveling down the busy street. It glided past cars and buses, until it landed flat against the face of a teenage girl wearing an over-sized winter coat.

The girl pulled the paper off of her face, revealing herself as the missing teen, Amani Turner. She took a look at the paper and saw her own picture.

"Yep. I'm in **big** trouble," Amani said to herself.

Joanie was still sitting with her head down when someone tapped her on the shoulder. She looked up and saw Amani standing before her.

"Amani!" Joanie screamed. "Thank God you're okay! Oh my, I was so worried!" She hugged her friend tightly, but Amani could hardly feel it as much as a normal person would have. "I printed,

42

like, a thousand fliers of you! Where have you been for the last two days?"

"Recovering from an accident," Amani said.

"You couldn't call?"

"No."

"Gosh! Well, I know you have your reasons, but you don't trust me well enough to tell me about it."

"And I'm glad you understand."

"Amani, come on! Not just a hint?"

"Nuh uhn."

"No? What kind of friendship is this? After all the searching I've done-"

"Joanie, I don't fully trust you, because you don't trust me."

"It was just a misunderstanding! Can't you get over it? I believe you, now. You never took steroids."

Amani listened closely to Joanie's heartbeat. Its consistency led her to believe that Joanie was being truthful.

"Okay," Amani said as she sat next to her, "but I'll tell you what's been going on when I am ready. Now is not a good time. I need to deal with my dad, first."

Joanie said, "Yeah, he's worried to death! The police were at your house, investigating the bushes beneath your window. They saw your library card that you left behind, too."

"Dang! I forgot it!"

"How are you going to explain that? That has me confused, as well."

"Okay, Joanie, you better not say anything about this to anyone. And I don't care how worried you are about me."

"I promise."

Amani looked at her sharply. "Okay. The other night, I went to the city in search of that rapist dude."

Joanie's jaw dropped like it weighed twenty pounds. "Are you crazy? You went after this guy? Who was with you?"

"I went by myself."

"What! What is your dad going to say?"

"How is he going to find out? Hey... remember what you promised."

"But, I have to tell! I didn't expect you to-"

Amani quickly grabbed Joanie by the throat. "Don't...you...dare." She released her. "This is why I can't tell you anything!" Joanie coughed with her hand over her neck. "I didn't want to have to go there, Joanie, but you annoy the hell outta me! You're too damn frantic! Scared of everything!"

Joanie gazed at Amani like she was terror-stricken by her. She would not say another word.

Amani got up and walked away, then after a few steps, she turned and said to Joanie, "Blame it on the PMS," then proceeded on her way home.

Joanie remained on the bench, stunned. She was too scared to tell on Amani, because she was not sure what would happen to her. She never expected Amani to ever put her hands on her, nor did she know Amani was even capable of doing such a thing.

❦ ❦

At the Turner residence, Mr. Calvin Turner was in distress over the worry of his missing daughter. Ivy, his youngest daughter, was also saddened. Eva Adams, Calvin's older sister, was there in support of her family, along with her son Lamont.

Someone rang the doorbell, then Eva answered it shouting, "Well, praise God!" She let Amani in.

"Sweetheart!" Mr. Turner shouted out. He stood up and went to hug his daughter.

Even though Amani's physical sensations were diminished, she still felt the warmth. She still found a way to appreciate the magnitude of her family's embrace.

Each family member hugged her tightly. There wasn't a dry eye in the house. Amani asked for their forgiveness, and all of them were receptive to her plea.

Mr. Turner chose not to discipline his daughter, at this moment. In his heart, he believed that whatever she experienced was enough to send her on a straight and narrow path. He was right. He taught Amani everything to prepare her for a life in the real world. She knew better, but there is no teacher like life itself.

◭

Today, the telephone rings at 5:00pm. Amani picks up to answer it. "Ms. Jett speaking."

"Hey, sis! It's me!"

"Hello, Ivy. What's up?"

"Are you watching TV? There is so much hype going on with your interview!"

"Yeah, it's too much. Ridiculous."

"I'm sayin'! I really need a favor from you, though."

Amani folds her arms. "What is it?"

"Plug my cook book for me, please?"

"Now, Ivy, you know I can't do that. And you know exactly why I can't do that."

"But, I need this to sell! I need to make money just like you need to make money."

"I can't have our family in the spotlight. I already told you, Ivy, that's a potential weakness that I cannot afford to have. Since they can't bother me, they might try to come after those who are dear to me."

"Nobody's going to bother us when they know who we're related to. Who has that much nerve?"

"You'd be surprised. There are a lot of people who are thirsty for power."

"Anyway, I need help with these bills. And I used up my government assistance." She put her hand over her chest.

"Ivy, you know you can't lie to me, right? I can hear your heart rate through this phone." This rattles Ivy. "And putting your hand in the way is not working."

"Dang! Well, look, I have some aid left, but it won't be enough. Is that better?"

Amani listens. "Much better. I'll see what I can do, Sis. How is that cousin of ours?"

"Lamont is Lamont. Don't concern yourself about that boy. This is just a phase he's going through."

"I hope you are right. Make sure he's watching the interview tonight, please?"

"I will."

The line clicks on Amani's phone. She checks the caller ID. "Oh, it's them. I'll have to call you back later."

Amani clicks over after they say their byes. "Ms. Jett speaking."

"Hi! This is Arnold Strong from BSC, calling you again. We're hoping you can arrive by the next hour, so we can get started on makeup and your attire selection.

"Would you like to be transported from our pick-up point, or would you prefer to go with your own means of transportation?"

Amani smiles. "Take a wild guess."

"Got it. Thank you, and see you soon!"

Amani hangs up and goes into her master bedroom. She takes her carrying bag and a pair of pumps.

She returns to the window where she can see the people of the media monitoring her house, and then she opens it. Cameramen lift their cameras and take numerous shots of her in clearer view.

Amani places her foot upon the window frame and leaps up. She takes off, soaring across the sky! The camera crews are excited! They flash on until Amani is beyond their view.

WEAPON
USA

CONVERSATIONS
with
Susan Dunn LIVE!

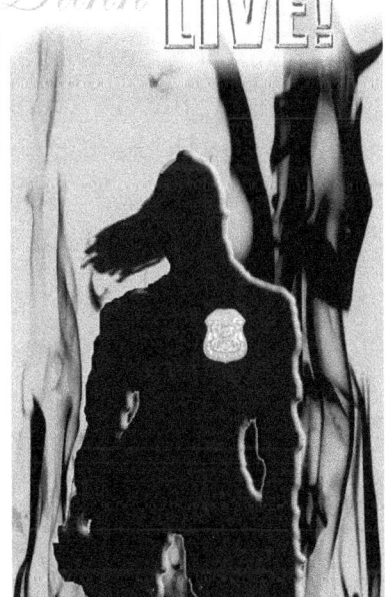

MIND OVER MATTER

here are two rows of people facing each other with a wide space between them. Security guards are regulating their distances.

One lady points to the sky. "Look! She's here!"

Amani Jett descends from the sky and lands between the two rows. When she lands, she jogs to a slow, and then brakes like an ice skater, skidding to the side. Right after her landing, she kicks off her athletic sneakers, places her pumps on the ground, then slides her feet in them one at a time.

The people cheer for her as she heads to the TV studio. Admirers are taking pictures of Amani with their mobile phone cameras. Those with posters and signs hold them up high. Some are chanting, "We love you, Amani!" She waves back at them.

This is her first formal public appearance. Amani never wanted the spotlight, being all about doing her duties as a "shero".

Amani is greeted by the crew that will assist her with everything she needs before the highly-anticipated interview. They offer her a drink of her choosing. She requests a bottle of alkaline water.

One of the crew members guides Amani to the wardrobe, where she must pick between the outfits she chose beforehand.

"I think I know which one I'll go with, now," Amani says. "The purple dress, with the matching stilettos. It reflects my mood."

Amani sits in her assigned dressing room. The makeup artists have their makeup tray ready.

Amani asks, "Now, that is organic and mineral makeup, right?"

"Yes, ma'am," one of the artists says. "Just as you requested. And nontoxic nail polish."

"Great! Thank you. And you don't have to worry about getting cut. I only sharpen my nails on special occasions."

"Yes ma'am."

"What are your names?"

"I'm Jean. Jean Parker."

The other artist says, "And I'm Samantha Kent."

"Nice to meet you," Amani says. "You can address me like you would anyone else. You can be comfortable around me."

"Sure. Thanks."

The show is in an hour. Amani meets with her interviewer, Susan Dunn, face-to-face for the first time. As they shake hands, cameras start flashing. Amani had never seen so many flashes before.

"It is such an honor and pleasure meeting you, Ms. Jett," Susan says.

"I am honored the same," Amani replies.

As they walk toward the set, Susan asks, "So, are you sure you don't want to go over a few preparations? No sample questions?"

"I'm sure. I am confident that I'll be able to compose myself well throughout this interview."

"Good! I believe you are, too. Fear doesn't seem to exist in your character at all."

"But, I'm sure you will ask me about that."

"Hey, that's part of the job." They smile.

Three... two... and the show begins. Susan Dunn and her guest, Amani Jett, sit across from one another in the plush seating of this home-style setting. The climate is cool inside of this state-of-the-art studio. Video cameras aim at both women.

Susan greets the home audience, "Good evening, America! We welcome you to a very special broadcasting of 'Conversations with Susan Dunn, Live!'

"Our guest tonight, I must say, is the most special of all the guests I have ever interviewed. I know that is saying quite a bit, because I have had many, including Presidents of the United States.

"But, how often do you run into a super being? The only one of their kind? Capable of doing things we can only dream of!

"I'm proud of the fact that she's a woman!" She laughs. "Look at me, I got goose bumps. My guest today has officially been named the 'Eighth Wonder of the World.'

"Here she is with us, this evening. I introduce to you, the incomparable, the one and only, Ms. Amani Jett. Welcome, Amani." They shake each others' hands once again.

"Thank you, Susan," Amani says, while sitting comfortably with her legs crossed.

"Well! Here you are, being still long enough for everyone to see you." Amani laughs. "This is not only your first interview, but the first time you allowed yourself to be in the spotlight. Tell me, why now?"

"Susan, I realize that when you keep your image concealed from so many people, they tend to create an image for you. I've seen some awful sketches of me." She giggles. "They would make my lips extra big and red. I don't even wear bright red lipstick. I was like, 'Who is that supposed to be?'"

"That's very funny."

"I know, right? But, it amazes me how some people need a physical image to look up to, while the most precious things you can find about a person are on the inside. Just honor my services, not necessarily my outer attributes and exaggerated drawings."

"And you know what, Amani? When you first landed, people were saying, 'She's like a regular woman! She carries a purse!' Then, I thought to myself, 'Where is she supposed to keep all of her lady stuff?'"

Amani laughs again. "Exactly. I was born a girl and I grew into a woman. That's what females do."

"What do you keep in your purse?"

"Same things every woman keeps in her purse. Lady stuff!" They laugh together.

"That was a question that you don't ask a lady, but I guess I did."

"Aw, please, I don't mind it."

"Good, because I have another question that I probably shouldn't ask you. How old are you?"

"Twenty-eight."

"You are still young! Wow, I thought it was your uniqueness that made you look so young and healthy. And you're so mature!"

"Thank you. Hopefully, my uniqueness keeps me like this for a long time. But if not, I can still live with that."

"So, when did you discover you had these unique abilities?"

"When I was in my teen years. Right when I hit puberty."

"Oh my. A double whammy. What was life like as a teenager with such powers?"

"It wasn't fun, as some would think. Not at all."

"Really? That was unexpected. What made it so bad?"

"I felt cursed. Like a freak. I couldn't share this with anyone, I couldn't compete in any sports... I just wanted to be a normal girl. So, what I did was restrain from using my powers. I managed to limit myself for two full years."

Amani was sixteen years old; a few inches taller and with no more baby fat. She was running on a treadmill at the recreational center during summer vacation. She spent a lot of time at that center for the many activities offered to people, young and old.

At this facility, Amani participated in every available sporting activity, from martial arts, to basketball, to swimming. She went there to learn, but not compete. This was not to gain more strength and power, but to learn how to ration her use of force. She needed to learn how to do things within her natural human limits without being extraordinary.

Amani made a vow to herself never to use her special powers again, after the night of the accident two years ago. But, as she was running on the machine, she couldn't help but hear the three guys who were watching her from a distance. These guys had no clue that Amani could hear them.

"Check her out," the first guy said.

Second guy said, "Damn! That's a ass, right there."

Third guy asked, "Would you hit that?"

"Hell yeah! I ain't gay!"

Amani was angry at herself for not having her earphones with her. She wanted to block them out, but at the same time, she was nosy.

First guy said, "I would have to see the front, first. She might look like a pit bull in the face."

"With a ass like that," second guy said, "she can't lose!"

"Man, you wouldn't know what to do with that."

"Shee-it, yes I do! Take them wide hips and be like," he motioned his hands, pulling, "**bang, bang**!"

Amani gasped. She can't stand to hear guys talk like that, even to this day. She hears this crude talk often, because most men are unaware of her super hearing, not knowing who she is.

Third guy said, "Yeah right, Kev, you wouldn't even last past the first stroke." He said to the first guy, "Look, he'll say **bang** one time and pass out."

"Whatever, man," Kev said, "I can hang with the best. You better ask somebody. I'll have her screamin' my name." He took another look at Amani's rear. "Just look at them ass cheeks! They jigglin'. Up and down..."

Amani had heard enough. She cut her run short, then headed to the weight scale, thinking, "They better not say a word to me."

The guys watched while Amani passed them by. The third guy grabbed his crotch and said, "Damn. She ain't bad-lookin'."

First guy said, "Aw man, that's jail bait. She look like she's about my daughter's age. Hell naw."

Kev said, "She looks ready!"

"Then, go holla, then," third guy said.

Kev submitted to the pressures of his peer and his hormones. He wiped at his face and strutted to the scale where Amani was.

Amani measured her weight at 144lbs. At this age, she stood 5' 9". As soon as she left the scale, Kev grabbed her arm with a light grip, just enough to get her attention. Instead of turning around, Amani kept her stride and walked away. In the process, she pulled Kev off balance, causing him to stumble across the floor. He accidentally bumped into a much larger man named, Armstrong.

"Oh, sorry sir!" Kev said. "I didn't mean to bump into you like that." Armstrong looked at him grimly without saying a word to him. The other guys were laughing at Kev for appearing to be so flimsy. Kev was too embarrassed to pursue Amani any further. This was also amusing to Amani, but she kept on walking. Served him right, in her opinion.

Amani made it home in time for dinner after leaving the rec center. She sat at the dining room table with her dad and younger sister, who was quiet this day. Ivy is normally talkative, but felt no reason to speak. Amani noticed this.

Amani asked her father, "How was work, Dad?"

"It went fine," Mr. Turner said. "How was your time at the rec center?"

"It went fine. So, Dad, what did you learn at work today?"

Mr. Turner chuckled. "Very funny, Amani. Let's see, I learned a lot about my coworkers' personal business, thanks to the gossip being spread around the entire plant. I learned that foreign cars still have a better reputation than the cars we build..."

"Do you agree with people when they say foreign cars are better?"

"Absolutely not! Look at what I drive."

"I understand. But, I thought you bought it, because of your employee discount."

"Hey, that's just one reason." He turned, facing Ivy. "So, Ivy, school will be starting soon. Are you ready for high school?"

Ivy hesitated to answer. "I guess."

"Then, you better find out for sure by the next time I ask you."

"Then, I guess I'll know by tomorrow." She rolled her eyes.

Mr. Turner said nothing after that. Amani could not believe how her father let Ivy get away with being sassy with him! She would have gotten in big trouble had she shown that much attitude when she was Ivy's age.

Mr. Turner was exhausted with the tough love parenting. He started to decline after Amani went missing two years ago.

After dinner, Ivy put her dish in the kitchen sink and went straight to her bedroom. Her demeanor was snobby.

Mr. Turner said to Amani, "Talk to your little sister, will you?"

"I sure will," Amani said. "I am **on** it."

Amani walked up to Ivy's door and knocked. She could hear her sister gossiping on her telephone. Unlike Amani, she had her own phone line. Amani knocked again.

"I'm on the phone!" Ivy shouted.

Amani shouted back, "Girl, don't make me tear down this door!"

When Ivy heard Amani's voice, she rushed to the door to open it. Amani was always tough on Ivy, unlike her father. Ivy knew not to get smart with her big sister, or there would be consequences. She ended her phone call to let Amani in.

Amani closed the door behind her. "How are you feeling?"

"Moody," Ivy said. "I just don't want to be bothered."

"I know the feeling. You're the same way I was. Imagine having a little sister getting on your nerves on top of that."

"Dang. Now I feel bad about that."

"It's cool. So tell me... have you noticed anything special happening to you? Besides the things I prepared you for?"

"Naw, what else is supposed to happen?"

"Nothing! I was just wondering how much your experience is like mine." She sat on the bed next to Ivy. "Do you feel aggressive? Like, you're able to move heavy objects and stuff?"

"I do when I throw a tantrum."

"For real? Let's see..." She pinched Ivy's arm.

"Ow!" Ivy screamed. "That hurt!" Amani thumped her head. "Ouch! Will you stop!"

"Okay. Just help me with one thing."

"What?"

"Don't use that tone with me. I need you to help me move my dresser."

"When?"

"Now. Come on, let's go."

Ivy dragged her feet behind Amani as they went into Amani's bedroom.

"We're going to move this dresser to that other wall, over there," Amani said.

"Why couldn't you ask Dad?" Ivy asked. "This is man work! You're going to make me break a nail!"

"Just help me with this. It'll be over before you know it." Ivy slumped to the opposite side of the dresser from where Amani was. "Alright, Ivy, lift up on the count of three." Ivy grabbed both sides of the dresser. "One, two, three!"

Ivy tried lifting the dresser, but it wouldn't budge. "I can't move this thing!" She checked her fingernails. "You left your clothes in the drawers? Why didn't you empty them, first? Or just take the dang-on drawers out before moving the whole dresser?"

"Never mind," Amani said. "I thought you were strong enough."

"I don't know any girls that strong! This thing is heavy! I didn't see your end go up, either! Did you even lift it?"

"I can take care of my end. Look, you were right. I should've asked Dad. Sorry."

Ivy stomped out of the room. This let Amani know that Ivy did not share the same gift that she has.

After hearing Ivy's bedroom door close, she opened her dresser drawers and removed the weight plates that were hidden beneath her clothes.

Susan Dunn's interview with Amani Jett continues. "I thought of so many ways to introduce you," Susan says, "but, there have been too many nicknames and titles put out there for you."

"Way too many," Amani says.

"I've heard names like, Turbo Girl, Mister Motown- before they knew you were a lady," Amani laughs at the ridiculous names, "Weapon USA, Super Sista..."

"That one wasn't too bad, but I'd rather stick with Amani Jett." She smiles.

"Now, that is what you go by, today. But, you know people searched school records and things, right? That's no surprise to you."

"Not a surprise at all."

"So, what made you choose a name like Amani Jett? And, is it legalized?"

"Yes. It is legit. It describes me better."

"And even though you have made your name nationally known on the net, you're still given nicknames. What do you think about that?"

"I don't let those kinds of things bother me. People like entertainment, so let them entertain."

"Such a good sport. But, those are the more endearing nicknames. Other titles or labels that were used for you, some you may have heard before, are very controversial.

"You have been referred to as Lady Savior, The Second Coming, Amani Christ, and even some less favorable; Angel of Death," Amani gasps, "Daughter of Satan, the Anti-Christ..."

Amani shows much disgust. "See, Susan, these titles and labels, or what have you, they are totally wrong and disrespectful.

"These people think they're doing me a favor by giving me a title that I never earned. And these others, they are just putting fear into the people, and that's not right.

"I'm doing what I think many would do if they had my gifts. And I'm doing it, because I believe it is just! The nerve of some people!"

"I believe there is a religious influence to most of these labels," Susan says.

"Yes, there is."

"Do you have a religion? What does Amani Jett believe in?"

"I'm sure the world wants to hear my answer to that question. That's what makes it such a good question.

"But..." Amani continues, "I will say that, yes, I study one particular faith more than I do others. However, I think that revealing this may spark an endorsement for that religion, which may result in individuals proclaiming this religion to be dominant among others, all because of me.

"Real faith shouldn't require my validation. That is not what I am here for."

"But, isn't that the purpose of religions?" Susan asks. "To convert those who don't follow them?"

"It definitely looks that way, Susan, but my beliefs are different. I embrace humanity in its many faces. In my research, I found good in most major religious practices.

"Of course there will be bad seeds. There are bad apples just about everywhere, but overall, I think most religions give valuable lessons and produce good people."

"So, Ms. Jett, you don't want to say what religion it is you're following. It's like you have a faith, but don't want to endorse your faith. How is that in any way beneficial to the religion you practice?"

"Susan, I endorse _having_ a faith. And I also believe in diversity. I favor the moralistic aspect of spiritual teachings over the historical value.

"So, whether Noah's ark existed or not, it doesn't really matter to me. I value the lesson I got from it. I value Buddha's words. I admire Muhammad.

"When I imagine Muhammad, Jesus, Buddha, and Moses in the heavens, I don't picture them fighting like earthbound people do.

"I imagine them talking and having a good time with each other, because their sense of morality were basically the same."

Susan says, "I don't want make a religious discussion out of this, Amani, but I can't think of one religion that is set up for its followers to not lure others into believing exactly what they believe."

"I agree. But, when you deal with different varieties of people who have good hearts, and they believe in something a little different than what you do, you can still appreciate what influenced them.

"And since there are people out here who are already thinking of me as either some godsend or hell spawn, I feel that I would only be adding to the religious hype surrounding me.

"With that being said; the day when the world stops sanctifying me, demonizing me, fanatically warring over religious differences, and executing those who see differently than they do, **that** will be the day when I announce my faith to the world.

"And hopefully, with this interview, they'll just see me as a good person."

"From what I can tell by sitting here with you, you are definitely that."

"Thank you, Susan."

"To do what you do... to be who you are... you must have not only tough skin, but a tough interior as well."

"Yes indeed. What I do is try to imagine if it was someone else with these abilities instead of me. And what I would think of them.

"If I were brought up very religious, then I might have been the same way. Some people respond to me the only way they know how."

Susan picks up a sheet of paper from her short stack of notes and says, "Very good. I'm not sure if you've heard about the comments made by the radio talk show host, Billy J. Marshall, but it made a lot of buzz. He had some interesting things to say."

"I've heard of him, but I never listened to his show."

"Would you mind if I read the transcript?"

"Be my guest."

Susan reads:

"'This obtuse malarkey they call, Amani Jett, is the worse lie I've heard in all of my life! This is prototypical US government bio-weaponry. She is not an evolution of nature, but a science experiment funded by our tax dollars.' He went on to say, 'A distraction to focus all of our attention on a phony, instead of the real issues at hand.

"Amani, you are here in the flesh for all the world to see. What do you have to say to this radio show host?"

Amani looks into the camera. "He deserves no mention. I don't want to remain a myth to anyone. Another reason for me being here, in this worldwide spotlight, is because I want a more personal relationship with the people. I want to be more of a positive influence for the next generations."

"That will make you a true shero, Amani." She turns to the camera. "And now, we are going to take our first commercial break. Stay with us for more live questions with Amani Jett after the break." Susan reaches over to her guest and says, "You're doing great."

NEW MOTIVATION

September 11, 2001. Amani was in the beginning of her senior year of high school. Things were going well for her. She was already ahead of the class, because she never took a break from studying during summer vacation.

Amani still never took the time to compete in sports, even though she became familiar with her body. She hadn't been using any of her special abilities except for super hearing. She heard every bit of gossip about her.

All rumors about Amani were ended very quickly, because she would intervene right away. Amani had no tolerance for lies told about her and her patience was short.

She didn't have any close friends, since Joanie graduated a year before. Joanie had already left for college.

Though schoolwork was easy for Amani, she had a hard time with one particular teacher named, Mrs. Gilbourn, who taught her Government class. She was mean, discouraging, and often fed into the negative side of things.

Amani did well in every class, except for hers. As a matter of fact, Amani never really cared for any of the history-related classes that were taught in school, since the discovery of her powers. Her new top interests were Science and Math. Becoming a defense attorney was no longer a desire for her.

It was the first hour of class for Amani Turner; the dreaded Government class with Mrs. Gilbourn. The students were seated at their desks, but some were late for class. Mrs. Gilbourn waited outside, monitoring the halls before the late bell rang.

Once the bell rang, Mrs. Gilbourn stepped inside the classroom and closed the door behind her. "Alright, class! Who did their homework? Bring your papers up!"

There was no greeting of "Good morning", or a "hello". The students who brought their work put their papers on her desk.

Mrs. Gilbourn called out, "Marcel, I didn't see you stand up. Where's your homework?"

"I didn't finish it," Marcel replied.

"That's a damn shame. Really, it is. I took time to walk this class through the whole chapter, and this is what I get from you?" Marcel was speechless. "What were you doing yesterday that kept you from finishing the work I gave you?"

"I... I don't know. I mean, I tried to finish, but I had a problem with some of the questions."

"Did you ask your parents for help? Then again, they probably can't tell you nothin', anyway. These parents out here, I tell you!

"They never put in any time with y'all, and obviously, they don't care enough about your future! And when I flunk your sorry behinds, that's when they want to get concerned!" She looked through the papers. "Makes no damn sense."

One student by the name of Eric James spoke out. "Any good news to start our day off with, Mrs. Gilbourn?" Amani snickered.

"What do you find so funny, Ms. Turner?" Mrs. Gilbourn asked Amani.

"Nothing," Amani answered.

"Then that's what I want to hear from you. Nothing!" She faced Eric. "And, Mr. Funny Man, I don't want to hear another word coming out of you, either. You want good news? Give me something to be glad about, instead of your big mouth."

This was an everyday thing from Mrs. Gilbourn. She hardly had anything good to say. Amani felt that once she could make it through this first hour, the rest of the school day was a breeze. But, this was a day that she and the rest of the country would never forget.

The intercom sounded. "Attention, all staff and students! Please turn your TV monitors on to channel one. There has been devastating news."

Each classroom in the school had a television mounted at a corner of the walls. There was a special channel that would be aired just for students. Mrs. Gilbourn hated it.

Mrs. Gilbourn said, "How are they going to interrupt my class for this TV nonsense? And it's never more important than what I'm teaching!"

She ordered one of the students to turn on the television, while she bickered on and on until the TV was activated. There is where Amani and her classmates witnessed the terrible attacks on the World Trade Center. Mrs. Gilbourn was horrified along with the class.

Amani felt deep sympathy. She hurt even more when it was reported that the planes were commercial passenger jets. This reminded Amani of her mother's death. Rosanna Turner, the mother of Amani Turner, was a victim of an airplane crash, five years before.

Amani cried when she saw the people who desperately jumped out of windows. She was heart-broken when she saw the reactions of those who came out covered in debris.

She was even more sickened when it was reported that firefighters and policemen went in to help victims, only to lose their own lives by trying to rescue others. This was the worst tragedy that anyone had ever seen.

Then, there were the people who stepped in and volunteered. Some were off-duty firemen, cops, and then you had regular civilians. This gave Amani a new desire.

Amani paid close attention to later reports. She knew that with her abilities, which she had been rejecting, she could be an excellent contributor in disasters like this. She wanted to leave her seat at that very moment and find a way to New York.

For two years, Amani had been beating herself up for the accidental death of the off-duty police officer and the injured mother with her child in the car accident. Fortunately, the latter two survived.

But, here you have people without super-human powers who stepped in and helped those in need. They put their lives on the line for these people. Some of them indeed lost their lives.

Amani had a change of heart. No more running from danger. She then chose to embrace the gifts and talents bestowed upon her and improve her methods.

This became serious business for Amani. Her plan, following high school graduation, was to pursue a career in law enforcement. She wanted to understand tactical strategies in the line of duty.

Amani decided to start her mission off with a change in her identity once she graduated. A name change...

"And we're back with the phenomenal, Amani Jett," Susan Dunn says after the commercial break. "When we left off, we were talking about the source of your power. There have been rumors of extra-terrestrial inhabitation, and genetic modifications... Have you discovered where they came from?"

"I honestly don't know," Amani says. "I stopped worrying about it a year after I first discovered them. But, I assure you that I am not a part of a government conspiracy. If I was, then why would they choose me?"

"Why do you think people, like the radio show host, accuse you of being part of a conspiracy?"

"Entertainment. The desire for attention. They feel the need to have answers, so they make up stories that they find most logical.

"It's just like what I said about my image. Those who never got a good look at me created their own image of me and did a bad job of it. Same goes with my origins."

"Understood. So, what is your relationship with the US government? Is what was said about our tax dollars paying your lifestyle true to any degree?" She extends her hand forward. "Not that I would be against it. You need to make a living by doing what you do."

"Yes I do, like everyone else who work their jobs."

"Then, are you a part of National Security?"

"No, I don't have a job salary or hourly wages."

"How do you manage in your mansion? It has to get expensive for someone with no regular income."

"Yeah it does. You know how they say crime doesn't pay?"

"Yes."

"Well, neither does crime-fighting, in my opinion. Early on, it was good. People made donations for me when I first started.

"But when the economy went from bad to worse, things changed. I didn't anticipate the drop in funds. I thought I would stay on top of the world."

"As most young people do," Susan says. "You're proving to be more normal by the minute."

Amani laughs. "That's a good thing."

"Do you get nothing from the United States government?"

"It's not like I'm on a contract or anything like that. I've been rewarded per duty. And that's not for all of the services I've done."

"Now, that is a **shock** that you've carried on missions for our country and have not been paid. Have you complained about the nonpayment?"

"No. Some things I do from the heart. It can be a charity at times."

"A charity? But, even some CEOs get paid by their charities. How is it possible that a service of that magnitude ever be considered a charity?"

"Because, I'm not putting my life on the line. It would be so for your average person, but not for me. It's volunteer work, because I just want to see the world as a better place than what it is now."

"And everyone, including me, thought you were on top of the world. You have hardships like the rest of us."

"Right. I am human. I've made mistakes."

"That sounds interesting. What are some of the mistakes you've made?"

Amani is a bit hesitant to answer. "Leaving the country behind for a war I didn't believe in."

"You're speaking of the Iraq War."

"Yes. I never believed there were weapons of mass destruction. I do believe Iraq needed to be reformed, but I did what every soldier did."

"If you did what every soldier did, then why are you blaming yourself?"

"I would have rather been here, defending people of my country. I was overseas during Hurricane Katrina. I was not there for the victims."

"I see, Ms. Jett. And, you can only be at one place at a time. I do recall the reactions of civilians when you were a no-show. This must have been on your mind for quite some time."

"Yes, it has. I've decided to stop thinking like a soldier and do more thinking for myself."

"So in other words, you take orders from no one."

"Not anymore, Susan. This is why I find it so ridiculous when people say I'm part of the US government, or I'm controlled by anyone. It couldn't be further from the truth."

"Do you oppose any of the decisions made our by US leaders?"

"I hate war. Period. I've seen too many young people die on both sides over things they do not understand."

In a dimmed room is a group of seven men and one woman sitting at a conference table. They look nervous as they watch Susan Dunn's interview with Amani Jett on a large LCD TV screen, which is mounted on the wall.

"I'm getting the feeling we're going to have to pull the plug on this interview," one mysterious man says.

"She won't expose us," another man says. "That would be sloppy. And I doubt Susan would drop the ball."

The lady of the group says, "The direction she's heading with her questions are quite daring. I hope she pulls back."

"Either way, I think Amani knows what is best for the country, whether she agrees with our strategies or not."

"Let's hope so," another man says, "for the sake of the free world."

On the television screen, Susan Dunn says, "It's already time for another break. When we return, we'll talk to Amani Jett about her astounding powers, and more personal questions, like, her view on love." Amani looks a bit surprised. "Stay tuned after these messages."

IN DAYS TO COME...

During the second semester of her senior year of high school, Amani worked at a local movie theater. She didn't like the job much, because it wasn't taking her in the direction she was headed for in life. However, she wanted the pay.

Amani's manager liked her a lot, because she was an excellent worker and finished her tasks quickly. This manager talked to her as if, someday, she would become a manager herself. Amani had no desire to stick with the company, let alone become a manager.

Amani's motivation was to buy a car, since the day she had acquired her driver's license. She worked diligently just for that, while knowing that her dad would co-sign for it.

One day, Ivy went up to Amani's job with her friends to watch the latest horror movie release. Amani was working the register at the recession stand at the time. She wasn't familiar with these friends of Ivy. Two were boys and one was a girl. It appeared to be a double date.

Ivy approached the stand. "Hi Amani!" She turned to her friends. "This is my sister, guys."

"How did you get here?" Amani asked Ivy.

"Jermaine drove us here in his dad's car."

Amani looked at Jermaine. "And, how old are you?"

"What?" Jermaine replied. "I'm sixteen."

"Do you know Ivy is fourteen?"

"Yeah. And?" He snickered.

Amani gave Ivy the you-know-better look. "Ivy..."

Ivy disregarded her stare. "We're just fifteen months apart. Can you give us a discount on some popcorn and pop?"

"You mean, give these boys a discount? Because, I know you don't have any money."

"Come on, Amani. Please! The movie is about to start!" Amani went ahead and gave her little sister's acquaintances the ten percent discount. "Thanks, Sis!"

Later that day, Amani arrived home from work. Mr. Turner sat at the dining room table calculating bills, when instead, he should have been eating.

Amani said, "Dad, you need to take your mind off of that stuff."

"How can I?" Mr. Turner asked. "There are things that need to be done around here and I got to figure out a way to do those things, while paying these bills. We're behind."

Amani sat down with him. "It'll get better. They'll call you back to work. I believe it."

"I admire your optimism, Amani, but let's be real. The industry is getting worse and worse. They will close more plants before they start opening them."

"Then, I will help with the bills."

"No, no, you keep putting your money aside for **you**. I don't want to put this burden on you. Not at seventeen."

"But, I'm just saving up for a car. That's not so important. I can help."

Mr. Turner gathered up all the paperwork. "I don't want you to share my responsibilities."

Amani couldn't understand why her father was so stubborn. She thought that maybe it was a man thing. When he started to leave, she stopped him.

"Wait, Dad," Amani said. "How well do you know Ivy's friends? Have you met any of them?"

Mr. Turner answered, "Sure. I met her friend, Christie."

"Is that it? You haven't met any of the boys?"

"Boys? No. What boys are you talking about?"

"I'll just let you have that discussion with her, Daddy. You sure have changed."

"What do you mean by that?"

"You are much easier on Ivy than you were on me at that age. She hangs out later-"

Mr. Turner leaned toward her. "And do you

remember where you ended up when you were her age? Missing for two days! So, I don't want to hear it from you."

"But Dad..." Amani couldn't come up with a clever explanation. "Okay, you have a point."

"I know I do. She may have a little more attitude, but you gave me the flux!"

"But, it wasn't because you stayed on my case. Don't you think you might be a little too lenient on Ivy? Who is she on the phone with right now?"

"Well, she's usually on the phone with that girl, Christie."

"Nope. Try again."

Mr. Turner eyeballed Amani strangely. "How do you know who she's on the phone with?"

"I have my ways. Go up there and check."

Mr. Turner waved her off. "Amani, I ain't studdin' you." Translated: Amani, I am not studying you.

This light debate went on for months. All the way near the ending of the school year. By this time, Amani saved up $2,600. This would have been a major help for her family's living situation, but her father would not accept it.

Mr. Turner tried to encourage Amani to put a portion of her funds toward her senior dues. He wanted her to enjoy the activities her school had for the graduating class, which he could not afford at the time. On the contrary, Amani didn't care about the senior activities. She was more concerned about her home and family.

❦ ❦

One night in the middle of spring, Amani, Ivy, and Mr. Turner were eating at the dinner table. It was silent.

"Why are you girls so quiet, today?" asked Mr. Turner. "Ivy? Amani?"

"I've been doing a lot of thinking," Amani said. "I might join the Armed Forces."

"What! Tell me you didn't just say what I thought I heard!"

"I'm really considering it, Dad."

"Amani, I did not raise you up with that type of mentality!"

"I knew you wouldn't understand, but my mind is close to being made up. They will pay for college."

"Hell, you would've been better off playing sports! The coach was right!" He gulped his water, then slammed the cup down. "You put off competing in sports, got your grades back up, and did all of that studying at the library... for this? I don't think so!"

"You say that, because you don't believe in me. You think something will happen to me."

"There is a war going on! Who in their right mind would go join the military **during** war? A long war, at that one!"

"I would."

"The hell you would!"

"It's my choice, Daddy!" Suddenly, Amani heard something peculiar coming from Ivy.

"No daughter of mine is going to join some wretched military forces! I can't believe you! After all that I raised you up to be!"

"You raised me up to think independently and not to simply do what I'm told. That's why I make these decisions!"

"And what do you think would happen in the military? You'll do what you're told! So you'll go against my wishes to be a puppet for people who will never respect you?"

"They'll respect me. Without a doubt, they will surely respect me."

Ivy stood up from the dinner table with her plate in hand, then she headed for the staircase.

"And where are you going?" Mr. Turner asked Ivy.

"To my room," Ivy responded.

Mr. Turner shook his head at Ivy as she went upstairs. Amani stared at her dad wide cycd.

"Don't even try it," Mr. Turner said to Amani. "You are giving me more hell than that girl is, so don't look at me with those big ole eyes."

"Dad, you are overreacting," Amani said. "I said I'm thinking about it, not that I'm one hundred percent sure."

"I don't like the fact that you're even thinking about it. And what is the alternative selection that you have in mind?"

"I was thinking about the police force."

Mr. Turner slammed down his fork. "Have you learned anything I taught you while growing up? Or, is this rebelliousness? Why are you doing this?"

"Doing what?"

"Running my pressure up!"

Amani took a deep breath before speaking. "Dad, you would be surprised by what I can do. I will let you know when you're not so excited."

Mr. Turner was lost by her words as he sat there bewildered. Amani got up from her seat and kissed her father's forehead. Mr. Turner had no clue to what Amani was talking about.

Amani went upstairs with her plate, but did not go to her room. She went to visit Ivy instead and knocked on her door.

"Who is it?" Ivy asked.

"It's me," Amani said, "open up." Ivy let her in, then sat back on her bed. "Anything you want to tell me?" She closed the door.

"No. Why?"

"Because, I think you do."

"I was asking you! Why are you doing Dad this way? You know how he is. You nearly gave him a heart attack."

"I can't help how he receives news."

"So, you're really going through with this?"

"Maybe."

"Why? Do you really think that's the best thing for you?"

"Ivy, I'll be straight up with you if you'll be straight up with me."

"Alright, but what do you mean by that?"

"You're pregnant. And don't try to tell me you're not."

"But... how do you know?"

Amani listened through the bedroom door to make sure their dad wasn't nearby. "You read part of my diary, right?" she asked Ivy.

"Yeah, but that was a long time ago. It was kind of funny. I remember that much."

"Do you remember me writing about how fast I was running in school?"

"Yeah, you were the fastest! Why did you stop?"

"Because, I was too fast. As of right now, I can outrun a car."

Ivy gazed at Amani, waiting for her to laugh, but it was not a joke. "Amani... did you bump your head?"

Amani scooted off the bed and lifted it over her head with Ivy sitting on it. When she let the bed back down, Ivy sat there with her mouth hanging open.

Amani checked on her. "Ivy?"

"I just peed in bed," Ivy said with a shocked expression.

"Sorry about that." She giggled. "Your big sister has special powers."

"Whooooa!"

"I know. That's why I asked you those weird questions last summer, and had you try to lift my heavy dresser." Ivy was lost for words. "And that's why I'm not afraid to be a soldier or an officer."

"What else can you do? Can you fly?"

"No. I just have enhanced human abilities. I don't have wings."

"Are you bulletproof?"

"That's a good question. I don't know. But, I can survive a car hit, a train hit, and I can swim the Detroit River really, really fast."

"How did you get like that?"

"I don't know, Ivy. Figuring all of this out seems impossible. I don't care anymore."

"Wow. Who else did you tell?"

"No one. Just you, so far. Who else knows you're pregnant?"

Ivy ducked her head. "Just you, Amani."

"Oh Lord... So, the boy doesn't know yet." She gasped. "He's old enough to work. And I won't be working at the theater for too long after the school year. I can refer him."

"Whatever you do, please don't tell Dad! I will do anything! I swear!"

"Really... How long do you think you can hide a pregnancy?" Ivy looked dumbfounded. "Look, don't worry too much about it, Ivy. We'll get through this. Okay?"

"I don't know anything about being a mother." She cried. "Mom left before I could learn from her."

Amani consoled her little sister. "I know, Ivy. I know. You got my support."

"Thank you, Amani!" She hugged Amani back.

Height= 5' 10"
Weight= 148lbs
Vertical= 29ft
Speed= 70mph(est)
Long Jump= 0.37km

Ivy showed Amani her results of the day. She was amazed by her jumps! This was her first time maxing out her leaping abilities.

"Now, how am I going to measure your super strength?" Ivy asked.

"I'm not sure," Amani responded. "I might have to first try the weight room at the school."

"They don't have enough weight in there. You are crazy strong! I wish I was that strong."

"Trust me, you don't."

"And, what about swimming? Do you know a pool we could use without anyone being there?"

"After some thought, I was thinking about going for the river, again."

"You are crazy! Don't try that again. They have Border Patrol riding through there!"

"They won't see me swimming underwater. I did it before and it was colder then."

"That is too dangerous, Amani. What if a shark comes and bites you?"

"Girl, there are no sharks in the river! You are trippin'."

"**I'm** trippin'? What were you doing in the river, anyway?" She shook her head. "I don't know about you, Amani. You're off."

~᷍~

The next day, Amani found a chance to get to the weight room without it being occupied, but the door was locked. Coach Pratt kept gym keys around his neck. Amani tracked him down in his office, where he sat at his desk, looking at a local newspaper.

"Hi, Coach Pratt!" Amani said with a smile.

"Oh, Ms. Turner!" he said. "How can I help you?"

"I think I may have left something of mine in the weight room. Can I borrow the key to search for it?"

"Shouldn't you be in class? I don't see a hall pass."

"A hall pass? I don't need a hall pass."

Coach Pratt grinned. "Why didn't you ever play in sports? You were very impressive and you still got the body for it."

"What do you mean by that?"

"You have an athletic build like you still exercise."

"Thank you. I do, sometimes."

Amani was flattered by Coach Pratt, being that he was a handsome man. She prided herself as being a mature young lady, so compliments from an older man like Coach Pratt was greatly appreciated.

Amani didn't bother with too many boys her age. She always said the guys in school weren't mature enough for her. Coach Pratt was twenty-seven.

The coach took the key chain from around his neck and handed Amani the key to the weight room. "Don't lose these," he said. "And don't lose that figure, either."

Amani giggled as she took the keys. "I won't."

"Then, keep working it out. When you take care of your body at your young age, you'll develop into a sexy grown woman. You remind me of my ex-wife, but smarter."

Amani laughed and said, "Thank you."

Coach Pratt checked out her backside as she walked away. "Um, um, um..."

The barbells in the weight room were no challenge for Amani. She managed to get eight hundred pounds on a single bar, using four one hundred pound barbells on each side.

She laid back on the bench press and picked up the bent bar. The first three presses were easy for her. On the next two reps, she tossed the bar up in the air and caught it on its way down. The next few reps were harder for her.

Someone tried opening the door, but it was locked. Then, this person started knocking. Amani quickly put the weights back where she got them from, then opened the door. It was Coach Pratt.

Coach Pratt surveyed the room when he entered in. "Why was the door locked?"

"A force of habit," Amani said. "And I didn't want to be disturbed."

"Disturbed by who? The only person who's around is me. You weren't locking me out, were you?"

Amani blushed. "No, Coach Pratt."

Coach Pratt stepped closer to her, then he put his arm around her. "Feel free to come around whenever you need to. Okay, baby?"

Amani eased from beneath his arm, "Sure. Thanks!" She had a shy grin on her face.

"Are you eighteen, yet, Ms. Turner?"

"I will be in October." She began to leave.

"Come back around, by then." He said from afar, "I'll mark my calendar!"

Amani was all smiles, because she liked Coach Pratt. She was very impressed with herself for getting a grown man's attention. She admired him since her sophomore year. As Amani passed by the girls' locker room, she heard the familiar voice of one of her classmates. She crept closer to the door to listen through.

"For real, San!" Tila said. "Coach's thang is even bigger than Derrick's."

"What?" Sandra responded. "So he's fine **and** he's packin'?"

"Yep."

Amani was sickened by this gossip! She had no doubt that Tila was talking about Coach Pratt. He was always friendly with certain female students, but she never paid it much mind. She became embarrassed and ashamed, because of how proud she felt just moments before.

The bell rang, then students filled the hallways. Soon after, Amani's name was called from a distance while she was at her locker. It was her classmate from the first hour class, Eric James.

"Hi, Eric," Amani said. "What's up?"

"I didn't see you in Government class," said Eric.

"Yeah, I didn't feel like going today. But, I'm surprised you noticed."

"I notice you every time you're there. And I was wondering, do you have a date for the prom?"

"Actually, I didn't plan on attending the prom."

"Huh? No prom?"

"I might not pay senior dues at all."

"Why would you have to pay? What about your parents?"

"My dad is laid-off and... my mother's not with us anymore."

"Oh, I'm so sorry. I didn't know that."

"Don't sweat it. But, if in some way I do go to the prom, I'd like to be your date."

"Really? Yes! Okay, let me see what I can do to make that a reality." Amani smiled.

Ivy walked up behind Amani and sang her name out. "Amani!"

Amani turned around and introduced Ivy and Eric, then asked, "What is it, Ivy?"

"I need a favor after school."

"Then, we'll talk about it after school. Is that alright?"

"Cool. Later, Sis." She walked away.

"I didn't know you had a sister," Eric said.

Amani replied, "There's a lot that you don't know about me." She smiled again.

～～

Amani waited for Ivy outside after school was let out. Ivy caught up with her sister.

"So, what did you want to talk about?" asked Amani as they began walking.

"Can you ask to borrow Dad's car?" Ivy asked. "I've made an appointment to get checked up."

Amani carried both of their books. "Wait. You can get checked up as a minor without getting a parent involved? Sounds shady."

"It's not shady, it's legal!"

"You must have bent the truth a little."

"No I didn't! I can get help without Dad's consent, but in some cases, they can still contact a parent for medical reasons."

"Why don't you just tell Dad?"

"Why don't **you** just tell Dad about **you**?"

"Okay, Ivy, you're right. I don't tell, you don't tell."

"Another thing, I got an idea for testing your maximum strength."

"Good. What is it?"

"Truck stops. Remember when we were on the highway testing your speed? And all of those trucks were off to the side of the road?"

"Yeah, I know what a truck stop is."

"But, did you know there is a scale that they get weighed on? They sit there for a while, too."

"That sounds like a lot of trouble."

"Well, you wanted to monitor your power."

"I just want know how much of my power is muscle, as opposed to some mystical force that allows me to move things. If exercise increases my strength, then that would show pure physical power. But, if I remain just as strong, then it must be something else."

"You said you've gotten stronger in the last two and a half years."

"Yes. And I don't have bulging muscles, either. Thank goodness."

"This is so weird, Amani. But, fun at the same time!"

"It's getting better, I must say. You know, I just <u>might</u> try that truck stop thing. That would be an adventure."

"That's what I'm talking about! Bench press a truck!"

"Yeah, I'll have to catch one without a pinwheel, so it doesn't detach. Too bad Dad isn't still working at the auto plant. We would be able to test everything in there."

"We sure would! Test your speed and strength more accurately! And even do the crash test!"

"I would probably skip the crash test."

On Interstate 75 was Amani and Ivy Turner, riding in their father's sports utility vehicle, with Amani at the wheel. They had just left from the clinic for Ivy's check-up.

"I gotta use it," Ivy said. "Real bad."

Amani replied, "Alright, we'll stop at the next exit."

The girls exited the next ramp, then rode down the road to the nearest gas station. Ivy went inside and used the public restroom.

Moments later, Ivy returned to the vehicle with snacks in hand. After driving out of the parking lot and onto the street, a policeman pulled up behind them and flashed his lights for Amani to pull over.

"Why is he flickin' us?" Ivy asked.

Amani pulled over. "I don't know."

"This is some bull!"

Amani rolled down the window. "It sure is."

"Did you hear him say some prejudice stuff?"

"Nope. I don't even need to."

The policeman leaned forward, looking through the car. "I'm going to need to see your license and registration."

Amani cooperated by handing over the items requested, including insurance. "Is there something wrong? Why am I being stopped?"

The officer looked like he had a problem with Amani questioning him. Then, he sighted a clear glass bottle of ice tea in the middle console. "Is that an opened bottle of beer?" he asked.

Ivy spoke up, "Naw! This is ice tea!" She picked up the bottle. "Look at the label! Dang!"

"You're going to have to watch your attitude. I want no more out of you."

Before Ivy could talk back, Amani said, "Please excuse my sister, she's hormonal."

"What is that supposed to mean?"

"It's a pregnancy thing."

The officer sighed. "That shouldn't surprise me at all. I'll be back after I run this paperwork. Stay put."

Ivy gasped. "The nerve of that punk! You heard what he said?"

"Yep, I heard him very clear," Amani said. "And it was uncalled for."

"He's profiling us! And he didn't even give us an explanation, like we don't deserve one!"

"Prejudice bastard."

"Amani, you should beat his ass down! That's what I would do."

"Girl, please. I wouldn't go there. That would start all kinds of problems."

"<u>He</u> started it! Shoot, I would beat him to a pulp, and then snatch that camera right out the car. Actually, I wouldn't even care if they **did** see me."

Amani shook her head. "Ivy, you are going overboard. Be cool."

"Naw, you're too nice! I'm telling you, he better be glad I didn't have powers like you!"

"Why do you keep saying that? Are you envious of me?"

"Who wouldn't be? Especially after some pig insulted me for being pregnant! And that was none of his business, Amani!"

"I do apologize for that. You're right. I just figured it was a good explanation, and maybe he wouldn't give you any more hassles."

"Fuck him."

"Ivy..."

"Naw, that dude pissed me off! He gonna say-"

"I know what he said! Just calm yourself down."

"Why are you being so passive?"

Amani turned in her seat to face her sister. "Ivy, I want you to start thinking about your future. Your <u>near</u> future." She pointed at Ivy. "Months from now, you're going to be somebody's mother! Do you understand? Do you understand!"

"Yeah."

"What?"

"Yes!"

"Okay... so you're going to have to grow up quick, and I mean **real** quick. And stop acting like you grew up in 'The D' when you know good and well you're Eastpointe!"

The officer returned to the driver's side door. "Everything is clean. Here's your ticket for speeding five miles over the limit." He pointed out a section on the ticket. "If you disagree with the citation, you can call that number and set up a court date, but you must call within this number of days for a hearing. Have a good day and watch your speed."

Amani rolled up the window and took off after the cop went to his car. "Bull! I was not speeding! We just left the damn gas station!"

Ivy asked, "When did they start pulling people over for driving five over, anyway?"

"Right! Forget this, I'm going back home."

"What about the truck stop?"

"I don't even care. I'll get under this truck and press it."

"And you said that you want to get into law enforcement. Still think so?"

"Don't get me wrong, I do. It's not for being a cop, but to understand their strategies. I want to make a difference in the city, but I first need to know it from an officer's view."

"Oh, I see what you're talking about."

"But, now I got to pay this stupid ticket. We can't afford this."

"Why not fight it?"

"I will, but just in case, I will have my payment ready." Amani exited the next ramp to turn the car back around toward Detroit. "I don't want you envious or jealous of me, Ivy."

"Amani, don't you see how good you got it?" Ivy asked. "You don't have to take nothing from nobody! You're unstoppable!"

Amani hesitated to speak, but she had to share her experience. "Remember when I was gone those two days?"

"Of course I do."

"I didn't just stay away because of my new strengths. I went to Detroit to catch a rapist. I was approached by a man who was armed." She sighed. "That man touched my shoulder and I reacted, thinking he was the rapist. I saw that man die. He was an off-duty police officer."

Ivy was stunned. "Amani! You killed him?"

"It was an accident. I couldn't tell how strong I was getting. I also caused an accident that nearly killed a woman and her little girl."

"That is jacked up! I didn't know you've been through that much! Now I see why you are this way."

"This is serious business. I got to keep a leveled head and gain wisdom. I don't want to make a mistake like that ever again."

"I can't believe you killed somebody. My own sister... murdered a man."

"Ivy!"

"Sorry, Amani. I really feel bad for you."

"I'll move on. Have to forgive myself. And I'll never make that mistake again." She slows her speed. "I do try to think of ways to make up for it. The best way I can think of is stopping as much crime as I possibly can. Him being a cop, I think he would appreciate that."

Ivy nodded. "There is good and bad in your case. I'm not sure I envy you anymore, Sis."

"Good. Do you realize this is the closest we've ever been?"

Ivy thought about it. "You know what? You're right. We barely sat and talked as kids."

"You pretty much got on my nerves most of the time. But, I always had your back."

"True. You were mean, but you were right about things, most of the time."

"I think things will be better between us, now that you're coming of age." She caught Ivy rubbing her stomach. "So, Ivy, what was it like?" she asked.

"What? What are you talking about?"

"You know..." She waited for Ivy to catch on.

"Sex? Is that what you're talking about?" Amani nodded. "Well, it was like... sex! Wait, you never did it?"

"No!"

"Wow! I assumed you had, since I did. And with all those boys hitting on you?"

"I have not had sex, nor do I plan to any time soon."

"I am learning so much about you, today! What are you waiting for?"

"Uh... marriage?" She looked at Ivy crazy.

"Oh. Yeah. Well, it was good, of course."

"Good how?"

Ivy snickered at her big sister. "I can't believe this! Now, I feel like the big sister."

"Yeah, and soon you're gonna feel like the big momma."

Ivy stopped chuckling. "It felt kind of strange at first. I only liked it as much as I did, because of my feelings for Jermaine. It was everything, not just the sex. Why?"

"Just wondered. I may never get the whole true experience."

"Why not?"

"I don't feel as much as I used to. Lost a lot of sensitivity. I would hear a shoulder tap before I would feel it."

"Oh no! Is this a result of your powers?"

"Yes. I consider it a side effect."

"That is so sad, Amani. I feel for you."

"I hope that wasn't a pun. But anyway, be glad for your sensitivity. It is more important than you know."

"Okay, Amani."

"And the pain? Embrace it. It's a sign showing that you're alive. Even the pain you will feel when giving birth to your baby; be proud of that pain."

"You're a good big sister, Amani. The best I could've asked for."

"Thanks, Ivy. I'm trying."

WHAT'S LOVE GOT TO DO?

"**A**nd we're back live with the one, the only, Amani Jett," Susan Dunn says, following the commercial break. "I am pleasantly surprised at how much of a lady you are! You have a good sense of style. Very elegant."

"Thank you, Susan," Amani says.

"And you're wearing stilettos! Who saw this coming?"

Amani laughs. "Yes, I like them. They keep me on my toes."

"So, Amani, now that you're in front of the entire world, and we see how beautiful you are, one must ask; do you have a love interest? Are you single?"

Amani smiles. "Yes, I am single. And no, I'm not seeing anyone at this time. As you can imagine."

"I have been wondering since I've been sitting here with you. For the men who knew who you were; are they intimidated by you?"

"Most definitely. But, who can really blame them? You're taught to be the protector of the family, and the one who's supposed to do the heavy work.

"How emasculating must it be to have a woman protect you and do most of the heavy lifting? We see it as ego, but it's awkward for them, considering their upbringing."

"So, you can even think like a man."

Amani giggles. "I was raised by my dad. He taught me a lot. I lost my mother when I was eight, to a plane crash."

"Oh, I'm so sorry to hear that."

"Yeah. My dad and aunt did a good job in place of my mother."

"Wait a minute, so... the renowned rescue of Flight 514. That had to be an epic moment for you, aside from the obvious reasons."

"Susan, when I managed to prevent that jet from crashing, I wasn't sure how I was doing it. I just reacted.

"I saw the nose of the plane pointed toward the ground at high speed, so I flew as fast as I could. I swear I had never flown that fast before in my life!

"I wasn't sure if I was strong enough to push the front end of the plane up like that. But, I had to try.

"And after it all... when I saw the landing gear touch the ground... I cried my heart out. I've never been so thankful for having such a gift. I looked up and said, 'Mom, that's for you.'"

Susan says, "You didn't stick around long after that, did you?"

"No, and I wasn't trying to be rude, but I wasn't ready for so much publicity. Or, for my identity being widely exposed just yet."

"It must have been difficult trying to live a normal life, while being a super shero. Do you have time for relationships?"

"Since I went nationwide, no I don't. I'm over with trying to live a normal life. I accept me as I am. No longer a freak of nature, but a real woman with a different objective."

"Well put. What are your powers, exactly?"

"I have enhanced human attributes, meaning, super strength and speed. I can jump extremely high and far.

"Acute super hearing. 20/4 vision, when focused. I have an ability that I call, 'x-ray discernment', where I can determine what is behind matter by the combination of sight and sound."

Susan covers her chest with her arm. "So you're saying you can see me sitting here naked?" They laugh together.

"Basically, when you move, I can figure out your bra size and type. Even the weight, after a while. I can't tell you what color it is."

"Very interesting. But, I know you wouldn't peek." Amani shakes her head, laughing. "And what else can you do, besides stripping us naked?"

"High current, close-range freezing with the

blowing of my breath. I rarely use that."

"Can I see you do that?"

"Sure. It only works within about three feet away. The closer, the more efficient."

Susan summons a glass of warm water, which an assistant brings on a tray in front of Amani. Amani leans in a foot away from the glass of water and blows. The water crystallizes into ice and the glass is coated in frost.

"Amazing!" Susan says. "I want you to zoom in on this, Mark." The camera zooms in. "This is solid ice!" She takes her pen and taps the ice in the frozen glass. "So, you never have to request ice for your beverage," she says to Amani with a smile.

"Haven't done it in years," Amani says. "I can also swim very fast, but I need more practice. And last, but definitely not least, I can fly."

"That may be the most enviable ability you have. What is it like?"

"Feeling free. Blessed, in spite of the challenges I face ahead of me. I rise."

~~

Back into Amani's high school days; A parked SUV went up and down, with the sound of Amani's voice grunting beneath it. Ivy stood there and watched with a pencil and notepad in her hands.

"That's twice!" Ivy cheered. "Curb weight of 3,935 pounds pressed two times! Oh my God!"

Amani slid from underneath her dad's SUV, wearing gloves to prevent her hands from getting filthy. She was short of breath.

"Looks like a truck would've been too much, after all," Amani said. "I'm pretty exhausted." She sat up against the vehicle.

"Do you have any idea how cool this is?" Ivy asked. "You're a beast! Who can stand against you?"

"I really don't want to get a big head out of this. That would be my first mistake."

"Amani, you worry too much."

"You're not careful." Ivy frowned. "So, when are you going to tell Auntie Eva about your pregnancy, since you're so afraid to tell Dad?"

"I was going to talk to her tomorrow. I'll be at her house all weekend. Did you tell Daddy about the ticket?"

"What for? I got enough money to pay it."

"I thought you were going to fight it."

"If I do that, then they'll send a letter in the mail for a court hearing. He might see it."

"Aha! You're afraid of letting Dad know!"

"I don't want him involved. And who's going to drive you to your appointments if he doesn't let me drive his truck after that?"

"I guess you're right. Can you hear what he's doing in there?"

Amani stood to her feet. "He's almost done with dinner."

"Good! I'm hungry." She paused. "So, you are going to the prom?"

"It looks that way. Eric was able to pull some strings and get me in."

"Wow, he must really like you! And wants you. What do you think?"

"He's a guy."

"So, do you plan to..."

"I'm afraid to have sex. I think I might hurt him." Ivy laughed. "I'm serious. What if I get carried away and sever his... you-know-what?"

Ivy laughed harder, then thought about it. "That **would** be messed up, though. And I can't say it's not possible. Dang, girl!"

"I've been reading up on the muscles of the pelvic floor-"

"How is that going to help, Amani? You need you some experience! Like a toy or something."

"Ivy!" She put her hands on her hips. "How do you know about all of this nasty stuff?"

"Because, I pay attention. And... I used to snoop around in Auntie Eva's drawers back in the day. Old women like to use those things."

"I should've known! You were the most snoopiest kid ever! Always up in my room, and apparently, always nosing around in other people's stuff, too!"

"True. You ain't lying. But, I stopped that a long time ago."

~⁓

In the next hour, the family sat at the dinner table. Mr. Turner glanced at Amani, making it obvious that he wanted to speak on something.

"What is it, Dad?" Amani asked.

Mr. Turner sat his fork down, then wiped his mouth with his napkin. "What made you decide to consider those career choices?"

"The nature of the job."

"Oh really? So, carrying a gun is your dream? Or, is being tough your dream?" Amani didn't answer. "Because, it's clear to me that being told what to do isn't your dream, if it's me giving the orders. No, you want to follow the orders of a man who tells you to arrest and kill, but doing what I say is nonnegotiable!"

"Dad, you raised us to be independent thinkers. But, every time we make a decision for ourselves, you have a problem with it."

"No, I have a problem with the poor decisions that you make. You are not fit for that line of work, nor does it do you any good to take on battles that are not your own!"

"That's where you're wrong, Dad!"

"You can't even handle it when your nails get dirty! You quit competing in sports!"

Ivy interjected. "Amani, why are you letting this go on and on? Just tell Daddy what's up." Amani didn't respond.

"What are you talking about, Ivy?" He faced Amani. "What is she talking about?"

"Nothing." Amani said.

"Something's going on between you two. What is it?" Amani and Ivy just looked at each other. "Okay, there's going to have to be something done about this."

Ivy huffed and said, "It's not a big deal! Tell him, Amani! If you don't tell, I will."

Then, Amani said, "Alright, then." She pointed at her sister. "Ivy is pregnant."

Both Ivy and Mr. Turner were stunned! Mr. Turner faced Ivy. She looked away shamefully. It was confirmed.

Mr. Turner leaned his head back and looked to the heavens. "Where did I go wrong? I failed you, Rosie." Ivy sat there teary-eyed.

"Dad!" Amani shouted. "That is so wrong!"

Mr. Turner sat forward. "It's the truth! This is not what I raised you two to be! As hard as I tried, nothing helped!

"I tried being strict, I tried giving you some room, I taught you everything!"

Ivy said, "Amani has powers! She's just too afraid to tell you! That's why she wants to be a cop and-"

"Go to your room!" Mr. Turner yelled to Ivy. "I can't believe you! You'll say anything to get out of this! And I want to know who this boy is!" Ivy left the table and went upstairs crying.

Amani battled with herself for keeping the secret from her father. It caused a lot of pain and damage to their relationship. At that point, she had to determine which was more important.

"I can handle this, Dad," Amani said.

"How long did you know?" Mr. Turner asked.

"A few weeks, now. You know, Dad, when you get excited, you get overly emotional, and then you start calling out to Momma. That hurts us, Dad.

"Then, we feel worse about ourselves than we ought to. We don't feel that we can come to you about anything. Anything!

"You go off on us, and then you send us to our rooms. I know that being a single parent is hard on you, but you're going to have to find a way to stand in for Mom's tenderness, just like single mothers do for toughness when the dads aren't around."

"Amani... I don't know how to make it without your mother," Mr. Turner said.

"Then, learn. And please listen to us. As crazy as it sounded, Ivy was telling you the truth."

"About what?"

"About me. Let's go outside."

THE SKEPTIC

Amani and her father were standing in the driveway next to his sports utility vehicle. She listened and looked around for any potential witnesses, making sure no one was there to see what she was about to do.

"What magic trick are you about to show me?" Mr. Turner asked.

"No magic trick," Amani said. "Power. As a matter of fact, I'll let you decide what you want me to do, then I'll do it."

"Show me your super go-to-college and not-the-police-force powers."

"Come on, Dad!"

"Alright. Lift my truck."

"How high?"

"Oh, lord... About two feet." Amani went to the front of the truck and lifted it at approximately two feet, then sat it back down. "You must've hidden a jack under there or something. I'm nobody's fool."

"What? Okay, give me something else to do."

Mr. Turner looked side-to-side. "Jump over this truck."

"I don't even need a running start for that." She hop-stepped and jumped right over the SUV with a spiral flip.

Mr. Turner walked to the front of the car and looked for a spring. "Do that again. I'm gonna watch you this time." He stood next to the spot where Amani took her leap. "Let me look at your shoes."

"I'll do it barefooted! This is easy." She kicked off her shoes, went right back to the previous spot, and did it again.

Mr. Turner scratched his head. "Maybe you... Naw!" He pressed the ground with his foot on the spot where Amani jumped. "Girl, I don't know how you did it, but that's some good athleticism."

"Dad, why don't you believe me? Okay then, walk away from me. Far away." Her father did so. "Now, whisper something!" Mr. Turner turned around and whispered as quietly as he could. "You just told me, I better get my butt in school!" she shouted.

"How did you... You put a microphone on me? Am I wired?"

"Of course not!"

"Don't you toy with me, young lady!"

"I'm not toying with you! Check your clothes!"

Mr. Turner patted himself down and thoroughly checked his collar. He found nothing. "Well, you knew I would say that!"

"Dad, you're more unbelievable than I am." She went and turned on the water hose. "Come here, please." Her father came to her. "Cup your hands together, like you're about drink."

Mr. Turner put his hands together as Amani poured water into his hands. After turning the water off, she blew a cold breeze into the water. When the water became too cold, Mr. Turner dropped the handful of slushy water and witnessed the results on the ground.

This was enough to convince him that there was something unique about his oldest daughter, Amani. He stood there wide-eyed and speechless. Ivy was telling the truth.

"Do you believe me now?" Amani asked.

Mr. Turner, bewildered, said, "Get in the house."

Amani, Ivy, and their father were sitting in the living room having a family meeting. Mr. Turner still had a concerned expression on his face.

"Your mother never showed any signs of... gifts like you have," Mr. Turner said. "She would've more than likely survived the plane crash."

Ivy said to her father, "You wrongly accused me of lying about this."

"You're still in trouble, Ivy!"

Amani asked, "Now do you see why I chose this path?"

"Amani, there are still other things you can be."

"Like what?"

"A magician?" Amani sighed. "Well, why not an entertainer?" Amani shook her head. "Well, if you really want to help, be a private eye."

"No, Dad, I need to learn protocol. I will be working with law enforcement, so it would help if I knew how they operated; same with the military."

"I do not approve of it!"

"I'm doing it anyway. It's my choice."

"You're still my daughter. Don't you forget that. I don't care if you could flip the car over-"

"I can, actually."

Mr. Turner was shocked. "I'm still Daddy!" He faced Ivy. "And you have a lot of explaining to do. Who is this boy?"

"His name is Jermaine," Ivy said.

Mr. Turner huffed. "Does this kid have a job, since he's out here making babies?"

"He's unemployed just like you."

Before Mr. Turner could explode, Amani cut in. "I plan for him to replace me at my current job."

"I can't believe this!" Mr. Turner shouted. "What else is going on?"

"I'm going to the prom, next month. And after I turn eighteen, I'll change my name."

Mr. Turner grabbed his chest and started faking a heart attack. "Oh my God... Oh my God..."

Ivy yelled, "Dad! Help him, Amani!"

Amani calmly said, "He is <u>not</u> having a heart attack. I would know it."

Mr. Turner stopped faking, then he sat up in his recliner chair. Ivy was disgusted at him.

Amani continued, "Dad, I'm going to need you to trust me. You've done an excellent job with us, believe it or not. Please don't stress yourself out." Her father had nothing to say. "We can work out all of this. It's not the end of the world."

"I need your help," Mr. Turner said to Amani. "I need you to take out that old stove in the basement and set it just outside the door. I'll take it from there."

Amani complained, "Dad, ever since I told you about my powers, you've been putting me to work. You always need my help with something."

"I see you still have a problem with taking orders from <u>me</u>. What do you think lies ahead of you? And with your strength, you shouldn't be complaining at all."

"I just feel like you're taking advantage of me."

"If I had a son, who would normally have the strength to do chores such as this, I would have treated him just the same. How would he look, complaining about hard work?" Amani had a smirk on her face. "Amani, no matter what or who you become, remember that it all started at home. If you can't take care of home, then you will get no loyalty elsewhere. Always remember where you came from."

"Yes, Dad."

Amani did what she was told to do by her father. She easily carried the old stove up the stairs and put it outside of the back door. In order to make the stove to fit through the exit, she removed the door after pulling the hinges out by hand.

Since the coast was clear with no one around, Amani carried the stove to the side of the house. Then, she heard a familiar voice from a far distance. She walked to the front of the house and looked down the street.

"Joanie!" Amani yelled.

Her best friend was back home from the university, which is located in Ann Arbor, MI, after the semester had ended for her. Amani went down the street to greet Joanie.

"Amani!" Joanie shouted when she spotted her. She went down her porch steps and hugged Amani tightly. "It's so good to see you!"

"Yes it is!" Amani replied.

"Look!" Joanie showed off the ring on her left hand. "I'm engaged!"

"Really? Oh my... well. Congratulations!" They embraced again. "What a big surprise!"

"I know! And he is so wonderful! He knocks me off my feet!"

"I'm so happy for you, Joanie!" She waved at Joanie's parents, then asked her, "They don't still think that I use steroids, do they?"

Joanie laughed. "No. They know it was a misunderstanding. Let's hang out later, if you're not too busy."

"Sure. I'm free."

Amani and Joanie ate in a diner that evening, then slurped on some milkshakes.

"I know you can't wait for next week," said Joanie. "I'll never forget my prom night."

Amani replied, "I already have my dress. His dad will be renting a sports car for us. I don't remember which one, but it's the hyped up car that everyone is talking about."

"Sounds expensive. That's awesome!"

"Yeah, but I'm not so excited about it. He went so far out of his way to make this happen, but I hope I won't mess it up for him."

"How? You're not saying you're not willing to, umm... you know."

"No, I'm not sure I want to sleep with him. It's almost a definite no."

"Why not? You're not attracted to him?"

"I'm very attracted to him. But, I'm lacking feelings. I hope that explains enough."

Joanie pondered. "You want love, I think. That's a good thing. That's what I have."

"Exactly. I want something more than just the physical contact. That won't be enough for me."

Joanie's face gleamed with enthusiasm. "I know just the thing for you! There's this book you need to read. It's actually a whole series called the Kama Sutra!

"I swear, it's the greatest piece of literature you will ever read! I have learned so much, Amani. Did you know that you can reach an orgasm without being touched?"

"A wet dream?"

"No, you don't have to be asleep. There's so much to the human body, you would be surprised! I've even taken up yoga classes."

"All of this while you were in college?"

"You know me, I'm just like you. I'm a study-holic! I hardly sleep, but with yoga, I am well rested and balanced."

"The only thing I see when people do that yoga stuff is them sitting down and doing nothing with their legs twisted all up."

"No, Amani, it's mostly mental. That's what you're looking for, mental stimulation. I'm going to show you the good stuff I've been learning."

"Okay. I'm willing to try it out."

"Cool! They have floating yoga classes in Grosse Pointe. That's a different type of yoga, where either you're on water or hanging on slings."

"That sounds interesting. Have you done the hands-free orgasm thingy?"

"Not quite hands-free, but the slightest touch did it for me. Tantric sex is wonderful!"

"I've got to get that book."

For the next few days until prom night, Amani practiced floating yoga with Joanie. It put her in focus of her mind and body. Her best friend was right! She eventually made it a morning ritual, with sun salutations.

Her readings of the Kama Sutra made her blush, but she didn't feel she was ready to use any of that knowledge, yet.

The day of the prom was also Ivy's fifteenth birthday. Instead of the usual cake and ice cream, there was something else on her mind; telling Jermaine about their unborn child.

On this day, Amani was at the hair salon, getting her look together for the night. She had already bought her dress, shoes, and accessories two weeks before.

Her hair stylist asked, "What do you treat your ends with? They never split."

"I don't use chemicals often, if at all, but I do use low heat."

"You're just blessed with good genes."

"Aren't we all?"

"Please, I make a living off of bad hair. I've seen enough toothless combs to know that there is a such thing as bad hair."

Suddenly, Amani received an incoming call on her cellphone. "What's up, Ivy?"

Ivy said, "I'm about to let loose on this woman! You need to come take care of this! I am so pissed right now!"

"Who are you talking about?"

"Jermaine's momma!"

"What? Girl, I'm at the salon, getting ready for the prom. I don't have time for that."

"You don't have time for your sister? Your niece or nephew? You're supposed to have my back!"

"First of all, calm yourself down. Don't make this between me and you. Now, tell me what happened."

"Okay, I told Jermaine about the baby. I finally did it, right? Why is this boy telling me, 'I want a DNA test just to make sure'?

"I ain't been messing around with nobody else! He's treating me like a hoodrat all of a sudden!"

"Ivy, he's trying to avoid facing the fact that he messed up, along with you. These are things that Daddy warned us about. Now you see."

"But wait, listen to this; His momma gets herself involved in the conversation. She was calling me all types of liars, talking about, 'I taught my son better than that!'

"She was talking more crap than he was! We almost got into a fistfight right there on the spot! Why can't she let him fight his own battles?"

"I don't know, Ivy, but I'm going to let you fight this one out yourself."

"Why are you leaving me hanging?"

"Ivy, what do you want me to do? Punch a hole through her? That is some ghetto hot mess that I'm not willing to participate in."

Ivy grunted, "Oh well, then, I guess I can't call on you for help. Go ahead and get all diva'd up for your little prom. Maybe you'll finally get lucky and find yourself in the position I'm in. Bye!" She hung up.

Amani thought out loud, "No that little girl didn't just hang up on me!"

The hair stylist said, "Uh oh..."

"You know what... I'm going to be cool, calm, and enjoy this wonderful day. I'll let her deal with her own garbage. That'll be retribution for me, and a lesson for her."

"Must be talking about family, huh?"

"Yeah, my little sister- Baby daddy drama. She turned fifteen today." The stylist sighed. "I know. And if things weren't stressful enough on my dad already."

Then the stylist said, "Well, whatever you do, love that girl the same. The last thing she needs to feel is abandonment. Believe me, I know. I was sixteen when I had my first."

Hours later, Amani was dressed and ready for her Senior Prom. It was intended to be a dual celebration between her prom and Ivy's birthday. Unfortunately, Ivy's confrontation with her child's father ruined the occasion for her.

Amani didn't let that get to her. She posed for pictures taken by her aunt Eva, who had demanded Ivy to take some pictures with her older sister. Reluctantly, she obliged.

Eric James, Amani's date for the evening, drove up in the flashy red convertible sports car. Mr. Turner gave him the watchful eye the entire time he was there.

After Eric pinned the corsage on Amani's dress, Mr. Turner took him aside for a short talk. Amani and the family knew what that was all about. Mr. Turner was giving Eric his warnings.

The senior prom took place at a luxurious banquet hall. Amani and Eric enjoyed their time spent together, with food and dancing. The two mingled with their friends and classmates.

Eric said to Amani, "Let's get out of here in a half an hour. That will leave us more time to get acquainted." Amani agreed.

They left out as planned, having until midnight for Amani to return home, in respect of Mr. Turner's demand. Eric was a very entertaining date with his vibrant humor and radiant charm.

They parlayed near the river at Chene Park, watching the water brush against the rocks by the dock. The winds blew lightly and steadily, the moonlight shined brightly. This is where Amani and Eric shared their first kiss.

The time was getting closer to midnight and Eric had an idea. "Want to drive the hot rod?" he asked. "Since you said you know how to drive a stick shift."

"Yes I do," Amani said with assurance. "I'll show you how to drive stick like a real pro."

"Is that right? Show me, then." He gave Amani the keys.

Amani took the driver's seat. She was not foreign to the manual transmission, thanks to her dad teaching her at a younger age. She peeled off and shifted like a seasoned driver. Eric was impressed. He let the top down while she drove up the street.

"Have you ever driven a car like this?" Eric asked. "This bad boy can go up to 200mph."

"No way," Amani said, "I already got a speeding ticket last week, so we won't be seeing anything close to that with me behind the wheel." They laughed together.

With the traffic being heavy, Eric advised Amani to take a different route. He didn't want to risk getting her back home too late. Amani was thinking that she could probably get home a lot faster by running. Of course that was not an option.

Once they arrived at a stoplight, Amani heard something suspicious. Footsteps were getting closer to the car. She heeded a man's heavy, nervous breathing. With these components, Amani foresaw an attempted car-jacking. She was not going to allowing him to be successful.

"Get out the car!" the car-jacker hollered with his gun pointed. "Hurry up, bitch!"

Here are the mistakes he made:

1. Car-jacking a vehicle with Amani in it.

2. Interrupting Amani's happy moment.

3. Calling Amani out of her name.

4. Choosing the B-word as the name to call Amani out of.

Amani was furious! She pushed the car door so hard, that it knocked the car-jacker on his back, causing him to skid across the asphalt yards away.

The gun went off at the point of impact with the swinging car door, causing the bullet to hit Amani's shoulder when the gun fired, but she was too angry to realize it at this point. It bounced right off of her! There wasn't a scratch on Amani's arm.

She rushed to the fallen gunman without using her super speed. When the criminal had regained his focus, he tried to aim the barrel at Amani again, but this time, Amani kicked the gun out of his hand.

Amani grabbed the man by his jaw. "Next time you fix your mouth to address a woman by that word, remember this!"

She snapped his jaw sideways. He yelled in agonizing pain, but she felt no remorse for him and considered her actions justified.

Eric walked up behind Amani with a gun in his hand. "Watch out, Amani."

Amani turned around and was surprised to see Eric armed. "What are you doing with that?"

"Move out the way. I'm about to blast this muthafucka."

"Eric! Are you crazy? Where did you get that gun from?"

This was not the gun that the car-jacker had. It was hidden in the sports car the whole time. Eric tried to move Amani out of his way, but she resisted. He couldn't move her one centimeter.

"Move, Amani!" Eric shouted.

Amani just stood there with her arms folded. "You are not about to commit murder, Eric. I won't let you. Don't ruin your future over this punk."

"What are you talking about? You want to let him right back out on the streets, so he could rob somebody else?"

"Call the police. But first, put away that gun." The car-jacker squirmed, then Amani pinned her foot down on him. "He's not going anywhere." She could easily puncture him with her high heel, but that's not her style.

Eric started to wonder how Amani out-muscled the man. He looked over and saw the man's mouth disfigured, but assumed it was from his fall. The car that the crook drove up to them with was apparently stolen. It sat in the middle of the street with the engine still running.

Headlights shined on the three from down the street. Eric tucked his gun under his belt and covered it with his tuxedo jacket.

"Let's go," Eric said.

Amani responded, "Huh? I thought we were going to get him arrested. He dropped his gun over there." She pointed to where the gun landed.

The car got closer and slowed down. It was only someone passing by. Eric was hoping that it wasn't the police. He pinpointed the dropped gun and picked it up with his silk handkerchief. When inspecting the weapon, he saw that it was loaded, not including the one shot that was fired.

"We should run his ass over," Eric said. "Give me the keys. I got to get you home."

Amani did so, then walked back to the rental car. Before heading toward the driver's seat, Eric pinned down the thief and pistol-whipped him.

"Eric!" Amani screamed. "Stop it!" One more hit and Eric was finished. Another car rode down the street, so Eric got back in the car and pulled off.

Amani asked, "Is he still alive?"

"Yeah, you saved his life after he tried to shoot you." He shook his head. "I don't get it. You actually have compassion for somebody who was willing to take your life for a damn car. Women."

Amani saw it differently, because she was never startled or intimidated by the level of danger. She began wondering more about Eric. How was he able to pay for her prom access? Why did he have a gun? Had he ever used it before?

Amani asked Eric while he was taking her home, "What does your dad do? This is an expensive car to rent."

Eric snickered. "My pops is a street pharmacist."

Amani thought for a second, then asked, "You mean a drug dealer?"

"Yeah, he's been in the game for a long time. If it was him in that situation back there, dude would've been killed. My dad doesn't mess around."

Amani was very disappointed and began to see Eric differently. He was a potential good guy, but was surrounded by darkness. This is the same story for many young men in the inner city. Eric, however, lived in Eastpointe with his mother.

"We're twenty minutes late," Eric said. "I really wanted to make a better impression on your father. This went bad."

"Don't worry about it," Amani said. "Good night."

Amani hugged Eric instead of kissing him, which he easily took notice of. Amani could tell he was disappointed in himself, but she felt that consoling him would have been misleading. She waved goodbye before going inside of her home.

As expected, Mr. Turner was waiting for Amani's arrival. He looked at the clock and saw the minute hand between the 4 and the 5.

Amani said, "Daddy, before you get too upset, we did not have sex. Of any kind."

"Then, I have no concern," Mr. Turner said in response.

"For real? That's all you were worried about? Me having sex?"

"Yep. Think about it." Amani realized there weren't many things that would threaten her safety. "In a few months, you will be old enough to go out and take care of yourself.

"My only concern is that you conduct yourself as the person that your mother and I hoped for you to be and not go by everyone else's standards.

"And please, talk to your sister. She needs you. I understand this was your prom night, but this was a special day for her, too.

"That nonsense with that boy and his ghetto momma should not have determined the outcome of her day. Be there for her."

"Okay, Dad," Amani said. "Good night."

Amani opened Ivy's door to see if she was asleep. Ivy was in bed, but wide awake eating ice cream, potato chips, and a banana.

"You are so... pregnant," Amani said. "Ivy, I do care about you. I just don't want to be a part of unnecessary drama. There are some things you got to experience on your own.

"And I want you to realize that when you get into these altercations, I don't want you getting extra hostile because you have a super sister. Do you know what I mean?

"I'm just asking that you think before you react. There may be times that I can't come to your rescue, so you're going to have to be wise and self-aware. Don't be too dependent on me, is what I'm saying."

Ivy replied, "Yeah, yeah, I got it. So anyway, did you get laid or not?"

Amani laughed. "No I didn't. And I'm okay with that."

"I wish I would've waited."

"I know, but you must move on. I'll help as much as I can. Just not fighting with baby's daddy's mommas." They both laughed.

Amani showered, then went into her bedroom. She reflected on the unforgettable, adventurous night she had with Eric. The good and the bad. She turned off her lamp and laid beneath the sheets.

Suddenly, Amani popped up in bed. "Hey! That man shot me!" Yes, she's bullet-proof.

Susan Dunn's TV interview of Amani Jett continues. "Most rumors that were spread about you, you deny. The source of your power, your background, the speculations of you being an extraterrestrial, and the list goes on. It is good that you're setting the record straight on this."

Amani replies, "Which is why addressing these topics are so necessary. I hope the clarifications will make people think twice about what others say and what they believe about me."

"I understand that you started your duties as a legitimate police officer in Detroit. What was that like?"

"It was educational. I learned a lot about the city and the law. I couldn't be who I am today without that experience.

"You'd be surprised at what goes on in a big city that is struck by poverty and crime. Being a Detroit Police Officer isn't a job for anyone who can pass a physical test. It can be emotionally draining."

"How long were you in the force?"

"Just over a year."

"Was it difficult gaining respect as a female police officer? Better yet, did you face any discrimination in the force?"

"Not from my fellow officers or my superiors. We were all like family, even to this day. As a matter of fact, we had our first female police chief during my days in blue.

"But, civilians? They showed less respect for women in uniform. The ones up to no good, that is."

"I can imagine, Ms. Jett. What made you leave? Did you just think it was time?"

"Soon after the Iraq War had started, that's when I decided to introduce myself to the Secretary of Defense, so I left my position."

❧ ❧

The year was 2003. Rookie police officer, Amani Jett, rode in the police car with her partner, Julio Vega. They received a radio message for a domestic dispute, then took the call.

When they pulled up to the scene, Amani didn't hear anything coming from the house, except for a child crying and TV playing in the background. Both officers noticed a lady briefly looking through the front window.

Officer Vega knocked on the door. "Police!"

The lady opened the door, airing out a putrid stench coming from inside the house. The two officers immediately covered their noses from the smell of crack cocaine mixed with death.

The lady answering the door was frantic. "I called, but it was too late! I had to do it!"

"Do what?" Officer Vega asked.

Amani looked past the nervous woman and saw the dead body of a man. Blood was everywhere and the crying child was there to witness his murder. Amani rushed to get the child out of the house.

The female suspect, who was high on crack, kept explaining. "H-He said he was going to kill me! He hit me in the face! Hit me so hard!"

Officer Vega spotted the rifle that the lady used to kill the man on the floor, then he immediately handcuffed her and called in his report. The lady pleaded, but she was being taken to the precinct, regardless.

The lady cried out, "What about my baby?"

More officers arrived at the scene to assist. "What's the news, rookie?" One of the officers asked Amani.

"I got my first year in, Sergeant Spencer," Amani responded with the kid held in her arms. "I'm no rookie."

"Still a rookie to me, and the academy doesn't count." He chuckled. "I say you are, because you're still not used to the job. You haven't acquired that tough skin, yet. You're as soft as they come."

"If having a heart for children like this is what defines a rookie, then I'll gladly accept the title."

Sergeant Spencer stepped closer to her and lowered his tone. "We all have a heart, Jett. It's just how you do your job that concerns me. Have you inspected the house?"

"I didn't do a walk-through, but I am for certain that no one else was inside. Vega's not in danger."

Sergeant Spencer and his partner gasped. "So you are for certain it was clear without checking," he said sarcastically. "We don't do hunches in this police force, officer, so you should do your duty and survey the home. Or would you rather babysit?"

Amani kept secret of her ability to scan moving objects beyond matter. She found no need to physically walk through the house.

Later that day, Amani and her partner were out on patrol again. Amani was clearly perturbed about the last situation.

"It's good that you care," Officer Vega said, "but you can't let every case beat you down. You've been here long enough to deal with this better. You've seen dead bodies before."

Amani replied, "It's not that, Julio. I feel limited. I hate this feeling."

"Then, what do you think is holding you back?"

"The very law that we represent. I mean, don't you see what's going on?

"Drug deals are made daily, Julio! Right under our noses! We know who the bad guys are, but we got to stay within our boundaries. We need search warrants, even though it is obvious who's selling and who's using."

"Amani, you know the format and, by now, you should know why you can't just go and start wars. It's reckless. Innocent people get hurt."

"But, they already started the war!"

"Look, none of us like it! But, we believe in our justice system. You, on the other hand, don't seem to believe in it."

"Maybe I don't."

"You are young. Very young. I have a niece your age. She's ambitious like you. Very emotional, yet fragile.

"But, this job requires cold steel veins. When you work in enemy territory, you adapt. It's not going to change for you, chica.

"So, get it together. You have unbelievable talent. I've never seen anyone hit targets like you, run like you, or take down bad guys like you do.

"If only you could harden up, like Jacobs and Haggler. Those two women are rough! That type of attitude with your talent would make one hell of a police officer."

An incoming radio message from dispatch gave warning of officers caught under fire in a nearby district. Julio and Amani took the call.

When they made it to their designation, Amani heard gunfire. "Let me out right here," she said.

"No way," Officer Vega replied.

"Let me out right now, dammit!"

"What are you trying to-"

"Pull over!"

Julio never heard Amani yell in that tone before. Not even toward the criminals. The glare in her eyes was piercing.

He pulled over and let Amani out. "Fine. Get out." He shook his head, then looked back toward her, but she was gone. He turned in his seat and faced every direction, but could not find Amani.

Officer Vega almost reported Amani's leave and requested more backup, but he chose to trust her and give her a chance.

Amani zoomed through the alley to the area where she heard the shooting, which was at a house near the middle of the block. Amani went to the back fence at the rear of the house where there were three armed men. Two were on the bottom back porch and one on the upper back porch. Most of the shooting took place in the front of the house.

Amani's strategy was to ambush the shooters from the back. Parked in the alley at the rear of the house was a police car with its lights flickering. Shielded behind this vehicle were Officers Spencer and Willis, who both were under fire and low on ammo at the moment.

The thugs guarding this suspected drug house were all armed with assault rifles. Amani poised herself behind the garage of the house next door to the house. She peeked over the corner and located one of the two armed thugs on the bottom porch.

Without much hesitation, Amani whipped out her pistol and shot him down with one shot. Her aim was precise. The recoil was no problem for her. Bullets came flying Amani's way, but she was not fazed.

With this distraction, Sergeant Spencer was able to get his last few shots in, while the two remaining thugs took cover. Since Spencer ran out of bullets, Amani tossed her gun to him.

"Are you crazy?" Sergeant Spencer asked.

Amani replied, "You can say that." More shots were fired by the enemies. "Just don't call me a rookie after this. Cover me!"

"You're insane!"

Another bad guy came out onto the top porch and threw a Molotov cocktail at the police car. Out of reflexes, Amani dashed for the bottle, caught it, then threw it back at the upper porch. The porch caught fire, then the two thugs ran back inside.

All who were left at the rear of the house was the other gunman on the bottom porch. Sgt. Spencer gave Amani cover fire as she approached him.

The gunman was behind a brick pillar of the house. Amani crept to one side of the pillar and the gunman heard her. He pointed his rifle around the edge and saw no one there. Sergeant Spencer fired at the exposed gunman, but missed him by a few inches.

Amani made her way to the opposite side of the pillar without the gunman knowing it. She crossed over to the side adjacent of the shooter and executed a hooked reverse heel kick behind her back. This knocked the gunman out cold.

Amani signaled to her fellow officers that the coast was clear. The two cops grabbed the rifles of the fallen criminals on the back porch.

Officer Spencer handed Amani her gun back. "Good work, officer! Damn good work!"

As Sergeant Spencer and his partner charged in through the back door, Amani slowly stepped back onto the lawn. She looked up at the flaming porch, then vertically leaped to the top. Then, she took two steps and kicked the door in.

Inside were drugs, money, and ammo shells. The first gunman who was nested on the upper porch ran in from the front and saw Amani standing before the burning fire.

The crook immediately starting firing his weapon, but Amani ran across with super speed, dodging the bullets until she got close to him. She yanked the assault rifle away from him and tossed it aside.

Another police car pulled up to the back alley. Once the cops exited the car and faced the house, they heard a man yelling as he fell from the top porch down to the lawn; a result of Amani tossing him through the upper exit. The officers in pursuit looked at each other, wondering how it happened.

Back inside, Amani took on two more bad guys with her bare hands. These thugs were no match for her combination of strength, speed, and fighting skills. After knocking out one criminal with a kick to the head, Amani rammed the other man through the plaster wall, leading into the next room.

Amani rose up and saw none other than her high school prom date, Eric James! He had two armed men with him who were shooting through the front windows.

Eric turned completely around after hearing the crash. "Amani?" He wore expensive jewelry and had tattoos on his neck. His pearly whites were replaced with gold fronts. This was not the same Eric James that Amani remembered from high school.

Amani couldn't believe it! "Eric?"

Eric saw her dressed in police uniform, powdered from busted plaster. His look became grim. Amani took steps back away from her former friend. Eric stood to his feet, then raised his gun to shoot.

Amani jumped backwards through the hole in the wall that she created, then rolled off to the side to avoid direct combat with Eric. She was saddened by the sight of Eric at this stage. It was clear that his father's ways had rubbed off on him.

"Come on out, Amani!" Eric demanded. "So, you work for the man, now? You're here to arrest me? After I helped you back in high school?"

Amani looked perplexed. "I didn't save you? Who knocked out the car-jacker?"

"Fuck that! Bring your pretty ass out here, girl!"

"The house is surrounded, Eric. Give up!"

"Nah. I ain't the submitting type, baby."

"Policemen have raided the first floor! They are on their way up the stairs right now! And your gunmen are being stalled!"

"I don't care! I'm going out fighting!"

"For what? Dirty money? Why are you being so ornery? "

"Fuck all this talk. Fellas! Take that wall out."

Amani distanced herself from the wall, while the two men fired as they were commanded. They kept shooting until their magazine clips were empty, then Eric stood there quietly, listening for sounds coming from the next room. He heard nothing.

Eric called out, "Amani..."

Suddenly, shots came through the wall! The piercing bullets hit one of Eric's gunmen head on, killing him instantly. Apparently, Amani got a hold of one of the assault rifles from one of the beaten thugs from the other room.

Eric tried to stall Amani. "That was a lucky shot, baby!" His remaining henchman began to reload his gun. His movement gave away his exact position, how he sat, and how he was holding his weapon. More straight bullets penetrated from beyond the wall. The second henchman; terminated.

"Damn!" Eric shouted. "How the hell? You just killed my boys!"

"Eric," Amani said peacefully. "Stop it."

"I ain't going out like that! I'm gangsta bred!" He put his pistol to his head. "See you in h-" Before he could pull the trigger on himself, Amani shot the gun out of his hand from behind the wall, breaking his index finger in the process. He screamed in pain.

"Where the hell are you?" Eric shouted. "Come on out, you bitch!" There is that word again. He slid downward, with his back to the wall.

Amani's fellow officers waited at the top of the staircase. Once they were in Amani's view, she held them back from barging in by signaling her hand.

"Eric," Amani said peacefully, "if you try to jump out of either of those windows, I will take out your legs just like I did your gun. You will do as I say. Now, you come out here, bitch!"

Eric cried from frustration, "I'm not going to prison."

Amani stepped in through the hole in the wall. Eric refused to show her respect by spitting on the floor before her.

"I actually imagined you doing something with your life," Amani said. "Not this. Maybe I should've returned at least some of your phone calls. For that, I am remorseful. But, I could care less about ya finger." She stepped away.

"Your day will come!" Eric shouted. "You know what they say about payback!" The cops charged in with their guns pointed.

"Officer Jett!" Spencer shouted. "How did you get up here? I didn't see you sneak by us."

Amani smiled and left the room while the other cops made the arrest. On her way down the stairs, she saw her partner, Officer Vega. He was surprised to see her! She just patted him on the shoulder and proceeded to their vehicle.

After all the remaining survivors were subdued, Amani and Julio took off without saying a word to each other. Julio had many questions to ask, but decided to hold off until their next day at work.

Amani wasn't thinking much about what was on Julio's mind. She was still in distraught over what became of Eric. She hated seeing him the way he was, behaving like any other hoodlum.

Once Amani made it to her apartment, she took a hot soothing bath with lavender and peppermint mineral salts. Soft music played from her crystal clear sound system as she relaxed in the tub.

Afterward, she oiled her body with black seed oil. Her favorite drink before a night's rest; dandelion root tea, sweetened with agave extract.

And lastly, she sat on her bed with her legs folded and meditated. This is how she ends her nights after intense days of work. This is what helps her sleep well.

THE INTIMIDATOR

On the day after the shootout, Amani Jett had checked in for duty. Everyone in attendance applauded her for her efforts on the previous night, including Officer Vega.

Although appreciated, Amani had other things on her mind. She knew that someday she would have to work alone. Being a police officer was just a stepping stone.

"Good morning, partner," said Officer Vega. "Can we talk?"

"Sure," Amani said. They went into a separate room to be in private.

"Why didn't you tell me you were going to the scene?" Officer Vega asked.

"I didn't want to debate about it."

"I see. And how is your leg? You seem to be doing fine."

"Of course my leg is fine. Why wouldn't it be?"

"I saw the bullet holes in your pants when you came down the steps from the second floor last night. I didn't recall seeing them earlier."

"Me either. Maybe moths got to them."

"Amani, I'm not trying to interrogate you. You can be upfront with me."

"Naw, my emotions might get in the way."

Julio chuckled. "This is my fault. I'm to blame for this lack of openness between us."

"Apology accepted."

"Listen. When I lost my partner, it was extremely difficult to deal with. We were as close as blood brothers. Johnny was irreplaceable.

"When he was killed in action, I felt like I lost a part of myself. And after that, I kept people at a distance. I never want to experience that again.

"So, I thought it would be easier not to get too wrapped up into someone. I decided to never allow myself to be so vulnerable."

"You're still vulnerable," Amani said. "You just try to hide your vulnerability. I do not.

"I embrace my feelings, because I'm glad to have them. It proves that I'm human. I have nothing else to prove."

"Very well," said Julio. "So... you knew that guy from last night?"

"Yeah. We went to the same high school. He was nothing like that two years ago."

"You're hurt about it."

"Very much so."

"Then, I'm sure you want to speak with him." Amani agreed.

Amani was let into the cell where Eric was being held. He was sitting on the concrete bench with his hand wrapped due to his broken finger.

"What the hell do you want?" Eric asked.

Amani asked a question of her own. "What made you this way?"

"I was born this way. What you talkin' 'bout?"

"You were born with gold teeth in your mouth? Those gang markings on your face and neck? Really?"

"You wouldn't know nothing about this shit right here."

Amani shook her head at Eric. "You changed, Eric. You were not like your father."

"Aye, what do you know about my father?"

"You told me he was a drug dealer."

"Look, he's doing his time."

"And you took over the family business. Now, you're about to do your time. This is not what your mother wanted from you."

Eric gave Amani an evil look. "What did you just say to me?" He stood up. "You gonna mention my momma like that? You have no right to speak for my mother!"

Amani refused help from other officers who were wanting to restrain him. "You're not the only one who dealt with the loss of their mother, but at least I'm making my mom proud. Look at you!"

"Oh yeah? How is that dad of yours, huh? I can't believe I allowed that old man to put fear in me. All because I was trying to get some pussy." Amani cringed. "What about your loose booty ass sister? Her name was a flower or something. Oh yeah, it was Ivy! She had that baby by now, right?"

Amani didn't like what message that Eric was slyly asserting. The look in his eyes showed that he was being threatening.

Amani responded, "You want to speak on my family? Want to push my buttons for real this time? Last night was nothing!"

"Officer Jett!" Captain Ted Nelson, Amani's superior, shouted. "That's enough."

Eric smiled and sat back down. "Look at you taking orders and shit," he said to Amani.

"That's enough from you, too, Mr. James."

"I'll say whatever the hell I want to! I know my rights! You tell her what to do, not me! I want my damn lawyer!" Amani left the area, followed by Julio.

"What was he talking about back there?" Julio asked.

"Nothing," said Amani.

"It seemed to me like he was threatening your family. How well does he know you? Does he know where you live?"

"He's locked up. What do I care?"

"Always be careful."

Captain Nelson stepped in and ordered them on patrol. He halted Amani and said, "You've done an excellent job, sharpshooter. But please, just try to keep focused, okay? Don't let that punk get to you. They all start off nice."

Later that day, while Amani and Julio were on patrol, Julio asked, "Why don't you ever hang out with the rest of the squad after a long day's work?"

"At the bar?" Amani asked. "I don't do bars. That's a place for people who like to drink."

"That's right, you're a kid." He laughed to himself. "We've been riding together for all this time and I'm just starting to get to know you. I apologize for being so stiff."

"Well, that makes two of us. We're both loners."

Julio paused before saying, "So... Amani Turner was your name. Why the name-change?"

Amani became upset. "What! So, you did a background on me?"

"Sorry, but yes, I did some time ago."

"I can't believe this." She glared at him.

"Again, I apologize. You are the youngest recruit I've seen in a while. I wondered how you got in at first, but now I see that you really got skills." Amani sighed. "I don't think I have ever seen you miss a target. That's not human."

"Then, what is it?"

"It's... spectacular."

"So, what else did you dig up on me?"

"You graduated from high school with a 3.8 grade point average, but didn't go to a college or a university. You came straight to the academy. Most young women I know took classes for at least two years before joining the force."

"I know my talents, so I took on a job that exploits them."

"You sure it wasn't the cost of schooling that held you back? They have funds for that, don't they?"

"Vega, you wouldn't understand." They sat quietly for a few moments.

"What motivates you, Amani? What is it that pushes you so hard?"

"My belief that good will prevail. I have no reason to doubt. But, I'm still frustrated."

"Why? You played a major part in a big bust, yesterday. You should be rejuvenated."

"You know how it goes, Vega. There will be another one to take Eric's place."

"And we'll keep putting them behind bars."

They rode past many abandoned buildings in their route. Uncreative graffiti tags over-shadowed former storefronts on the avenue.

"What are your goals with the police force?" Julio asked. "Being a chief someday?"

Amani answered, "I would take whatever position that allows me to make a difference in this world. As long as I'm fighting."

"I asked because of your ambition. You seem very driven to become more than a cop, from what I can tell. You feel the need to control situations."

"I guess you can say that."

Julio hesitated before asking, "Do you ever date?"

"Why?"

"Because, I'm trying to imagine the type of man... or woman, you would end up with."

"I'm not lesbian, Julio. Anyway, I don't think much about dating. The last guy I went out with has a broken finger now."

Julio pulled the car over and slammed the brakes. "Are you telling me that guy was your boyfriend back in high school?"

"No," Amani replied. "Just my prom date." Julio stared at her for a moment. "We did not have sex."

"Oh, shit." He laughed to himself. "That would've been awful." Amani chuckled also.

A car passed by them, going about fifteen miles over the speed limit. Julio followed after it. Obviously, the speeding driver didn't detect the police vehicle at the curbside.

Julio flashed the lights while trailing the car, but the speeder would not stop. Amani reported the occurrence.

Eventually, the law-breaker slowed his car down, then got out and ran off. He fled with his pants sagging, trying to pull them up.

"And we have a runner," Julio said. "I like this part. Giving him a head start, Jett?"

"If that's what you want to call it," Amani replied. "Be right back."

Amani ran after the fleeing man. He cut through an alley, then hopped a fence and cut through a yard. He took strange routes to stay out of their sights.

Once Amani ran into the alley, she knew no one was around to spot her, so she used her special abilities. She zoomed three times the speed of any normal human being, then jumped directly over the fence. The runner could not hide from her.

When the running man became exhausted, he hid in a shaded spot between two houses. He panted hard, slumping over with his hands on his knees. After catching his breath, he made a call on his cellphone.

"Pit!" the fleer said. "I'm on the run, man. I need you to meet me somewhere. Where you at?" He listened. "Well, meet me at the dairy shop in five minutes. The po-pos got my car, man. Alright." He hung up, then took out his handgun. "Come on," he thought out loud. "I'm waiting for you." There was no sign of either cop.

As soon as the man left from the shaded area, Amani tackled him, cuffed him, and then called her partner. "Got him. And more on the way." She shoved the crook's gun out of reach.

"Excellent job, once again," said Julio. "I think we have another dealer in our hands."

Amani scanned the crook without patting him. "He was armed. No ID on him. Yep, a dealer no doubt."

Ten minutes later, police cars surrounded a nearby ice cream parlor. Suspects' hands were behind their heads as they knelt to the ground. The runner's associates had been caught. Apparently, Amani heard the man's whole phone conversation.

"Another job well done," Sergeant Spencer said to Amani. "I see medals coming your way." He saluted Amani and she saluted back.

Then, Amani had an incoming phone call from her sister, Ivy.

"What is it, Ivy?" Amani asked.

"There's this van that's sitting outside of the house," Ivy said, before describing the make, model, and color of the van. "I'm feeling suspicious."

"Can you identify the driver? Are there any passengers?"

"Not really. It's too dark to get a good detail of him. It looks like four of them."

"How long have they been there?"

"I don't know, but I first saw them when Auntie Eva dropped me and Lil' Maine off. I can tell they were looking right at me and my baby!" She peeked through the window very briefly. "I don't feel safe here. Dad is at work, and Jermaine won't take off of work. What should I do?"

"In the meantime, you should call Eastpointe police. They'll be there quickly. I will get there as soon as I can."

Ivy took Amani's advice and called the police in her city. Amani wondered why anyone would stalk her sister and who were these people.

Amani and Julio were heading back to the police station. "It is always drugs," Amani said. "What would you do about the drug epidemic if you had to make the call? Would you pick at the leaves or deal with the root?"

Julio answered, "Well, I would yank the stem and expose the root. But, when it's pollination season, I'd be more concerned about the spreading.

"No matter what you do to one plant, root, stem, or whatever, another plant will sprout. What we do in our position is eliminate the spread. Pollination season is in full effect."

"Give me a shovel and I'll dig the whole yard."

"Amen to that, chica."

Amani received another call on her phone from Ivy. "Someone just called on the house phone and threatened us!"

"Us?" Amani asked.

"Yes! He said, 'Your asses are marked!' then he said, 'Payback, bitch!' I didn't even know what he was talking about!"

"Is the van still out there?"

"No, they took off!"

At that point, Amani considered the possibility of Eric James having something to do with these blatant threats. He seemed simple-minded enough to do such a thing.

He knew where Amani resided two years ago, he remembered certain details about her family, and he arrogantly thought he had an advantage.

Plus, Eric is a spoiled, immature, sore loser. He had promised payback before he was put under arrest. Being that he was still fresh with rage, he was more than capable of threatening a police officer's family.

"Oh, the police just pulled up," Ivy said. "Thank goodness!"

Amani said, "Just be cooperative with them, Ivy. I'm going to look into this, then after that, I'll be there." The phone call ended shortly after.

Eric James sat in his holding cell, wondering what he was in store for; how many counts and how many years. His lawyer couldn't promise him a get out of jail ticket. His assets were gone.

Amani stormed in alone. "Get up, punk!" she demanded.

"You again?" Eric responded. "What you want this time?"

"You sent people to threaten my family?"

"I don't know what you're talking about."

"Say that again."

Eric got up and stepped closer to her. "I don't know what you're-"

Amani quickly reached and pinched his esophagus. "You're lying to me. You would be so **dumb** to make threats to my family?" Eric gasped for air, attempting to unclamp her fingers. "I can rip your throat out at any time I want to. Take note of that." She let go.

Eric stumbled back, coughing. He looked up at Amani in disbelief, barely able to say a word. "Y-y-you crazy!"

"Worse," Amani said. "I'm mad as hell! At first, I was disappointed in you, but now? Oh, you just pulled the lever!"

Eric backed against the wall. "You can't do nothing to me! I'll be out of here by Monday!"

Amani grabbed two parallel steel bars and pulled them apart. Eric, for the first time, had total fear in his eyes.

"What... How the hell?" Eric asked. "Are you

possessed?" Then, Amani squeezed the bars back, close to how they were. "Ain't no way!" he shouted.

The glare in Amani's widened eyes showed just how serious she was. Her voice trembled as she said, "Before they send you away, you will give me names. All of them. Or else, I will break all two-hundred and six bones in your body.

"I will not be stopped. I will not let anyone get in my way. Not even my partner.

"You will tell me what you know about that lawyer of yours. The dirty cops. Every damn thing." She squinted sharply. "Don't make me come in there."

Moments later, Amani barged into a room where detectives were examining a criminal map. She took a good look at the photographs, the names, and the strings connecting the affiliations.

Amani pointed out. "That's wrong, that's wrong, that's wrong, and that's wrong." Then, she walked out.

PHENOMENAL WOMAN

T his was a special day for Amani Jett, as she stayed at her family's home. On this day, she reached a new height. Literally. Staying with her family overnight gave her rejuvenation. Just being in her old bedroom reminded her of the values she gained as a youth.

On the day before, Amani had lost her cool. When Eric threatened her family, she had felt rage and was willing to torture him, forgetting that she ever knew him. Amani was even willing to harm anyone who would stand in her way. This was something she had to overcome.

Initially, Amani wanted her family to stay with her, for the time being, but her father is a proud man. He refused to let any man drive him away from the place he called home. He is old school.

Ivy would have liked to stay with Amani, but Mr. Turner wouldn't allow it and wanted to stay on her case. So, Amani stayed with her father, sister, and baby nephew.

In the morning, Amani did something she hadn't done in months. She prayed. Amani realized the limitations of her special powers. Clearly, she is not omnipresent, so she had to pray for protection over her family for when she can't be there for them.

Amani also prayed for the wisdom to use her abilities justifiably, and not let her power go to her head. She has to stay humble to some degree.

She ordered everyone not to disturb her for hours, unless it was a real emergency. This was to get herself centered again.

Amani requested time off from the job, because of her family's emergency. She used this time to refocus. Working in the force demanded most of her attention. She had gained a lot of experience, but hadn't gotten any stronger. Her nighttime ritual was not enough to make her elevate spiritually.

She was doing her Tai Chi exercises, which was something she had been practicing more recently. Every time she performed Tai Chi, she felt herself expanding, feeling the air around her with every steady movement.

When Amani finished, she went on to her yoga positions. This brought her to a significant sense of stability. She envisioned herself doing floating yoga with Joanie from the days they went to the lake to channel themselves above the waters.

Strangely, the thought of her five month old nephew, Jermaine Jr., came to mind. There was something about his gentleness, his peacefulness, and his undoubted innocence that brought her joy.

Then suddenly, Amani bumped her head. She opened her eyes and witnessed herself physically elevated! After a loss of concentration, she fell to her feet. From downstairs, her dad looked to the ceiling, wondering what was going on.

Amani was totally excited! She had never dreamed human flight could be possible. Then, she began to think to herself, "Expansion... stability... visualization... joy?" Siting with her legs folded, Amani tried her best to channel that same energy, again. She would not get up until she did.

Two minutes passed and there she was floating again. When she opened her eyes this time, she did not fall. She understood.

Her power did not come from physical strength. It did not come from wishing on a star. All of Amani's abilities came from the expansion of her mind. It is indeed a gift!

Therefore, the stronger Amani's mind, the more powerful she becomes. From that point was where Amani decided to quit the police force and pursue something of greater importance to her. As she once said to her partner, she felt limited. Amani felt jailed just like Eric was.

Amani remained elevated in her old bedroom. She moved around in air by pushing off the ceiling fan and walls.

She looked to the window and thought to herself, "Pushing off of trees wouldn't do me any good. I'd be better off jumping."

Amani lied horizontally in midair. She visualized herself strapped to the ceiling with slings, like she was in earlier floating yoga classes. She stopped wobbling in the air. This qualm, aerial balancing helped Amani tremendously!

Next, she applied her focus level of Tai Chi to guide her movements. With one wave of her arm, her entire position corresponded. Then, she waved in another direction, delivering the same results. Amani was able to rotate in every direction, even to the point where she could execute multiple midair somersaults while floating in place. She was greatly pleased!

Finally, she focused her sights to where she wanted to soar. The focal point that she chose was a picture on the wall. It was framed art with a poem titled, Phenomenal Woman. Amani rubbed her hands together, ready to fly like an eagle. And that, she did. Too fast!

Amani hit hard against the wall and fell to the floor, causing a bump loud enough to wake the baby. Mr. Turner got fed up and charged up the stairs to Amani's old bedroom.

"Amani!" Mr. Turner yelled. "You done woke the baby! Cut out all that noise!"

Amani shouted back, "You're breaking my concentration, Daddy! Please! I wanted no disturbances!"

"This is <u>my</u> house! You don't come in here making the rules, I do! That police stuff don't mean a thing up in here!" He walked off and mumbled, "Girl ain't even old enough to drink and got the nerve to be telling me what I can't do in **my** house..."

Amani opened the bedroom door and said to Mr. Turner, "I love you, Daddy."

Mr. Turner turned around. "I love you too, honey. Now, you keep it quiet in there."

"Yes, sir." She smiled.

There is no place like home. Here, Amani felt no limits. She wanted to learn more about thought processes and how she could improve her flying.

Hours later, Ivy was almost done with cooking dinner. Mr. Turner called Amani downstairs, so she could eat at the table with the family like she used to do. Amani came floating down to the living room.

Ivy was walking back to the kitchen when she noticed Amani hovering just below the ceiling. "What are you...? Dad!"

Mr. Turner walked in from the dining room. "What is it, Ivy?" Ivy pointed to the ceiling, then he looked up. "What in the world is going on?" he asked.

"This is called flying, Dad," Amani replied.

"I know what it's called, but why are **you** doing it?"

Ivy screamed, "She can fly! Oh my god!" The baby woke up crying again.

Amani showed off her ability to get around in air. "What do you think?"

Mr. Turner asked, "How long have you been able to do that?"

"I just learned it. That's why I needed time alone."

Mr. Turner shouted. "Get from over my glass table!"

Amani moved swiftly. "Dang, Dad. Aren't you happy for me? I can soar!"

"What's holding you up?"

Amani gasped. "Not this again."

Ivy yelled, "I have never seen anything like this!"

"Ivy, your baby is crying."

"But, you're flying! I mean, you are really up in the air while I'm right here talking to you! Let me get on your back."

Mr. Turner yelled, "No!"

"Come on, Dad, let's see what else she can-"

Amani pulled Ivy up and flew her across the room. Mr. Turner was nervous, as he was astonished by this whole phenomenon. He saw no hook or rope attached to Amani.

She brought Ivy back down, placing her in front of her child's bassinet. Ivy gave "Lil' Maine" his bottle. Amani descended from above them.

"I just reached a whole new level," Amani said. "And I did it with concentration."

"Either way," Mr. Turner said, "I'm proud of you. All of my children." Both Amani and Ivy kissed him on his cheeks. "Now, let's get ready to eat. I'm hungry."

Just like old times, the family ate at the dinner table. Amani was going wild over Ivy's cooking! She hadn't eaten a meal this good since her mother was alive.

"You got me on this one, Ivy," Amani said. "You can cook your tail off!" Ivy thanked her.

"Yes she can," Mr. Turner said. "So, what's next for you, Amani?"

"I plan to infiltrate the Mexican drug cartel scene." Mr. Turner choked on his food.

Ivy was also excited. "Go for it!"

"Wait, wait, wait," Mr. Turner said after clearing his throat. "Now, Amani, you're a powerful lady. But, you are only nineteen years old. And you're my daughter."

"Dad, what can they do to her?"

"They have powerful guns, Ivy!"

Amani said, "Dad, I got shot in the legs with an AK and didn't feel it until the next morning."

"What are you made of?"

"My point is, I can do this. There are other things I got to take care of, too. Like crooks in the force."

"And how are you going to do that?"

"I'm not sure, yet. I've only known about these things since yesterday. I made Eric spill it."

Ivy asked, "Why are you so hesitant? Just go in, pull the bad guys outside, and whip their behinds!"

Amani sat her fork down. "It's not that simple. Some people do wrong, because they are being forced to. Some are repaying a debt and can't find a way out.

"There are some bad guys tied into the system that protects our way of living. And after taking them out, you have to replace them.

"The system has failed many. There are people in jail right now who are wrongfully accused. They shouldn't be locked up.

"Then, there are people roaming the town who should be in prison for life. And if you lock them up, they'll be in a comfortable cell for just a few months.

"Basically, no one's hands are clean. The only difference is, some are exposed and some are not.

"Can I tell when someone is lying? Yes I can. Can I prove it in a court of law? No I can't.

"And if I take the law into my own hands, because I'm big and bad enough, then that would lead to a whole new list of problems. The most effective thing I could do is have a full thought-out plan to rearrange the entire system."

Mr. Turner said, "That sounds even more difficult than what Ivy was talking about."

"It is. But, I'm willing to try. It's going to take years under my belt as a public servant and a soldier."

"You're going to be famous!" Ivy said.

"I'm not ready to show my face to the world yet, but they will know my name."

Then, Ivy asked, "Will you have a mask? What about a costume?"

"No. I'm not doing that."

"Why not? You said you don't want everybody to know your face."

"I'm just saying that I won't be making grandiose appearances. I won't hide, either. I'll do my job and bounce."

"It sounds like you're quitting the force," Mr. Turner said. "I was looking forward to this day."

"Yeah, yeah. I know you were."

The telephone rang and Mr. Turner answered the call. It was Eastpointe police informing him that they found the suspicious men who were lurking around their area. The vehicle was confiscated and the men were arrested for stupidly carrying illegal firearms.

Mr. Turner spread the good news. Amani couldn't believe how careless the crooks were! Ivy was disappointed that Amani didn't get her chance to deal with them herself.

☞ ☞

On the following Monday, Eric James was visited in jail by his attorney, Richard Twain.

"What happened to your neck?" Richard asked after seeing the bruise that Amani left.

"I had an accident," Eric said. "Don't worry about it."

"Police brutality is a serious offense. I'm going to report this-"

"No!"

Richard sees that Eric is terrified. "This is not like you, Eric. What did they do to you at that precinct?"

"You don't need to worry about that. I'm safe here."

Richard laughed to himself. "They really did a number on you."

"They? No. Her."

"And who is this 'Her' you're speaking of?"

"You'll see. She can't be explained, man. I advise you to move your ass out of state. She's coming."

"Are you trying to get an insanity plea? You will serve some time, Eric. We just have to try to-"

"I don't care about that! I'm safe here."

"Eric... I respect your father..." he rubbed his chin, "but, if you ratted us out... it won't be safe for you here. Or anywhere else, for that matter. Remember that." When Richard left, Eric had a concerned look on his face.

WRAPPING IT UP

S usan Dunn asks more questions in her sit-down interview with Amani Jett. "There is a question that I've been craving to ask you, Amani. Being that you are so fast, powerful, and impenetrable, still, do you fear anything?"

"Absolutely!" Amani answers.

"Tell us about them."

"Well, anything to do with outer space, I'm not in it. There's no way I'm flying way up to the moon. That's too much for me."

"So, are you afraid of being that high, or is it the idea of being so distant from earth?"

"Both. And I don't care how much NASA is willing to pay me, I won't do it."

"Very interesting. And I don't blame you."

"I don't see the point in going to the moon, anyway. There's enough going on down here.

"They have all these millions to pay me for space exploration, but yet there are still people with no shelter in this country."

"You make a good point. Any other fears?"

"I can't do rats. They gross me out."

Susan laughs. "You too? You are such a girl!"

"Look, if you lock me in a room with one, I just might fly through the ceiling." Susan laughs again. "The faster I ever swam was in Colombia, where I was investigating the importation of cocaine.

"I was spying low-key, so I took this route where I had to swim across a body of water. I don't remember if it was a lake, a pond, or whatever.

"Then, I sensed something behind me. I looked back and saw this big, red-eyed rat with its long, ugly tail! It was swimming with its buddies!"

"Oh my god," Susan says, "I'm getting freaked out just by listening to this."

"Let me tell you, I could've parted the Red Sea the way I got up out of there."

Susan cracks up laughing. "Now I don't feel bad about my reactions to those pesky creatures. Thank you, Amani."

"Wait, there's more. Alligators." She frowns and shakes her head. "Can't stand'em. Those things look like they're up to no good. Always smiling with them sharp teeth." Susan can't stop laughing. "But, they make good purses."

"It is so refreshing to see this side of you! I see that you're fun to be around."

"Thank you, Susan. More serious fears I have are like, making the wrong decisions and flying over the oceans for hours on my own."

"What makes the flying so difficult?"

"I worry about losing concentration after the first two hours. I'm afraid that I might doze off or lose direction, because if I'm not near land, I can't tell where I am."

"Radar is not one of your gifts."

"Unfortunately, my radar is limited." She giggles. "But some day, I <u>will</u> overcome that fear. I have to, because there is so much going on in the world. I want to be global.

"Right now, I am dependent on the Air Force for missions overseas. And, missions governed by the US don't always coincide with my aspirations."

"And where do you differ?"

"When we went to Iraq, I wanted to be in Afghanistan. And like I said earlier, I wish I had been in New Orleans when the levees broke. I want to go to the Congo whenever I please, but I need to do more research on their government structure."

"What would you do in the Congo? What would be your mission?"

"First of all, protect the people from the long, vicious war. But, my specialty is going straight to their leader. Not killing a bunch of misled soldiers, or blowing things up, but getting right to the guy who is running things."

Amani speaks on this passionately. Apparently, it has been on her mind for a long time.

"You were instrumental in both the Iraq and Afghanistan captures," Susan says, "so I agree, you do find your target."

"Finding them is not as hard as people make it seem," Amani replies. "It's a matter of getting to them and at just the right time."

"How did you persuade the Secretary of Defense to put you on board? Was it by a demonstration of your abilities?"

"A bit more than that. I carried out my own personal mission in '03, soon after the war began. It was in Tijuana, Mexico...

TIJUANA, MEXICO 2003

"I HEARD RUMORS OF A CARTEL ALLIANCE. A FORCE NEARLY IMPOSSIBLE TO STOP. IT WAS MY OPPORTUNITY TO MAKE MY PRESENCE KNOWN. I SEARCHED THE SLUMS."

"TATTS ARE DEAD GIVEAWAYS. LED ME STRAIGHT TO..."

"...THE BIG GUNS."

"I SCANNED THROUGH THE WALLS. IT WAS BLURRY FROM THE FAR DISTANCE. I NEEDED TO GET CLOSER."

AYE! WHO IS IT!

IT'S A MAMACITA WEARING A VEST, HOLMES. KIND OF WEIRD,

NOT GOOD, ESE.

PABLO'S NOT ON LOOKOUT?

MR. THIRD-EYE-DOORMAN IS TAKING A NAP.

HE'S NOT ANSWERING HIS PHONE!

WELL... SINCE RAUL'S AFRAID OF GIRLS...

...VATOS, LET'S TAKE THE WALL OUT. WE'RE RELOCATING.

IT AMAZES ME HOW THE CRAZIEST PSYCHOPATHS MANAGE TO FIND IDIOTS WHO ARE WILLING TO FOLLOW THEIR ORDERS.

WOW. THEY ARE ACTUALLY SHOOTING THE WALL OUT.

VEGA WAS RIGHT. THESE MANIACS ARE TRIGGER-HAPPY.

OKAY, AMANI, THIS SHOULD BE PRETTY QUICK. 3 GUYS WITH GUNS. PIECE OF CAKE. THIS WON'T BE A BLOOD BATH. WATCH YOUR MOMENTUM. SHOWTIME...

CRACKLE

EH?

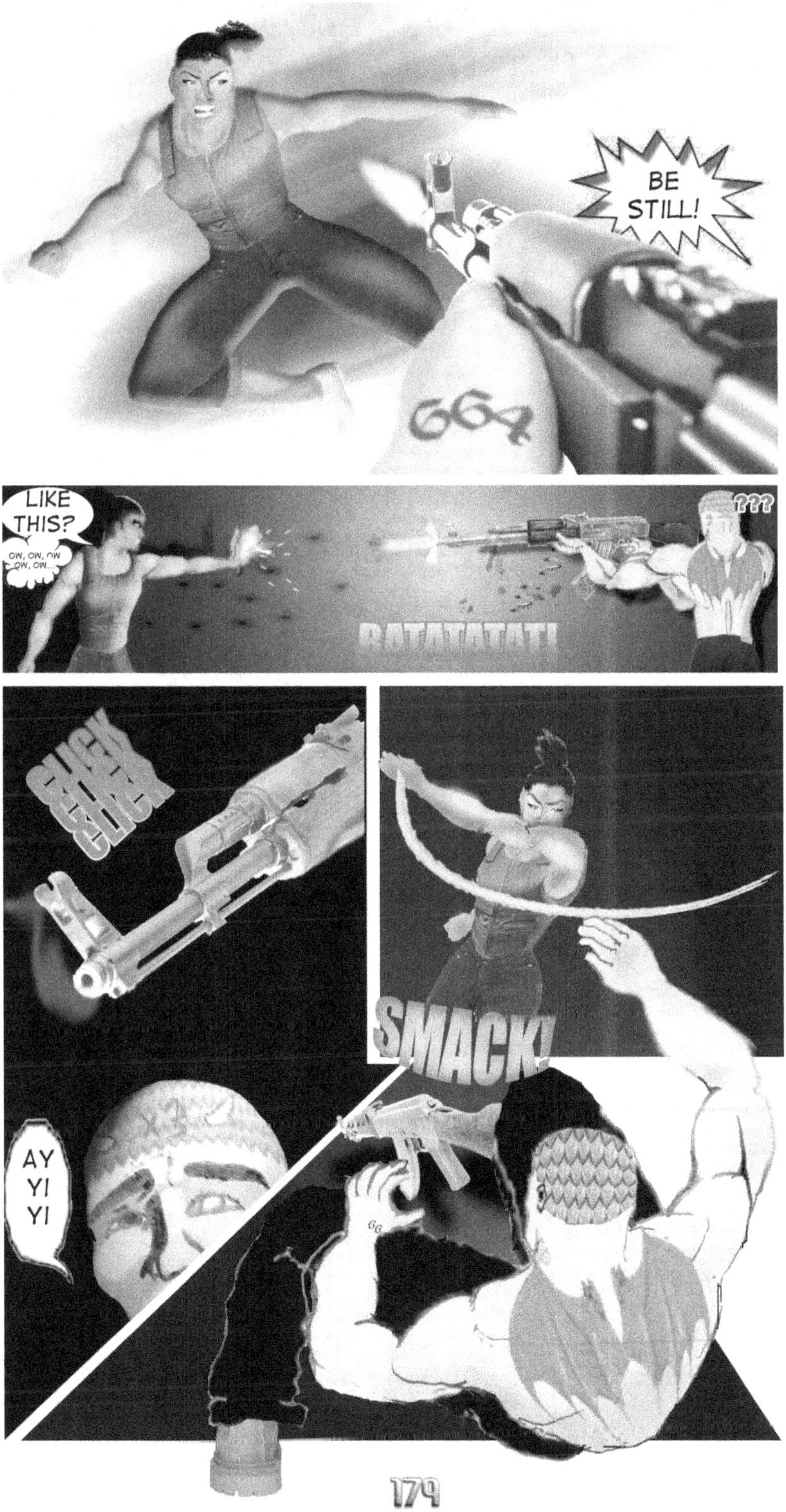

THE BOY WITH THE DRAGON TATTOO IS KINDA RIGHT. I AM A WOMAN, AND PROUD OF IT. NOT A SICKO WHO'LL RIP OFF LIMBS TO GET THE DETAILS I WANT, BUT I FIGHT WITH INTEGRITY. HE IS GRINNING AS IF THIS IS A SIGN OF WEAKNESS. HE'S TESTING ME, BUT HE KNOWS THE RESULTS. I'M PROUD OF BEING THE WOMAN I AM, AND NO, I AM NOT THAT DESPERATE TO GET WHAT I WANT. BUT, I WILL BREAK BONES.

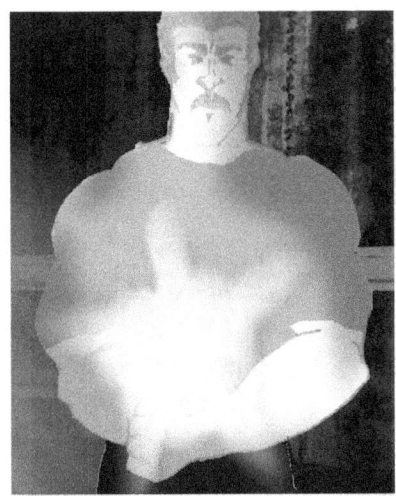

I SLIPPED UP BIG TIME.

I FELT THAT!

WHY DIDN'T I HEAR HIM GET UP?

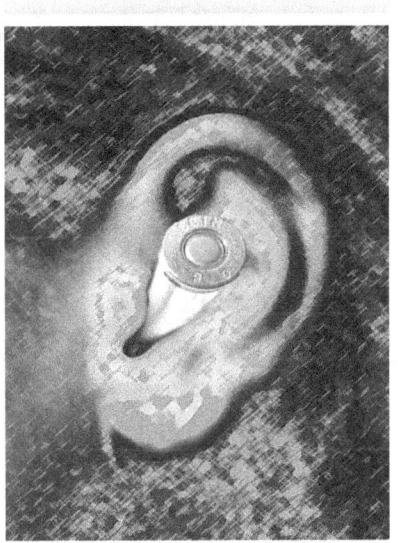

DIE! DIE!

WHAT DOES THIS ONE-EYED FOOL THINK HE'S DOING?

TIME TO GO

"I GOT OUT THE SAME WAY I GOT IN, WITH SOME EXTRA BAGGAGE. HE SCREAMED THE ENTIRE TIME."

AAAIIIIIIIIEEEIIII

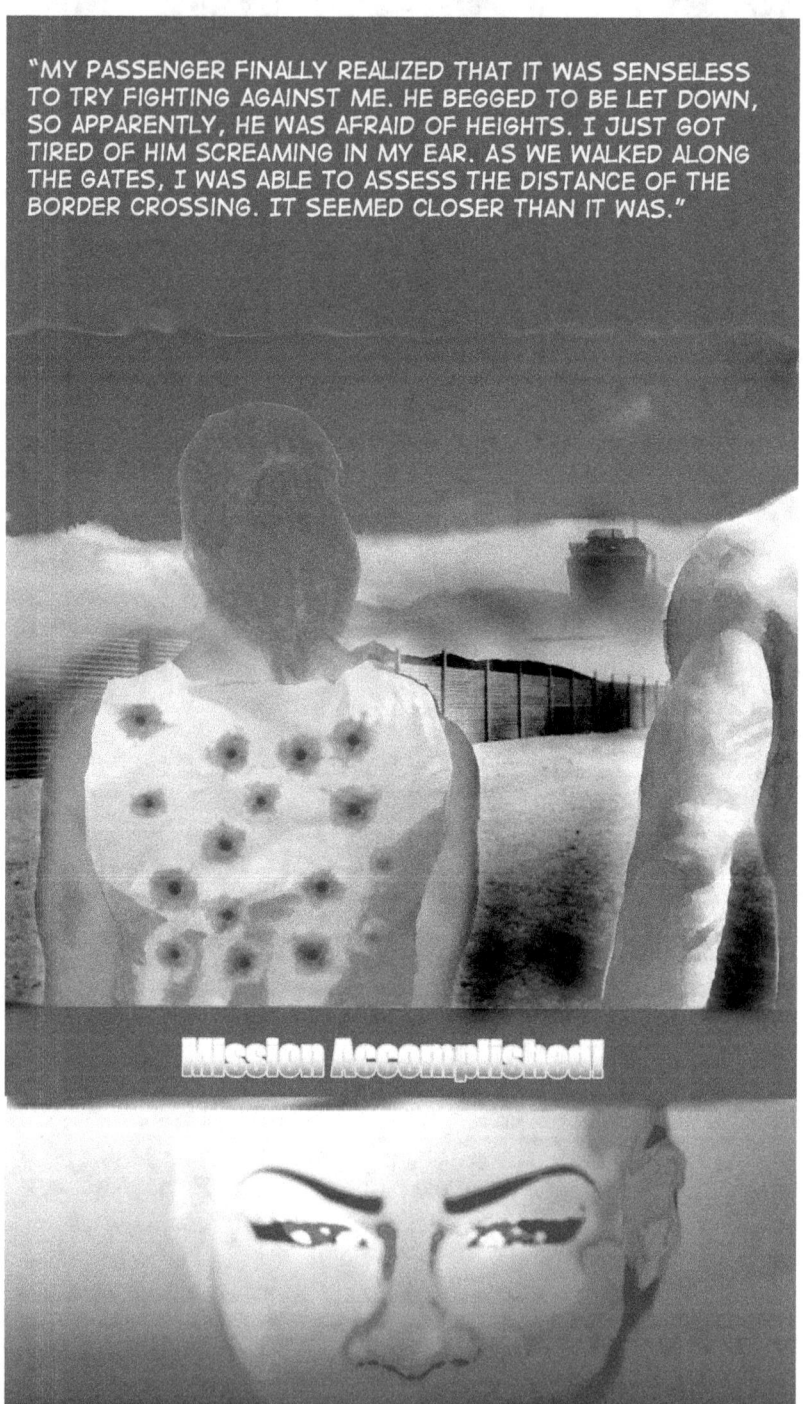

"MY PASSENGER FINALLY REALIZED THAT IT WAS SENSELESS TO TRY FIGHTING AGAINST ME. HE BEGGED TO BE LET DOWN, SO APPARENTLY, HE WAS AFRAID OF HEIGHTS. I JUST GOT TIRED OF HIM SCREAMING IN MY EAR. AS WE WALKED ALONG THE GATES, I WAS ABLE TO ASSESS THE DISTANCE OF THE BORDER CROSSING. IT SEEMED CLOSER THAN IT WAS."

Mission Accomplished!

"I made my accomplishment known to the National Guard, and then, Washington DC. I agreed to fight the war, as long as my identity wasn't publicized. I never officially joined any of the Armed Forces, but I still followed orders.

"My first time in Iraq was short. Hussein was captured, then I left soon after. That was my clear intent, to help put an end to the war as quickly as I could.

"There were too many dying over there. And sadly, even after I left, there were still shootings and killings. Shows how much I knew about what was going on."

Susan asks, "What made you return? Your mission was complete."

"The continuous fatalities. I believed in the democratizing agenda for that country. And to be honest, that was a point in time when I was down on my luck, financially."

"Oh, I understand now. So, technically, you were a mercenary."

"Yes. Though I hate that word."

"And, that is where the Weapon USA moniker was established, am I correct?"

"Yeah, I wasn't crazy about that either."

"If you were asked to carry out an order that you totally opposed, then what would you say to that?"

"Ask somebody else to do it."

"And what if you witnessed something that appeared to be a war crime done by our own military personnel, but was not confirmed? Would you intervene?"

"I need an example."

"If you were present during the air raid on Fallujah. One of the targets was a medical clinic. Would you have interfered with that bombing?"

"That's a definite yes. I can detect what is going on beyond thick walls, and that clinic should not be bombed."

"But, the order was given by an official and was being carried out. Wouldn't that be a crime on your behalf to interfere?"

"Some may see it that way, but I know better. I believe in fighting for what's right, more than anything."

"In such a case, would you stand trial?"

"I sure would. I'll give the courts respect."

"And if the courts found you guilty, would you adhere to the court's ruling?"

Amani pauses. "Hell no."

"In any case, if you were considered to be a flight risk, would you allow to be contained until the trial is concluded?"

"Nope."

Susan repositions herself in her seat. "If you don't mind, Amani, I'd like to play devil's advocate."

Amani sits attentively. "Sure, go ahead."

"Amani Jett thinks she's above the law. The only reason she agrees to be on the show is because she needs money. She doesn't love America." She adds, "These are not my words, but they may be words coming from some of the people watching. What would you say to that?"

"I would say they must have not watched this interview from the beginning. And, that they are ignorant. I started my journey ten years ago with no attempt at getting rich or famous.

"I only requested money when I needed it. Will I prosper after this interview? I'm sure I will, but I stated my reasons for it.

"And I love the peaceful, noble American people. Actually, I love peaceful, noble people everywhere."

Susan says, "There is no doubt about that." She reaches for Amani's hand. "Thank you so much for sitting with me, Ms. Jett. It's been a real pleasure talking to you."

"Thanks for having me."

Susan faces the camera. "And so, that does it for my interview with the wonderful Amani Jett. Thank you for tuning in. Good night, America." The studio lights dim. "That went well," Susan says to Amani.

"A piece of cake," Amani says. "Except for the religion part."

"Aw, you did great."

"Thanks, Susan. It wasn't half as bad as it could've been." She removes the small microphone from her top.

"Just know that you will get tons of attention from now on. That's the real doozy." They walk away from the set.

"Yes, that will be an adjustment for me, but I think it'll all be worth it."

～҂～

After the two separate, Susan gets a phone call. She picks up.

"Good job," a mysterious voice says. "We are pleased with the interview."

Susan replies, "I could have done it just as well without your influence, whoever you are. I've been doing this for many years."

"But this time, it was for National Security. You should be proud."

"As I am every time I give a meaningful interview. Listen, that young lady is not a threat to us or any other..." She stops when she notices the call was disconnected. "Jack-ass."

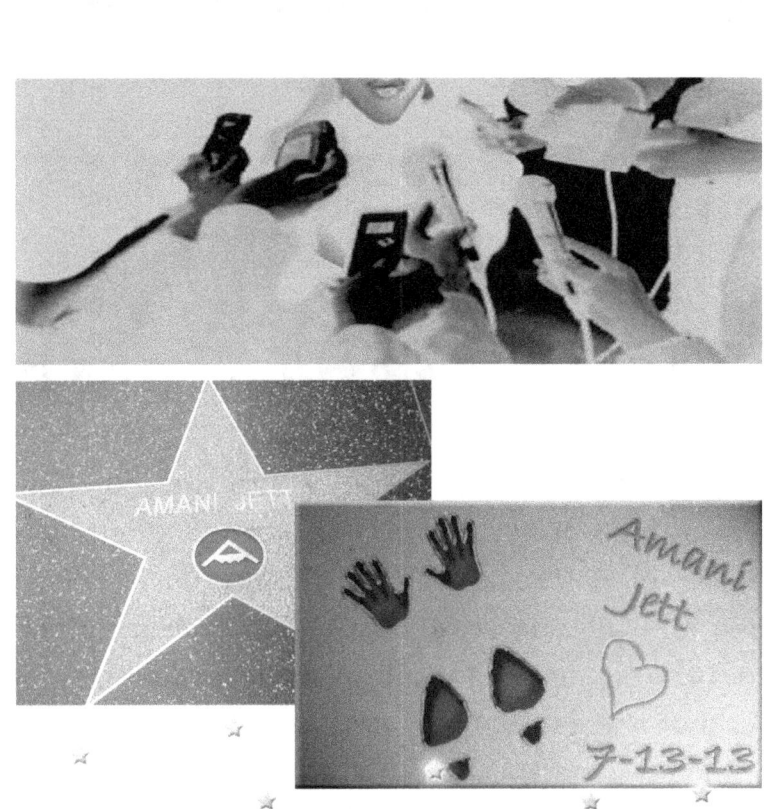

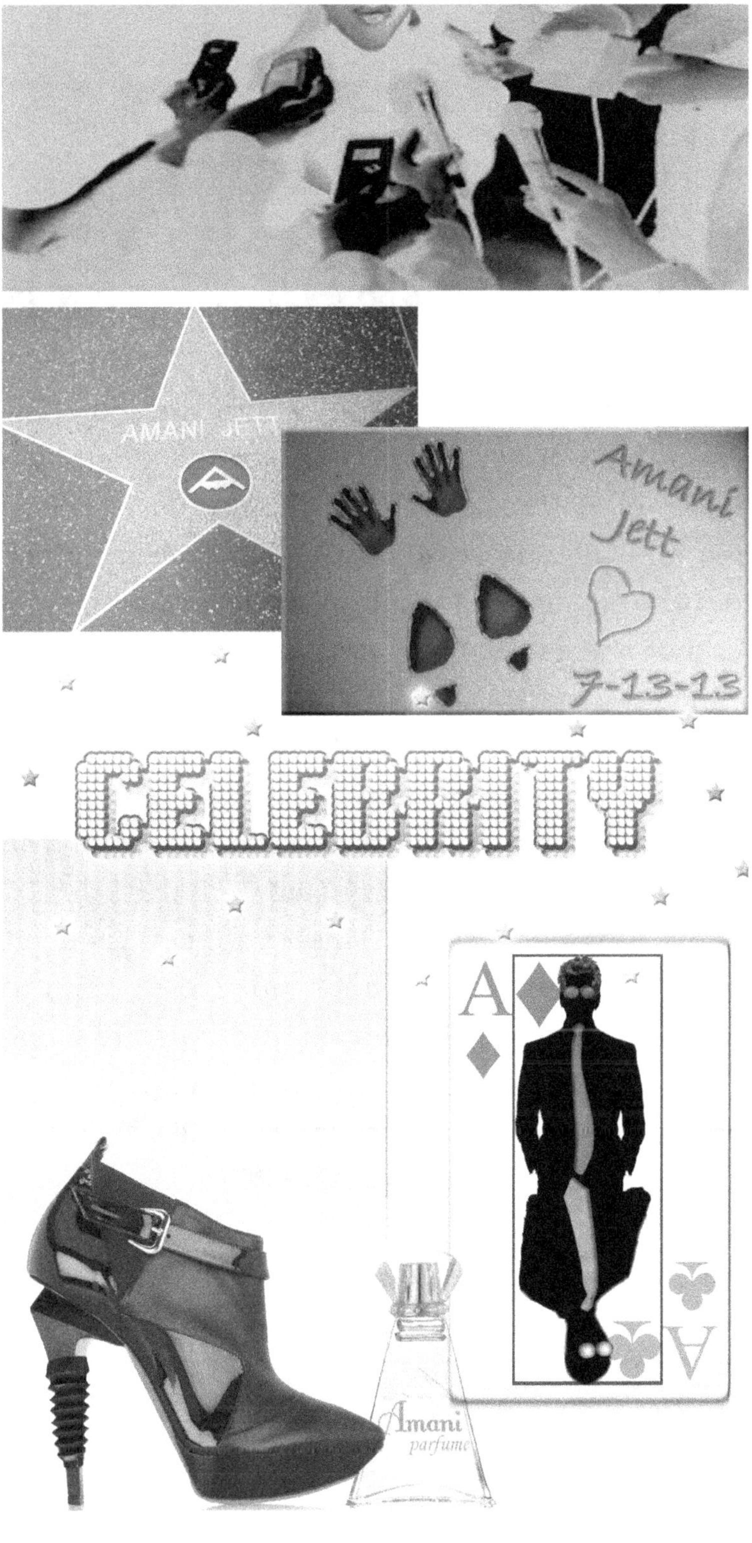
AMANI JETT
Amani
Jett
7-13-13
CELEBRITY
Amani
parfume

MEDIA HYPE

Outside of the studio, where the interview took place, Amani Jett is surrounded by a huge crowd of desperate reporters and admirers. Cameras are flickering from every angle. There are so many questions being asked at one time, that she can hardly get to any of them.

Somehow, fans already have T-shirts with Amani's picture ironed on them. They cheer her name, some cry even. Amani didn't expect this much hype so soon. She has no bodyguards. The reporters move with her every step.

Amani stops and says, "This excitement is a bit overwhelming, so maybe I'll set up a few events to reach out to the people. That is, if things are going well enough and I'm not needed elsewhere."

A reporter asks, "How will we be notified?"

"The internet, I guess. Social nctworks."

As news reporters bombard Amani with more questions like, "Any upcoming missions?", "Do you agree with the use of drones?", "Do you really have a religion?", "What brand of shoes do you prefer?", and "Who designed that dress for you?", she shoots straight up into the air and flies away as the people look on.

Amani makes it back to her home and sees there are still people outside of her property with their cameras. Amani ignores them and flies in through the window she flew out of earlier. After she closes the window and curtain, the people start to leave.

Following a quick hot shower, Amani goes into her mini-theater. There, she watches the news to see what is going on in the world. But instead of world news, the world is talking about her!

Every news channel is nonstop talk about Amani Jett. Speculations concerning every aspect of her.

The first news channel Amani turns to has four panelists debating about the nondisclosure of her prime religious study. It goes like this...

"I got a sense that she is leaning more towards Islam, because when describing the prophet, Muhammad, she used the word 'admire'. That is a stronger emphasis than 'value', like she used for the other religious figures."

"I disagree, because she doesn't wear the head wrap. And come on! The lady wears stilettos!"

"I think that with the biblical references, she has more of a Christian background. She mentioned Noah's ark, and when she talked about her fear of mice, she said that she could've parted the Red Sea."

"Well, she clearly stated that she studied most major religions, but I don't think she belongs to any religious group."

"Then, why study one more than the other? Or why even admit to that? It seems rather pointless."

"Maybe she wants to be accepted by all people and just said that to keep everyone interested in what else she has to say."

"While that could be true, I really doubt it. She's Amani Jett. How could anyone not be interested in what she has to say?"

"Right, the ratings were going through the roof before the topic ever came up. But, I do think she is a Christian."

"But, she made no mention of the word 'Christ' and the biblical references you spoke of were both from the Old Testament. She might not even believe in Christ."

"That's a good point. Maybe she studies Jewish teachings more than anything. We don't know and may never know."

"If I can make a statement, all followers of Islam do not necessarily go places wearing their head wraps all the time. That is a blatant stereotype, and occasional stilettos aren't disproof, either."

"I believe what Amani did was protect the faiths of the people she serves. She doesn't believe in one ruling practice."

"Then, that would mean that she has no belief. No allegiance. I totally disagree with that notion."

"And if she is denying Christianity, then what makes her any different from Peter when he denied Christ in front of the enemy? Is she not doing the same thing?"

Amani changes the channel after she heard enough. She didn't think her words would lead to more religious debates. That was not her intent.

On the next station, the two hosts are talking about her growing celebrity fame...

"Did you see that dress?"

"Oh, yes! She looked absolutely stunning in the all purple with those stilettos!"

"People can't get enough of the shoes ever since Susan mentioned them! They were designed by the world-famous designer, Pierre Gazelle." They show a close-up of her shoes. "Just look at those heels."

"Yes, and she is so beautiful in them."

"Isn't she? Good thing she cleared up those alien rumors. I didn't expect this!"

"So elegant, with a body that is physically fit. I guess that comes from fighting off the bad guys." They laugh like pompous rich women.

"This just in, the shoes that Amani wore is already up for auction! Wanna know the starting price? 2.5 million dollars!"

"Whoa!"

Even Amani says to herself, "What?"

"Yes, and that particular design by Pierre Gazelle is in high demand. It's only been two hours since the interview!"

"Where can I find those?" the other host asks.

"It's rumored to only be available at the online store, and they have few in stock."

"Then, expect to spend some change if you want a pair."

"That's for sure."

Amani switches to a more serious news network. Here, they are discussing politics. These people are overly expressive with their discussions. This is a reputation that the network has.

"That's preposterous! You can't say you respect the courts, then say you will not serve your time if found guilty!"

"But, if she's not guilty-"

"It is her obligation to prove that to the court!"

"Exactly! If you respect the court, that means **you** must show that the charge was in error! And if **you** fail to do so, then **you** must serve **your** time like every other US citizen!"

"Is she even a US citizen? We don't know! I would like to see her birth certificate! We the people should demand that she shows us her birth certificate before the government gives her another check paid for by our tax dollars!"

"There are a lot of things I want to say, but I don't know what America may look like in upcoming years. It may look like Amani-ca.

"For the first time as an American, I am afraid to use my freedom of speech. I don't know how long our rights will be in effect."

"God as my witness! As long as this is the United States of America, I will exercise my rights to the fullest! I will not allow a so-called super-being of any kind to take away my freedom of expressing the truth! So help me God!"

"How is this young lady threatening to you? Help me understand."

"Not just threatening to me! Threatening to you! Threatening to this whole country that I love so much from the bottom of my heart!

"She has shown that she is a clear threat to our nation! If you don't respect the law, you don't respect the country or anything it stands for!"

"That's not true."

"It is true!"

"This is a woman who fought for us. And did it voluntarily at times, so that makes her someone to be respected."

"Would you say the same thing about the one American soldier who turned his back on this country and joined the Taliban? He fought for us, too! Then, he turned on us!"

"Don't put so much trust in this woman! She already showed her true colors! Even disrespected animal rights, by showing her hatred of alligators out of **fear**! So, anything she fears is better off dead!"

Amani is very disgusted by the constant fighting on this news channel. She changes to a more entertaining station...

"So, what type of man would be good enough for an Amani Jett? We have dating expert, Dr. Mark Scot, here with us, tonight. Welcome, Dr. Scot."

"Hi, Cathy."

"So, what would you say is the perfect match for a super-woman?"

"I would say he has to be a powerful, wealthy man-"

Amani changes the channel.

"And, what can be expected for these public appearances that Ms. Jett considered?"

"I would expect it to be a press conference of sorts..."

Amani thinks out loud, "Who is this dude and what does he know?" She changes the channel.

There is more hype about Amani, but there are no reports of anything valuable to her. No updates on the missing children reports. No report on the progress in Afghanistan. The best thing to do for now is get rest. She has many meetings tomorrow.

PROPAGANDA

It is a bright and sunny morning in a Detroit neighborhood that is quite peaceful. No loud music playing from parked cars, and no loose dogs roaming the block. It's actually uncommon.

Flying in from the sky is Amani. She does her usual landing with the slowing down to side-skid. She isn't dressed to impress, wearing her jogging clothes, sneakers, and a scarf on her head. She stands before a tall apartment complex, which is where her sister, Ivy, lives.

A neighbor calls out, "Hello, Amani! Good job on the interview!"

Amani waves, "Hi Rachel! Thanks." She walks to the building and rings the buzzer.

Moments later, Amani follows Ivy into the apartment suite. She immediately goes to pick up her niece, Amber, who is Ivy's third child with her longtime boyfriend, Jermaine.

"Hey, Amber!" Amani says, then gives her a kiss on the cheek.. "How's my niecey-poo?" She dances with the baby in her arms.

"Bad as ever," Ivy answers.

Amani sits Amber down. "She's not bad. Parents love to say that when their kids are just being kids."

"She's been crying all morning."

"Yeah, babies do that. So, anyhow, I want French braids this time. The same way you did it back in February, with the pigtails."

"I think I can pull it off in two and a half hours." She sits on her living room sofa with a comb in her hand.

Amani sits on the floor between Ivy's legs. "That means three hours."

"Whatever. Your hair is easy to deal with and that was my first time trying that style." She removes Amani's scarf, then parts her hair with the comb. "You know you could've plugged my book, but I ain't mad at ya."

"Please don't keep bugging me about that book. I have a lot of things coming up, so you, Dad, Auntie, and the kids won't have anything to worry about."

"I didn't hear you mention you-know-who."

"Who? Lamont?" She gasps, then looks across to the bedroom door. "He should be out looking for a job."

"It's not like that anymore. These places want you to apply online. You really don't get a chance to represent in person, so you got to have one hell of a resume."

"That's different."

"Then, you got jobs that do a credit check on you. And some of these places won't even hire you if you don't already have a job! How much sense does that make?"

"Not much, in my opinion. What is he doing now?"

"He's probably in there sleep. When the boys left for school, he got up off the couch and went to their room." She picks up the remote to change the channel.

"Please don't turn it to the news stations. I don't want to hear another person talking like they know me. These people in television are downright crazy."

An hour passes by when Amani and Ivy's cousin, Lamont, steps out of the bedroom to get to the kitchen. He passes by the two ladies and greets them. "Hey, Ivy. Morning, Ms. Jett."

"Don't you 'Ms. Jett' me," Amani demands.

"That's your name, ain't it?"

"What's your problem, Lamont? Are you still part of that online congregation?"

"Very funny. And, I find it interesting that you wore that triangular symbol on that belt across your dress during the interview."

"Lamont, what in the world are you talking about?"

"You know what I'm talking about."

Amani looks confused. She asks Ivy, who is not yet finished with her hair, "What is this fool talking about?"

"Girl, I don't know," Ivy says.

Lamont says, "It's symbolic of the Great Pyramids, which symbolizes-"

"Lamont!" Amani shouts. "It was a belt buckle to a dress I picked out for that one single interview! It doesn't symbolize a damn thing! Man, I don't believe you!"

"Then, how come when you waved your hand to the crowd, you were posing like the goat man on your way to the studio?"

"Boy, you need to stop messing around on that internet. Whatever you're watching, it's making you crazy! You're letting these people tell you about your own cousin?"

"Why would they make all this up?"

"Are you fooled that easily? What do they know about me?"

"They were right about you working for the government."

"To save lives!"

"Not when you took part in that shootout at the mosque in Fallujah."

"What! Who the hell told you that? And you believed it?"

"Okay, maybe they got that part wrong."

"Damn right they did! And who are 'they', anyway? Do you know them personally?"

"In a way I do. I chat online with some of them."

Ivy stops her braiding for the moment and says, "Oh shit..."

Amani points down to the floor in front of her. "Sit down, Lamont. I want you to listen up." Lamont sits on the floor. "Stop listening to that garbage!" she says. "It's not true! Now, tell me. These things that you call Truth and facts. Do you swear by them?"

"What do you mean?" Lamont asks.

"Just what I said! Do you swear by them?"

"I'm just saying, I believe what I believe."

"I didn't ask you that. I'm not telling you or anybody else what to think or believe, but I have a serious problem with idiots who go around preaching stuff that they wouldn't even swear by!

"There are things I believe, and I know a whole lot more than you do. But, I wouldn't swear by them, as if they were infallible! Just like I wouldn't stand before God and affirm what I think and be so arrogant to call it Truth!

"So, Lamont, know that you don't know a damn thing. All you know is what somebody came up with, and then made a video out of it. They have theories based on information they were <u>allowed</u> to see.

"I have acquired information that the rest of the world, except for a handful of people, don't have access to! And let me tell you, your 'online leader guys' are way off! If they knew what I knew, then they would shut the hell up!

"Is there a shady side to the government authority? Absolutely! But, you won't find anything accurate on the internet, stupid!" She points at Lamont. "Do you think you're a threat? A rebel?"

Lamont says, "Yeah. I know I am."

Amani laughs at Lamont. "You are a joke to them. No one can tell you better than I can. You treat life like a TV murder mystery, guessing at things like it's entertainment.

"That website you follow? It will always be up and running as long as its web host is paying its taxes. Not a threat, even in the slightest.

"If anything, you're doing dirty politics a favor! With your outrageous theories, you ruin the validity of damn near any legitimate argument against them! You go too far!

"What you're doing is crying wolf. With your daily rants, you're just teaching people how to ignore you. A babbling fool!

"You all are no different from those religious fanatics, calling me Christ this and Satan's child that! I can't believe you're judging me by a belt buckle! My own cousin!

"These people got you that scared? So every time you see a triangle, that represents the pyramids? It can't just be a shape?

"These people you follow are only good for amusing people who are already fearful of what may come. They have to foresee every damn thing, because they're worried.

"Whatever may go down, you will not be warned about it. You will not expect it. You will not see it coming.

"You need to accept the fact that you don't know jack, and you're better off getting **your** stuff together. Find you some damn work! Get your priorities straight!

"You got too much time on your hands, Lamont! Get off of those stupid websites and get on a payroll!"

Ivy says to Lamont, "You really do need to find work, cousin. I know it's hard, but at least get a hustle."

"Okay," Lamont says, "I'll try harder. And Amani, I apologize for accusing you of being associated with the Underworld Society."

"The who?" Amani asks.

"You should really check out this video. I know you don't really get into-"

"Lamont! I'm not about to waste my time with that mess!"

"Why not? It's very informative!"

"I'm done with this. Don't bring it up again."

Lamont gets up, goes back into the boys' bedroom, and closes the door. Ivy shakes her head.

"So, big sister," Ivy says, "how's that paycheck for the interview looking?"

Amani says, "The contract is a huge one. I think it's a new record."

Ivy stops braiding. "Then, why am I doing your hair for free?"

"I don't have the money yet, Ivy. You'll know when I get it."

Ivy happily proceeds with the braiding. "I can't wait! My sister is finally rich!"

"It just amazes me that I'm getting paid for talking more than I did for fighting."

"Why complain now? Be happy about it!"

"I can't celebrate, yet. There's a lot of work to do. This is only the beginning."

"Well, I'm going to celebrate! Can't wait to get the car that I always wanted." Amani frowns. "And, I can finally have my dream wedding..."

"What?"

"Don't worry, Amani. I'm going to make some investments, too."

"Investing in what exactly?"

"I don't know. I'll have to check around. See what's out there that is worth investing in."

"You need to learn about becoming a venture capitalist. Having a substantial amount of money overnight is not going to make you successful at investing."

"I know that!"

"But, you sound like you are more interested in a car and an extravagant wedding. What about some rental property in this buyer's market?"

"That sounds like something Daddy would say. I guess I could do that."

"Plus, you're renting! Why not first invest in a home for your own family?"

"I'm not sure I want the responsibility of owning a house, anyway. With all of the maintenance, that can be a headache."

"What do you think rent is? Every month, you pay for roofing, plumbing, and property taxes through rent! And you're overspending."

"I don't see it like that."

"Why not think about the future, when your kids grow up? With property, you'll have something you can pass down to them. You can't do that with rent."

"Yeah. You're right, Amani."

"I don't want to give you money just for you to use it up on things that won't last. A dumb investment from you is a dumb investment from me."

"Okay, okay. You can stop with your preaching, 'Calvina'."

"Whatever! Dad says 'hell' too much to preach."

"I admit, we were blessed with a good father."

"Speaking of fathers, Jermaine should've married you years ago. I'm just saying."

"You're not just saying, Amani. You never just say."

"I have **never** gotten involved in you and your man's business. Not even when you wanted me to, back in the day, so don't even try it."

"Then, why start now? Oh, because your money is involved."

"You got that right! But really, I hope you get more out of my contributions than what you're allowing yourself to have."

Ivy is skeptical. "Sure, Amani. You have control issues."

"Ivy, haven't you seen my mansion? When I bought that place, I was thinking on your level. I thought money would keep flowing in.

"There were so many other investments I could've made, but I wanted what I wanted. And later, I realized that my plan could only work for two years.

"You are obviously making the same mistake by not thinking far enough ahead. Stretch your dollars! You're talking about spending chunks of money as if you'll be paid like this regularly."

Ivy says, "Being a hair stylist for a super woman is serious business." She giggles.

Amani laughs. "I think the cook book is a good idea, though. I'm proud of you for that."

"Thank you. So does that mean you will plug it?" Amani doesn't answer. "People are going to know who I am, eventually. You can't hide us, silly. Not forever."

"You remember the last time you all were threatened?" asks Amani.

"Yeah, I remember."

"That was the last time I lost control. I can't let that happen again. Not if I can help it."

"You probably can't, Sis. Everything is not in your control."

COMMERCIALIZING A LEGEND

New York City. Amani has arrived with her freshly-braided hair. Her change of style will definitely have the people talking. She lands on the helipad of a tall skyscraper, where a group of people in business attire meet with her. They walk her into the building.

Amani has meetings lined up that will fill the rest of her day. She takes a seat at the head of the table in a conference room. By noon, they let in the first presenters.

The main host brings in three fashion designers, including Pierre Gazelle, the designer of Amani's famous stilettos worn in the interview. "These high-profile fashion designers have teamed with NASA to create the best quality uniforms for your choosing, Ms. Jett," the host says.

Amani looks at each of the outfits after listening to the designers' presentations. She likes them all, but finds them to be a bit too revealing.

"These look very tight." Amani says.

One of the designers says, "But, you want them fitted, no?"

"I want my clothes fitted, but I don't want them so tight to the point where the crack of my behind is showing. You guys are trying to give me a yeast infection!" One of the hosts snickers. "Guys, I know 'sexy' is your usual go route, and there's a lot of buzz about me being this and that, but I don't want to be exploited in that way. I'm not a sex symbol."

"We will make these adjustments for you, Ms. Jett. Right away."

"Good," Amani says as she takes a closer look at one uniform. "Now, what is with these logos? This outfit looks like a race car driver's suit."

The designer of that particular suit says, "I had to get sponsors to help with the cost of creating this suit. It is state of the art with a reflective material."

"Keep in mind, I go into serious battles. I want to be taken seriously." She puts down the logo-loaded suit. "I'm not trying to take you out of your element, gentlemen. I requested your help, along with NASA, so I could have a durable set of suits with a sense of style for a woman. I plan to wear each of your suits."

The designers show relief. "Thank you so much, Ms. Jett! This is a surprise!"

"It's cool. I like variety. And you thought I was going to choose just one." She winks.

The designers feel greatly appreciated. They thought Amani was going to choose between their outfits, but she chose them all. She just wanted the best from them. They left happy.

Next, Amani meets the graphic artists who are there to display their concepts for her own emblem. This is not something that she cares much about. It is a simple roll of the dice for her. In the back of her mind, she wonders what else is going on in the world.

Amani wants to establish good relationships, so she sits through the demonstrations, anyway. She has to let law enforcement do their duties without her.

She chooses her emblem, which is the letter "A" in the shape of a stealth fighter jet. There wasn't much enthusiasm in her selecting.

Now entering in, is a man who has his own introduction. "Greetings to the Eighth Wonder of the World, Ms. Amani Jett! Today, I'm going to give you an opportunity to make a substantial amount of money! This dollar figure will surpass what you made from last night's interview. How does that sound?"

Amani lights up. "That sounds great!"

"Good! My name is Herman Schwartz, and I am representing as Vice President of the world-popular, Hooty Magazine. I'd like to-"

"Wait... hold on. Did you say Hooty? As in the nude magazine?"

"Ms. Jett, we get accused of that, but we are so much more than just a magazine with a bunch of pictures of naked women." Amani shows disgust with her head in her hands as Herman continues, "If you're uncomfortable with being topless, Ms. Jett, that would be no problem with us. A cover photo and article is all we'll ask for, but the pay will decrease significantly."

"What's the nature of the article?"

"America sees you as the out-of-this-world woman, yet you are so down to Earth. There is a lot of buzz about your non-love life, so we would like to put more focus on that. This is another way to connect with the public, and as you know, we have one of the biggest followings in the world."

"And what would the front cover consist of?"

"Ms. Jett, you are super-strong, super-powerful, super-beautiful, and super-sexy! King Kong ain't got nothing on you!" Amani chuckles. "So, I came up with this idea. Here in New York City, we put our photographers in a chopper... We fly high, to the top of the Empire State Building... You're there at the top of the building, up against the lightning rod..."

"Hold it, hold it, hold it." She chuckles again. "You want me to simulate a pole dance on the lightning rod of the Empire State Building?"

Herman is hesitant. "Virtually."

"And what would I be wearing?"

"Hopefully, nothing. But, you will be in a tasteful position that will cover up your lady parts. It's art."

"Oh, with the leg up and the arm across, right?"

"Yes! You got the idea!"

"No."

"Huh? I mean, is that a 'no' for the pose, or a 'no' to the-"

"Everything, Mr. Schwartz."

"What did it? Was it the part where the rod came into play? Because that would just be photo edited, being that it's so wide. We also want to insert lightning."

"I'm not excited about posing for that magazine or doing the article. I'm not one of those women who always had dreams of being in that book or meeting the founder. I could care less about a pimp.

"This is the second time this afternoon where someone tried to make me into a sex symbol, then make money off of that. Can a woman just be a woman?"

"Thank you for your time," Herman says, then leaves embarrassed.

Amani says to the hosts, "That guy's heart was racing extra fast!" They laugh.

Amani has no publicist, just popularity. The hosts who accompany her are people who represent the corporation which owns the building where she is having her meetings with various people.

Throughout this week, she receives offers from plenty of companies for endorsements. Here are the types of offers:

Food industry: Cereal box covers, Weight-loss diets, Energy drinks, Sports drinks, and Fast food restaurant kid's meal themes.

Sporting: Gym shoe brands, Athletic wear, Workout equipment manufacturers, Workout video productions, and a fitness magazine spokeswoman offer.

Retail: Clothing lines, Fragrances, Hygiene products, Makeup advertisements, Action figures, and Video games.

Everyone is trying to jump on the Amani Jett bandwagon, but she has no knowledge of most of these products or brands. Each company has excellent representatives who are very confident and persuading in their promotions.

Amani turns down every endorsement of the food industry. She is totally against the blatant genetic modifications of foods. She is absolutely against fast food chains and how they target children.

Also, Amani turns down all athletic wear, feeling that their products are overly priced, shoes in particular. She had heard enough about foul play involving expensive sneakers to make her sick.

Amani vows to try out the many workout contraptions presented to her within the next year to determine if she will endorse either of them. And the same with exercise videos. However, there is uncertainty about the salability of these products.

As much as Amani likes clothing styles, as proven in her selections of the uniforms, she does not want a clothing line. It does nothing for her image and what she is representing. It is cliché, in her opinion.

Though Amani likes the scents of the fragrances and hygiene products, she doesn't use them, nor does she wear the makeup. Amani only uses oils and natural hygiene products. She would feel like a hypocrite to endorse these types of products, since she wouldn't purchase them herself.

There is an inner battle going on within Amani. On one hand, the money sounds great. With her name being in high demand, her fame can make any product sell as a brand. There is a lot she could accomplish with these huge financial offers.

On the other hand, Amani must value her image. She would love to build a school, or homes, or reopen the recreational center that she used to attend, but at what cost? Amani must decide if earning millions is worth selling out her humble, green, and natural image. She needs a little help to decide.

"A hundred million?" Mr. Turner asks, sitting in his recliner. "A hundred million! Did I hear that right?"

"Yes, Dad," Amani answers. "What do you think about it, Auntie Eva?"

Eva Turner-Adams, Amani's aunt, says, "I think you should take it. Screw what other people think. They're going to criticize you in one way or the other."

Mr. Turner says, "That is a lot of money, sweetheart. You have really good ideas, but those things take a lot of time and a lot of effort."

"Who would you get to help you run the school while you're out saving the world?"

"Would it be private? Public? Charter?"

"Which grade levels?"

"Is this truly your passion? I don't mean a passion just for having a school or a bunch of properties, but in order for it to be successful, it must be driven by someone who put their heart into it."

"That's why you need a staff that you can depend on. Your time is limited."

"Are you going to hire property managers? Picked any accountants, yet? Lawyers?"

"If you think you've been busy this past week, you'll be very busy opening up any type of school. And real estate, too?"

Amani says, "I know there will be a lot of steps to take, but I can do it."

Mr. Turner says, "Amani, I believe you can do anything you set your mind to. But, the challenge is setting your mind to one thing and sticking with it."

"Yes, sir."

"You wanted to be a lawyer, then a soldier, then a cop, and then a soldier again. Now, you want to be worldwide. Settle down."

Eva adds, "None of us have been where you are, Amani. We can only imagine. You have every reason to believe that there is no limit for you, but you got to give yourself a break."

"You're still human, Amani. Take care of yourself, first."

"Even the Lord rested on the seventh day! My goodness, girl!"

Mr. Turner sits up straight in his plush chair. "My dear, you are still young and are ambitious. You're thinking of ways to spend money before you even get it. Pace yourself, Amani."

"Please do!"

"Be true to yourself and listen to your own heart. You know who you are. Your mother and I raised you to think for yourself, and now is the time to do just that. I believe in you, Amani. You'll do what's right."

Amani smiles. "Well, I'm definitely going with the action figures and video games!"

Eva says, "Be careful with that. You already got people making churches out of you. They might use your doll as an idol."

"Ma'am?"

"You know." Amani does not know what her aunt is talking about. "You haven't been watching the news?"

"No, ma'am. I got sick and tired of all the hype surrounding me."

"You better pay attention! There's this church in Tennessee called, 'Grace of Amani'. Something like that."

"That is crazy! Are you sure?"

"Yes, girl! Look into it." Amani sighs. "And what about those things that the rapper said about you?"

"Rapper? What rapper? You heard about this, Dad?"

"No I haven't," says Mr. Turner.

"What did he say, Auntie?"

Eva says, "Lamont said that he was saying something like, I want to put my super *blank* in her super *blank*."

Both Amani and her father shout, "What!"

"Lamont didn't tell me this!" Amani says. "Okay, I'll find out who this guy is and deal with him."

"Now, don't go doing nothing crazy," says Eva.

"I won't, depending on your definition of crazy."

"Oh, Lord..."

"Those guys get away with too much! I'll just make an example out of him. I'm not worried about a lawsuit."

"Is he the one who likes to call women B's and H's?"

"One? Just about all of them do that."

Eva sits back with her arms folded. "Well in that case, kick his butt."

"I'll get him alright. Please believe. But first, I got to make a trip to Tennessee."

ATONEMENT

In the outskirts of Memphis, TN sits a mid-sized building called, "Church of Her Grace, Amani Jett".

Amani flies into town on the day after she learned of the place's existence. There is an angry look on her face as she stands before the "church".

When Amani steps inside, she sees all sorts of pictures of her, mostly taken from the night of the interview. Then, there are some paparazzi shots. This setup is more of a storefront than a church.

There are postcards with her pictures on them, holiday cards, greeting cards, T-shirts, and many other unofficial products. This creeps Amani out.

A middle-aged lady steps to the front to greet the church's guest and can't believe her eyes when she sees Amani. "You're here! Thank the heavens! I knew someday soon you would come!" She hugs Amani tightly, who is even more flabbergasted.

"My name is Lucy Stallworth," the peculiar lady says. "I'm so excited to meet you!" She yells out toward the back of the storefront, "George! Our Grace has descended!" Amani is speechless!

George walks in from the back office. "Oh my!" He falls to his knees and Lucy does the same. "We humbly present ourselves to you, our Grace. We come before you as servants."

Amani says, "If you don't get up from your knees..." The two look at each other surprised. "What in the world is wrong with you?" George and Lucy get up from the floor.

"But, I don't understand," George says. "Have you looked inside our hearts and found something that is not of your ways?"

Amani realizes that she can't treat these people like she would common people, understanding that they are truly ignorant. They really believe her to be something that she is not, so she chooses to soften up on them.

"Lucy, George," Amani says, "I want you to no longer address me as your Grace. I'm just simply Amani. That's all." The two look at each other confused again.

George says, "Yes... Amani."

"That's better. So, what is this place? A souvenir shop?"

Lucy replies, "No... Amani. This is the church which honors your name. We give reverence to you and-"

"Please. That is not necessary. Haven't you seen my interview?"

"But, of course," George says.

"Then, you should know that I'm not who you're saying I am. I'm no different than either of you."

"Bless you for your humility, but your secret is safe with us."

"What secret?"

Lucy says, "That you are the Messiah."

Amani gets fed up. "That's it! Who is in charge of this place? This has to stop."

"Pastor Kyle Vance is the founder of this ministry. Please show him great Favor. He works diligently for you."

George says, "Just beyond that door in the back is the sanctuary. I think he is in there. He will be overjoyed to see you."

Amani wastes no time to walk through that rear door. George and Lucy follow behind her. The first thing that catches Amani's eye when she walks in is a shrine in her honor, which is a big painting of her on the wall, surrounded with candles. The setting is actually a traditional layout with rows of pews and a pulpit.

"So, this really **is** a church," Amani says. "I don't believe this."

Pastor Vance comes in from his office, which is just off to the side of the sanctuary. "Our prayers have been answered!" He walks up with opened arms.

Amani halts him when he gets within a few feet of her. "Wait a second. Don't come any closer. I have questions."

"Yes, our Grace."

"See, that right there. Where do you go off calling me your Grace? What's that all about?"

Pastor Vance smiles. "That's who you are to us. Because of your solemn mission, we understand the need to keep your true identity confidential."

"Interesting. You're the Pastor, right?"

"Yes, our Grace. And proudly so."

"How did you become such? Who ordained you? Because, I sure didn't."

Pastor Vance grins. "I'll give you the history of this ministry. This church has been here for thirty-five years. I've been the Pastor ever since.

"But when you appeared, doing miracles that were never done before, I decided to go in another direction. I changed the name of the church and based it around the second coming of a Savior.

"We have a small congregation, as of now, but I'm sure new saints will be rolling in, in days to come."

Amani says, "If this church is legit, then that would make this organization a non-profit, right?"

"Yes, our Grace."

"So what's with the storefront? Isn't that for profit?"

"The church needs to be able to cover its own expenses."

"And you collect tithes and offerings, don't you?" Pastor Vance nods. "And what do you do, Pastor? You represent me? Can you truly speak for me?"

"I... I try to search my heart. And discern in the Spirit."

"What Spirit is that? Because, this shrine over here," she points toward the painting of herself, "I'm not happy about that. I'd like to know what Spirit is responsible for making you do that, so I can have words with it."

Lucy says, "The three of us should pray, like we do during service. The Spirit always shows Pastor Vance the way."

George says, "That's how we knew you would be here someday soon, our Grace."

Amani is totally angry with this so-called Pastor for taking advantage of these naïve people. She looks him right in the eyes, but he keeps calm without swaying. There is no way he'll come clean about his scam.

Amani puts her hands on her hips. "If you believe in me, then take that shrine down."

Pastor Vance says, "Certainly you don't mean that, our-"

"Yes I do, and I'm not your Grace. You know that you're manipulating these people."

George asks the pastor, "Why is She saying this, Pastor?"

"I'll tell you why," Amani says. "He's a conman. He's playing you and the rest of the church members as fools." She walks around him. "He appears to be cool, calm, collective, but his heart rate is hopping all over the place. He's simply taking advantage of you."

George inquires. "Pastor?" But, Pastor Vance will not speak another word.

"He's a false prophet for profit," Amani says. "He never expected me to pop up in here and expose him like this. He's overconfident.

"There are rumors and propaganda about me everywhere, and he found a way to make money off of it. He knew people would buy into it, so he used my name to shine.

"I am not your Messiah or anyone else's. I am just a woman with a gift."

Lucy asks, "But, your gift must come from God Himself! Why are you taking what He's given you for granted?"

Amani replies, "Why are you taking what He's given **you** for granted? Use your head and stop letting people like this crook use it!" She walks to the shrine, falsely dedicated to her, and destroys it. She looks to George and Lucy and says, "Find yourself a real temple."

Amani proceeds with the destruction of the place. What a relief she feels! Afterward, she tells George and Lucy to stay in touch with her via internet. She believes they are very nice people and doesn't want to see them taken advantage of again.

George and Lucy stand there in awe when Amani takes off flying. They still believe that she is a godsend in one way or another. The shamed Pastor is visibly upset. He actually thought Amani was a myth. Like she said, he never expected her to show up at the church. Pastor Vance plans to reopen the church under a different name. Again.

꿋ꞈ

Late night in Atlanta, GA, there is a party going on at a popular nightclub. This event has a special guest; a rapper who goes by the name, "Big Rich". He and his crew are seated in the VIP section.

The Hip Hop star is popping expensive bottles of champagne with his "homies and hoes". The girls were picked out of the crowd to hang with him and his entourage. These girls are considered "lucky" for being selected.

When others pursue Big Rich to take pictures with them, they are stopped by his security. These guys are very strict and are on top of their job.

In comes Amani, who's not in her best mood. Her presence was not expected. Those who recognize her freeze in their place, having a hunch on why she is there. The look on her face tells it. They know those lyrics.

The DJ announces, "Oh snap! You never know who might pop up at his club! That's why it's better than the rest!" Big Rich stands up to see who it is. "It's the one! The only! Amani Jett!"

The place goes crazy! Big Rich stands to his feet and claps for her. Amani isn't enthused, as she heads straight for the VIP, where Big Rich is waiting to greet her.

Once they are face-to-face, Big Rich says, "What a surprise! I'm glad you came. Want a glass of this champagne?" Amani does not say a word. "Oh, you're probably mad about what I said on my track." He giggles about it. "You know how the entertainment industry is. I meant nothing by it."

Amani slaps Big Rich in the face, sending him to the wall. He spins spirally until he lands on the floor.

The DJ says, "Damn!"

Amani eyeballs security, daring them to do something about it. They won't try it, nor would Big Rich's company. One guy turns away, scratching the back of his head.

People in the crowd become afraid of Amani. This is not what she wanted, so instead of a cold, mean exit from the club, she goes to the DJ booth and asks for the microphone. The DJ obliges.

Amani says, "Just had to teach him a lesson, y'all. Keep the party going!" The crowd cheers. "Oh, and another thing... all of that talk he does about him being well endowed? Well, you know about my X-ray discernment, right?" She points at Big Rich. "Dude has a baby penis!"

The crowd taunts Big Rich. They insult him by chanting "Big Bitch," repeatedly, then Amani leaves soon after. Many in attendance had their video camera phones on, recording the humiliation. This is sure to get the media's attention.

THE AMANI THREAT

The newly-appointed Director of the Central Intelligence Agency(DCI) is led quietly into a mysterious location within the nation's capital. This building is heavily guarded.

The secretary walks him into a dim room, then leaves him with those who arranged this meeting. He is greeted by a few familiar faces, and some new.

"Good morning, sir," one of the persons says. "Before you speak, we are addressed by different code names in these quarters. And everything said in here is kept confidential."

The DCI shows his curiosity. "What is this meeting all about? I wasn't expecting to see you three here. What's going on?"

"This is a secret sector, only known of by the President, Vice President, those sitting here, and now you. Please, have a seat."

The DCI looks around at everyone before taking his seat. "Is this sector under my authority?"

"At this moment, no. It was headed by your predecessor, before his resignation. This meeting will be a briefing of our agenda."

"And what would that be?"

"Regulating the potential threat of Amani Jett."

The DCI is surprised to hear about this! He had no idea that there was such a group within the organization. He starts to doubt. "This is a prank. Surely, you guys are pulling my chain."

Another group member says, "Not at all, sir. This is very serious."

"Then, why was this sector kept hidden from so many of us in the agency?"

"Do you realize how powerful Ms. Jett has become?"

"Of course!" the DCI shouts. "And it's been to our benefit!"

"But, what if that changes, Director?"

The DCI is disgusted. "So, this is basically a what-if operation. How long have you been doing this?"

"Since her first discovery."

"Ten years? Oh my god."

"Director, you are aware that she holds valuable information. She has shown that she could disrupt sensitive operations. She even admitted she would resist punishment if anyone tried to subdue her."

Another group member says, "Amani **can** be an extreme danger to our way of life. All of us had questioned at some point; what if she turned on us?"

"But, she wouldn't," the DCI says. "We met her before and we know well enough that she is a reasonable troop."

"I agree, sir, but would you bet your life on that? Or better yet, do you really want to risk the country for your faith in her? Who can govern her?"

Another group member says, "Our soldiers pledge. We have laws for our soldiers. We have penalties for our soldiers. Why would it be any different for Ms. Jett?"

"Mr. Director, I love Amani. Dearly. But she, just like myself and any of us, would need to be held accountable if anything harmful results from her doings. Without the vision of this group, we are giving her a free pass to do as she pleases."

"We have to have a defense against her, in other words. And you know just as anyone else, sir, sometimes to defend means to eliminate." The Director ponders. "We're not asking you assume the position as the former Director. Had he not resigned, he'd still be a part of this group."

The DCI asks, "Is this still considered CIA? Or is this another covert alternate?"

"Yes, it is a covert alternate. All standard rules do not apply to our operations."

Another group member says, "Please don't look at this as a plot to get rid of our friend as we know her. But, she's still human and she has impulses."

He takes a remote control and lowers a video monitor. "Have you heard about the incident outside of Memphis? She allegedly destroyed a church."

"I've read," says the DCI, as he watches footage of the destroyed Church of Amani.

"The pastor of the church is going to press charges and sue for his injuries. What do you expect Ms. Jett to do?"

Another group member says, "And there are people of the public who are going to demand law enforcement to take action against her. But how?"

"Then, you have the video of the slapping incident that occurred that same night. Mr. Director, clearly you can see that she is doing what she wants at her own will, with no regard."

"This cannot continue. She may have good reasons to act out, but in the process, she is making us look weak. She's showing the world that she can do as she pleases and not face any penalties."

"She has been a life-saver since we've met her. She foiled a large number of terrorist attacks on American soil. I salute her for those acts and will never forget what she's done for our country...

"However, we would be irresponsible to do nothing about her conduct, or try to prevent future acts."

"I understand," says the DCI, "you don't have to explain any more to me. Citizens of our country need to be able to depend on us as a nation, more than they do one gifted individual."

"Good! I knew you would understand. This is a difficult conversation, but necessary."

"But, why this level of secrecy?"

"Amani has access to everything. As you know, there is no easy way to hide from her. This group was carefully selected and was intended to have a small membership."

"So, after a decade of brainstorming, what have you all come up with?"

The group members appear to be short of solutions. "We've studied her for years," one of the members says, "but we cannot track the source of her powers. Therefore, we can't discover many weaknesses."

Another group member says, "But, Amani is a human being, that's for sure."

"Yes, she needs air. She is affected by weather. Not sure what she may be allergic to. Her immunities don't seem much greater than the average person. She ages, obviously."

"If she travels to continents like Africa on her own, then we must find a way to have her quarantined upon every reentry. No matter what the case. She cannot take any injections, because she is impenetrable."

"The only vulnerable spots she has on her body are on the inside. She refuses to take any type of pill or drug. For every sickness she obtains, she only uses natural, herbal remedies."

"God forbid if we would have to take her out. But if so, CO poisoning might be our best bet. Carbon monoxide is non-detectable, even by her, and would neutralize her without her even knowing it."

The DCI asks, "And how would you isolate her?"

"That became complicated ever since she proclaimed her independence. Whatever we do, it would have to be done perfectly. Amani is skillful enough to figure things out if a plan failed. There could only be one attempt at her life."

The DCI asks, "And what about her family? If push comes to shove, shouldn't we put ourselves in a position to negotiate?"

Another group member says to the DCI, "That was something I asked one time, and our former Director ended that idea quickly."

"He believed that it was too dangerous," says another member. "Said it was a sure way to start a civil war. He sees Amani a little different than we do."

"That, I do recall," says the DCI. "But, now that he's no longer in charge, I advise you to consider it." The group members look around at each other.

"We have many tactics in that area, so let's keep them in mind. Now... what do we have on her background?"

"She was born Amani Rena Turner. Father; Calvin H. Turner, blue collar worker in the automobile industry. Somewhat of a militant type, which would explain Amani's defiance at times.

"Her mother; Rosanna Turner, deceased, as we already knew. No close contacts from that side of the family.

"Younger sister; Ivy Turner. Mother of three, lives with boyfriend. Attends school part time."

"That's Amani's immediate family, and we have information on other family members as well. This cousin of hers, Lamont Adams, is a character. He spats anti-American rhetoric on the internet. A sure embarrassment and humiliation for Amani."

"Humiliation is much needed. Anything to discredit her from the American public can be useful. That would turn them away from her, making her absence more tolerable and would appear to be karmic."

"She's ruining her image on her own, but it's good to have that added advantage."

"So, what do you think, Director?"

The DCI says, "I completely understand the purpose of this group."

"We would be careless not to have it, sir."

The group member with the remote control plays video footage of Amani in action. The DCI can't believe his eyes! In the video, Amani is taking on Taliban forces by herself, unarmed.

"I've never seen this video!" the DCI says. "When was this?"

"Back in October of 2010. This footage is top secret. We use many videos like this one to study her.

"Look at how she rips through vehicles." He plays the video in slow motion. "Look at her form. She has studied martial arts. Highly skilled."

"She's not even using her gun!" the DCI says. "Unbelievable! And you've been hiding this footage from me?"

"Until now. Had you not supported our agenda, it wouldn't have been disclosed."

Another group member says, "Amani is much stronger than she was when we first met her. It's like she gets better with every battle. Definitely more than a seek-and-find mercenary."

"She is a one woman army."

The video screen shows Amani standing victoriously over beaten Taliban soldiers. She has bullet damage to her clothes, but no physical bruises.

The DCI says, "When she first came to the National Guard after capturing the Cartel boss, she had small bruises on her body from the gunfight. But after this battle, she doesn't appear to have a blemish!" He is in total amazement.

Another group member says, "This battle was called in after recording the biggest loss of Marine soldiers in the year; the deadly month of October. Amani was sent there to assist the soldiers.

"As you can see, she punished them all. But, her orders were to terminate them. Kill them dead.

"Instead, she left us with a large number of P.O.W.'s, refusing to finish the job. So, our soldiers gladly executed the Afghan soldiers that she left as prisoners. Amani wasn't too excited about the decision of the military."

Another group member says, "She fails to understand the premise of... war."

"And, the other concern we have is the danger of her releasing secret information, which is unlikely, but still possible. This is why we carefully monitored her interview with Susan Dunn. We must keep an eye on her."

"I agree," the DCI says. "My duties will remain as they have been. I will not assume any position in this group, however."

"We respect your choice, Director. And we were glad to have had you in our presence, today."

They all shake hands with the DCI before escorting him out of the building. The DCI attended the meeting alone and in secret, leaving the same way he entered.

Back inside the dim room, the group members are having a short discussion:

"You were right, Agent Blue. It is better that we run this group with those who were present from the start."

"Yes, but at least the Director is aware of us."

Agent Black asks, "But, to what benefit? That it keeps us legit?"

"Legitimacy is important in the eyes of the President, Agent Black. When in question, the Director will vouch for us, seeing that we have significant purpose."

"I didn't know the group was in danger of not being obligatory."

"Obligatory, yes. But, it has yet to be proven worth funding. Washington is trying to cut as much spending as possible.

"It was also a good idea not to brief him on the other plans. Speaking of the other plans, Agent Red and Agent Gray, is there a report on the scientific developments?"

"At a standstill," says Agent Red. "But, there is hope in the international market."

Agent Gray responds, "The manufacturing of new drones are set to start in sixty days, Agent Blue. Looks promising."

Agent Blue says, "That's good to hear. As for the international market, Agent Red, I'd like to avoid that path. Clone technology is not to be established outside the US." Other group members agree. "That would lead to a compromise which is definitely not in our best interest. And I doubt the President would be open to a worldwide debate on something that is historically controversial.

"This will be our last meeting at this facility. Our other locations will continue to be accessible." This meeting is adjourned.

THE COMMITTEE

D aytime at the Turner residence, Amani gathered people who she trusts. They are there to meet with her for something very important. In attendance are Mr. Turner, Ivy, Auntie Eva, and Lt. Julio Vega of the Detroit Police Dept. The meeting is being held in the basement.

"First of all, I'm glad you made it," Amani says. "As you know, I will be having my first public press conference this coming weekend in downtown Detroit." Eva finds the need to applaud, so everyone else follows. "Thanks. I realize that in order for me to be effective in my future endeavors, I will need assistance. I'm asking for help from the people I trust.

"In the past ten years, most would say that I've done a lot. Yes, I put in a lot of work, but I'm not totally satisfied with the results.

"I put away crime bosses, dirty cops, a dirty lawyer, and exposed some crooked politicians in the city. But, what became of it? Did it become a better city afterward?" Everyone denies it. "I was thinking the same thing. Not much has changed.

"Some of those top bad men had special connections and served sentences much shorter than what they deserved, even the bad cops. Violence in Mexico is now at a new high, since I've crippled the one cartel in '07.

"That lawyer, who was Eric's guy and who had clearly helped put you in danger at one time, is now campaigning to be a judge!

"Lieutenant, you were right about me. Back when we were partners, I was young and didn't know the game. Now, I can understand it very well.

"You can't tear down without a plan to rebuild. That's something we should have learned from the riots that took place in the sixties, or as Dad calls it, the rebellion.

"I was discouraged at one time, thinking I was just wasting my time. Maybe I should have gone to school to become... I don't know.

"But then, I had to remind myself what was most important. The many lives that were saved as a result of my actions.

"This is what keeps me going. Not severe punishment of the bad guys. So, I want to make that clear to you.

"As you know, I have opposition coming from every angle. And the one I'm concerned about knows as much about me as I do. I've worked for them.

"They wanted blood samples from me. They wanted locks of my hair, saliva from my mouth. They want more like me. They want me to be expendable.

"If you ask why, it is because they fear me. Mom and Dad taught me to think for myself, so I couldn't possibly be the soldier that they wanted me to be.

"I found information. Deep, dark secrets kept by our own Government. Understandably hidden, I admit. So, I know that they'll be watching my every move.

"They think I'm foolish enough to exploit them. But, that would be reckless. There are more ways to hurt them than putting more fear and anxiety into the people than there already is."

"Will you tell us?" Mr. Turner asks.

"No, Dad. Never."

"Then, what are we to do when things go bad?"

"They won't. And if they did, there would be nothing you could do but keep living.

"As long as you have fear, any and all of your enemies will have an advantage over you. Stop worrying! We are all equipped with the instinct to survive.

"Keep in mind, these government factions are not all about destruction, but there are cases where some geographical locations could be a lot more safer than others.

"What I need from you is to frequently gather reports. It's very simple. I am going to divide databases between you.

"I hope all of you will accept being my exclusive reconnaissance team. I really need you."

"How much are you paying?" Ivy asks.

"Ivy, I don't have a consistent income where I can calculate an annual budget. I'm asking you to trust me like I'm trusting you."

"Okay." Everyone else accepts as well.

"The database will be in four categories. The first category is Background. Lt. Vega, I will need you to pull your resources for information on suspects in question."

"As always," says Lt. Vega.

"Auntie Eva, I will need you to be my dispatcher, which is the second of categories. You'll have the maps, state laws, and soon, international laws ready for me. You will be my main guide during my missions and you will keep us all connected."

"I can do that," Eva says. "It'll be like my secretary days."

"Great. The third category is public relations, which will be overseen by you, Ivy. I need you to stay on top of what's being said in the press, on social media, and all other networks that I **know** you use often."

Ivy says, "Yeah, that's what I do anyway."

"And, Ivy, you should stay connected with the lieutenant. His information and yours go hand-in-hand. People reveal themselves a lot on these social networks."

"They sure do. Tell all of their business."

"Mr. Turner... Dad... I need you to study the system like never before. For as long as I can remember, you have always stayed on top of the news. Whether local, national, or worldwide.

"Even while I'm on missions, I want you to monitor special interest groups and their agendas. Watch where the money's going. Every move of the military. Give me the dots to connect."

"Piece of cake, sweetheart," Mr. Turner says.

"Aren't you missing someone?" Vega asks. "A certain scientist you used to tell me about when you first started?"

Amani ponders. "Who? Joanie? Oh, no."

"Why not? You once told me how she kept up with everything that had to do with science and technology."

"Joanie is my friend. But! She's a scaredy-cat."

Lt. Vega throws his hands up. "What is that supposed to mean?"

"Okay, here is Joanie..." She impersonates Joanie. "I think you should work things out with the CIA. They are here to help you. You shouldn't hire your family members to do your business." The family members laugh. "If they want you to do something that you don't approve of, then I'm **sure** there is a good reason behind it. You shouldn't go against our leaders." She stops imitating. "And when she sees that I won't do what she thinks is right, she would call authorities, exposing this whole operation out of fear. She will never be a part of this committee."

Lt. Vega says, "Understood. I can't work with people who can't keep their mouths shut, either."

"You did make a good point about her, though. I could use her help when it comes to technology and bio-technics. I'll make a special trip to Illinois to see her."

"What are you going to tell her?"

"It'll be easy. All I have to do with Joanie is ask her questions and she'll go on and on. She gets excited in her line of work." Lt. Vega nods. "So! Now that we're all on the same page, I feel a lot better. And Ivy, I will you take care of you. Don't you worry about it."

"Thanks, Sis," Ivy says. "I'm on top of the job, already."

"I bet you are."

"Me too," says Mr. Turner.

"Same here," Lt. Vega replies.

Amani smiles confidently. "I really do appreciate this. Someday, this will be a bigger operation, but

I'm glad to start things off with trustees."

"There's another person missing," Eva says. "Where's my boy? Where's Lamont at?" Ivy tries to signal her aunt to quieten her. "Naw, we're in this together, right? Lamont could use the work."

"And I cannot use Lamont," Amani says. "No use whatsoever. Not for what I'm trying to do."

"Now, that's not fair, Amani. He's your cousin."

Ivy shouts, "Auntie! Please! She does not need his help."

"I just don't see why Lamont can't be a part of-"

Mr. Turner cuts in. "Eva, let's respect her choice and move on. Okay?"

"Alright, alright." She pauses. "Maybe if-"

"Eva!"

"Okay!"

Amani says, "Then, that's that. We are a solid unit. No newcomers, unless I appoint them myself." She speaks in a stronger tone. "This is more than a family affair. This is serious business. Lives will depend on us. I don't want to hear another word about money and who needs it." She looks at each of them in their eyes. "Are we all clear?"

Everyone says, "Yes."

Amani smiles. "Perfect."

BULLY

Amani lands in front of a beautiful house in Springfield, IL. This is the home of Joan and Dylan Jacoby. The couple moved from Michigan two years ago and found solace here.

This is only Amani's third time visiting. She rings the doorbell, but no one answers. She knocks on the storm door, and still, no one answers. Next, Amani tries calling Joanie on her cellphone, only to get Joanie's voice mail greeting.

Amani leaves the message, "Joanie... open the door. You know I can hear everything. You can't blame it on the loud TV or radio, because neither of those are playing. Just answer the dang doorbell. I didn't come all this way for nothing."

Moments later, the door is opened. Joanie ducks her head and says, "Come on in."

"That's no way to greet your friend!" says Amani. "Give your girl a hug or something."

As Joanie reaches out to hug, Amani notices the blackened eye on her face.

"I'mma kill him," Amani says.

Joanie pleads, "No, no! Please don't hurt him!"

244

"Why not?"

"He's my husband! Don't hurt him! We worked things out!"

Amani sits with her friend on the sofa. "He shouldn't pay for what he did, because he's your husband? Tell me, where were your wife benefits when he gave you that black eye?"

"Please, Amani! He really is a good man."

"You don't even believe that. Why do you insist on telling me what you think you want me to hear, instead of telling me the truth?"

Joanie looks ashamed. "I just don't want you to do anything to harm him. I mean, if I wanted vengeance, I would have called the police."

Amani nods. "You are right. I can't force you to take action against your husband. I do believe that a warning would be feasible."

"Or, do you mean a threat?"

"Same word, different spelling."

"Come on, Amani."

"Look, Joanie, I've been involved in plenty of situations like this. Wives who get physically abused by their husbands, or girlfriends by their boyfriends.

"I don't recall one case where that man never violated the woman again after she took up for him. Not one case! Unless she was the aggressor, and I know for sure that you weren't.

"So, let me talk to him. I'm surprised that he even had the nerve! Has he hit you before?"

"Yes," Joanie says.

"In front of Justine?"

Joanie sniffles. "Yes."

"Did he threaten you with what he would do if you told me or anyone else?"

"...Yes."

"Then, I must do what I must do. Your husband is too dangerous-"

"No, no-"

"Too dangerous to be with you two!"

Joanie cries, "You're ruining my life!"

"No, I'm saving it. I'll offer you protection. I could use your help in return."

"What do you want from me?"

"Keep me up to date on modern science and technology. Wherever you get your info, I'd like to have access to it. A good look into the future."

"Why is that so important to you?"

"I just might invest. Even make some big contributions to science."

Joanie finally shows a sign of happiness. "Really? That would be great! There are so many things taking effect in the near future!

"You might not have to fight another war, with these new unmanned tanks and drones. It would be a smart investment for you!"

Amani says, "That is the most I'm going to tell you. And take note, I said I <u>might</u> invest."

"Don't worry. Your secret is safe with me!"

"Thanks. So, do we have a deal?"

"Yes indeed! This is going to be awesome! I can't wait to see what happens!"

"That's the Joanie I remember."

Hours later, Joanie's husband, Dylan has returned home from work. He opens the door from the garage entry and announces his arrival, then he wonders why there is no food cooked.

When Dylan enters the dining room, he sees his luggage packed. Next, he goes into the bathroom and sees the bathtub unfilled. This infuriates him!

"Joan!" Dylan yells. "Where are you?"

Joanie patiently sits in the den, watching a movie with a glass of wine. The film she watches is about a woman who stands up for herself after years of abuse by her husband.

Dylan enters the den, smelling of liquor. "Joanie! Why isn't there food ready for me and why-"

Joanie shushes him. "I'm watching this movie. You're loud."

Dylan can't believe the nerve of his wife! He marches toward Joanie and pulls her up by the hair. She screams out loud.

"Hey," the calm and distant voice of Amani resonates.

Dylan releases Joanie quickly. "Who's there? Come on out, you coward!" He grabs Joanie by her throat. "I'll fucking choke her out! You better show yourself!" He looks left. He looks right. "I'm not fucking kidding!" There is no sign of anyone. "Stay still," he demands Joanie.

Little does he know, Amani is floating right above the two, upside down. Her eyes are locked in from the aerial position.

Dylan yells, "Bring your ass out-"

Quickly, Amani chokes Dylan from above and says, "There are six bones in the neck." Joanie signals seven. "That's right. Seven. Let her go, and I'll only break two of them." Dylan tries to break away, but it only hurts to do so. "The longer you wait, the more I'll break."

Dylan instantly releases his grasp of Joanie, causing her to fall to the floor coughing. Once she catches her breath, she asks for Amani to show mercy for her husband. Even with all the abuse, Joanie has much compassion for Dylan.

From the head locked position, Dylan tries to gouge Amani's eyes out with his thumbs. Amani laughs at him with her eyes widely opened, merely affected by his attempt.

Amani tosses Dylan across the room. She takes him by the neck again, but from the front this time, lifting him above the floor.

Amani says to Dylan, "It's funny how you questioned your wife about your food not being done, but asked nothing about your daughter and her whereabouts. Don't you think that's a bit backwards?

"Say yes or no, or shake your head." Dylan can do neither. "Oh, that's right. You're in an uncompromising position." She faces Joanie. "Joanie, how does that feel, being in an uncompromising position?"

"Well, Amani..." Joanie replies, "it feels pretty bad."

"I kind of figured that. What do you think, Dylan?" Dylan tries kicking her. "See? Still no compromise." She faces Joanie again. "I forget, how many bones in his neck was I supposed to break?" She squeezes tighter and says to Dylan, "That's for trying to hurt me."

Joanie says, "Let him live. Besides, I don't want Justine's feelings hurt."

Amani says to Dylan, "You have a great wife. You know that? She just saved your life. I'm going to let you down, because I'm not a bully like you."

Amani slams Dylan to the floor with big impact, startling Joanie a bit. This put the much needed fear in Dylan. Amani had to let him know just how serious she could be. As folks from the old school would say, she knocked some sense into him.

Joanie says to her husband, "I will return to work again. I want my independence back from you! Now, pack those bags and get out of here."

Amani gets into Dylan's head by saying to Joanie, "I still don't trust him. There have been too many murder-suicide cases I've witnessed."

"You think he would try?"

"He might be stupid enough. I think I should paralyze him, so he'll be harmless. It won't be the first time I broke the law."

Dylan pleads, "Please no! I'm not psycho! I just made foolish mistakes and I need help!"

Joanie begins to tear up. She can't hold her emotions back when seeing her husband defeated by his emotions. She is glad to hear him admit that he needs help.

Joanie asks Amani, "Is he telling the truth?"

"See to it that you get some help," Amani tells Dylan. "And know that there will be a restraining order against you for abusing your wife."

Dylan takes what he needs before leaving the house. "I'll be at my brother's, Joan. So, when you change your mind, I'll be there for you." He makes his exit.

Joanie says to Amani, "I am so glad you came back to see me! And I'm so sorry for not letting you be the best friend that I know you are! I should've told you what I was going through."

"As long as you're fine, now," says Amani. "We should go pick up Justine from-" Her mobile phone rings. "Just a second, Joanie. It's my aunt."

Amani speeds to a different room to talk on this phone line. Her aunt is calling as her dispatcher. Amani wants to make sure that her words won't be overheard.

"Ready for report," Amani says.

Eva shouts, "Girl, these folks out here are crazy! They done lost their minds!"

"Please keep it professional, Dispatch."

"Oh, sorry. Listen to this; there's a man... a young White male in Minneapolis, MN... who just made a bomb threat."

"We're going to have to go over these routine phone calls. Please give me the exact location, first."

"Okay, 1283 Buckingham Ave at the Community Center. There is a bomb threat. Where is your location?"

"I'm in Illinois, approximately three hours away. I don't think I can make it to that one."

"You're going to have to. This man wants to see you. He's an obsessed fan of yours."

"You have got to be kidding me."

"I kid you not. And they're saying this boy ain't got no clothes on!"

"I am on my way."

Amani pardons herself from the house and tells Joanie to keep her updated on the rocky marriage. Joanie agrees to do so. She goes to the front door to let Amani out, but Amani already flew right outside through the window.

Joanie says to herself, "Oh."

Amani soars through the skies, heading west from Illinois to Minnesota. She is in contact with Lt. Vega.

"The man's name is Andrew Hardy," says Lt. Vega. "As you would guess, he has a history of mental illness. He's been in trouble for arson, and has been labeled a pyromaniac."

"Thanks, Lieutenant," Amani says. "What a day."

Soon after, here is an incoming call from Ivy. "Hey, girl!" Ivy shouts.

"Why are you calling me on this line?"

"Why else? I have a report."

"Haven't you seen the emergency in progress?"

"This **is** the emergency in progress!"

"What? No, this is not your department. You are to target media coverage about me."

"That's what I'm doing! You're being talked about on Hello Entertainment News! They're showing the inside of the Community Center in Minnesota!"

"That's not entertainment!"

"With your name involved, yes it is. One of the hostages was recording with his camera phone.

"You can actually see the guy with his clothes off, holding a detonator! He has tattoos of you all over his body. They blurred his privates, of course."

"That's disgusting. So, what does he want from me?"

"I hope you're not trying to get a logical answer for that question. Just show up! He might want your autograph."

"Just great," Amani mumbles.

"And check this out! Before the hostage's phone battery went dead, he got a good view of that bomb. It has your picture taped to it and it says, 'Amani is the bomb'."

"Well, I'll be damned. Watch the media blame me for this, somehow."

"And Lamont's friends will blame you, too." She laughs.

Amani laughs. "I know, right! Crazy so-and-so's. So, this guy is really naked. I don't want to have to deal with him."

"Tough job you got there. I like my job a lot better. Just use you super speed and tackle him."

"Yuck! I don't want to go near him. I can't believe that my first experience with a naked man is going to be this." Ivy is hysterical! "It ain't that funny, baby momma."

"Aye, don't get mad at me because you got a date with a nut case!"

Inside of the Community Center in the city of Minneapolis, MN, is a group of young people, mostly teenagers, and two adults. They are lined up against the wall, along the floor wearing handcuffs. They are hostages of a crazed maniac who is running around naked with an explosive device in his hand.

Outside of the hijacked building, a news reporter addresses her live audience. "It was a special event at the Community Center; The March of Heroes, where children observed who they consider as their most influential heroes. Needless to say, there have been many praises surrounding the super-powered vixen, Amani Jett.

"People gathered to watch the children's displays for their heroic stars. But, something unfortunate occurred. A lone gunman barged into the building, demanding everyone to get on the floor.

"He initially wore a trench coat with a backpack strapped around his back. This backpack was later revealed to contain a bomb.

"Most of the people made it out of the place, but there are still some trapped inside with the lunatic."

Amani crosses the border to Minnesota and checks in with Lt. Vega. "Almost there."

When people see Amani passing by, they cheer for her. There is a new trend starting dubbed, "Amani-watch", where civilians search the sky to spot Amani en route to her destination. Knowing where the trouble lies ahead, some watchers anticipate her passing by, so they make sure to keep their cameras ready.

Back inside the center, the crazed man is running around, toying with the spotlight that is tracking him. "Can't catch me! Can't catch me!" The assault rifle he used to take over the facility is sitting next to the bomb that has Amani's picture taped to it.

"Who loves Amani!" Andrew, the crazed man, shouts. "I do! Eighth Wonder of the World! Super soldier!" He marches to the big windows, facing the fleet of police cars to show off his tattoos of Amani. "She saved my brother! A true American! I'll die for her!" He turns around to face the hostages. "I'll kill for her."

Finally, Amani makes it to the scene, landing behind the rows of policemen whose guns are aiming toward Andrew. They are positioned behind their vehicles.

The commanding officer says to Amani, "If you are who they say you are, please end this nonsense, so we can get the hell out of here."

Amani approaches the Community Center at a normal pace. As she walks, she scans out the entire building and spots Andrew Hardy right out in the open with nothing on but his boots. Amani wants to throw up when she sees drawings of herself on this maniac's body.

A hostage speaks out, "It's Amani!"

Andrew looks over his shoulder and sees Amani walking toward the building. A tear drops his eye. He lifts his arms and says, "I knew she would come! No mountain is high enough!"

Amani enters through the double glass doors. "Okay, fella, what's with the indecent exposure? Put some clothes on."

"Like my tattoos? They're for you."

"And why the bomb, Andrew? Why are you threatening these poor people? What did they do to you?"

Andrew becomes frustrated. "You ask too many questions! Say you like my tattoos! Or I will blow this place up!"

Amani reluctantly says, "I like the tatts, now give me that detonator."

"I like your hair. I want a tattoo with your-"

"Andrew. The switch. Hand it to me."

Andrew spreads his arms apart. "Come to me. I want a hug from you." He starts to cry. "I love you. Not like these people, but I've always loved you from the bottom of my heart!"

"That is very sweet-"

"Don't patronize me! Come here. Tell me you love me, too!"

Amani looks around. "I love all of you."

"Not them! Me!" He becomes extra fidgety. "I will blow this place up! Say it!"

"If I get too close..." she points behind her, "they will start shooting. I don't want that, so let me tell them it is okay. Alright?"

"You got one minute! You're fast! You only need a minute!"

Amani smiles at him. "Thanks!" She looks to the hostages. "Sit tight, everybody." She zooms over to the commanding officer. "Give me a sharpshooter, so we can go home. We have less than a minute."

The commanding officer speaks on his walkie-talkie. "Hauser, come in."

"I'm here, Sarge," Hauser says.

"The young lady wants a sniper rifle. She needs it pronto. You're the nearest shooter."

"Yes, sir."

Amani locates the sniper and immediately flies to him. She takes his rifle and says, "Thank you," then returns to her original spot next to the sergeant. Next, she removes the rifle's scope.

"What are you going to do?" the sergeant asks.

"Take his knuckle out," Amani says. "I got this." She aims the weapon.

"That is... that's insane! You'll set the bomb off!"

"No I won't. I only went in there to get a closer look at the detonator. It'll be safe."

Nearby officers who heard this look at Amani as if she is as crazy as Andrew. Amani locks in on Andrew's thumb, which sits over the bomb trigger. He won't stop moving, but she is not worried.

Amani takes her shot through the glass window. She hits her target! The shot was right on the knuckle of Andrew's thumb. The detonator falls from his massively wounded hand, spinning on its way down.

Amani is poised with a lock on the button. On its way down, the trigger nearly hits against the floor, which would set the explosives off. Amani aims exactly where she needs to, then fires. She hits the detonator before it touches the floor, preventing the bomb from going off.

Andrew is curled on the floor in the fetal position, yelling in pain. "My hand!"

The Bomb Squad and other policemen rush in. They inspect the detonator and witness just how accurate Amani was. She totally avoided the hot wire!

The sergeant says to Amani, "Yep. You are what they say you are." They shake hands.

"What was your name again?" Amani asks.

"It <u>was</u> Sergeant Paul Orton, but now, you can call me amazed!" They laugh together.

Moments later, Amani meets the freed hostages. She takes pictures with them, along with police

d on my way here."

super."

being super isn't enough. Your

aught you... never mind." She hugs

is Dylan's sister. Justine stayed

Amani and Joanie confronted Dylan

cted this from him," Rebbecca says

"Our father was that way at times,

oint of..." She begins to cry.

to get weary. She craves a drink of

nk of choice is alkaline water, but

tever she can get. As Amani heads to

machine, someone asks for her

if you can get me a bottle of this

Amani says to the admirer.

young lady says. "Gladly! But, why do

to get you water? Don't you have

I think. It doesn't... quite..." Amani

sh. The young lady catches her from

he wakes back up.

gotten any sleep, Ms. Jett?"

ut that. No I haven't."

he hands Amani the bottled water.

o rest. Drink the water." She walks

nearest waiting room.

officers, and signs a few autographs. The news reporters hurry after Amani to get a story. She gladly talks about the success of this mission and thanks the police department.

This is good for her reputation, which was starting to get questioned due to the pastor's claim and the slapping video. Amani does not want people to be afraid of her, but she certainly wants to be respected.

Amani receives another emergency call. "What is it now, Dispatch?"

Eva says, "Good job, Amani. But, there's some bad news. Joanie was just rushed to the hospital."

"What!" She flies off right away. The people of Minneapolis wave goodbye to Amani as she soars faster than ever before!

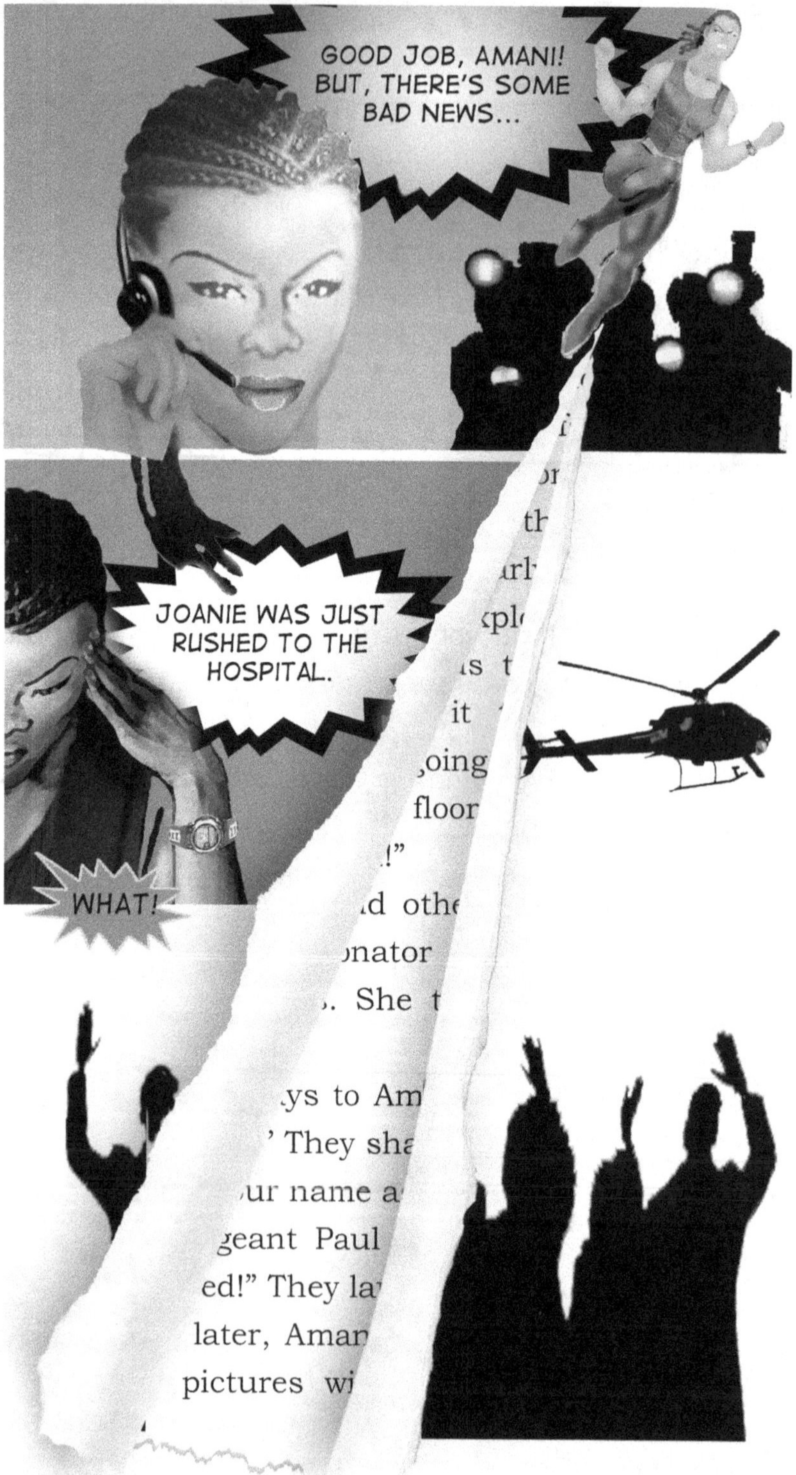

GOOD JOB, AMANI! BUT, THERE'S SOME BAD NEWS...

JOANIE WAS JUST RUSHED TO THE HOSPITAL.

WHAT!

The n
head
parer
This girl hav
1 operator. T
This girl seei
This girl not l

Amani mal
time she made
of the hospital
landing, Aman
pushed hersel
she did. She w

Amani scans
to find out whe
Amani along th
through the wal

"Justine!" Am
squeezes her snu

"Please help m
"It's in the doc
"No." Justine
never part of her

"Well, I praye
"Why? You're
"Sometimes,
parents never t
Rebbecca, who
with her while
earlier.

"I never exp
of her brother.
but not to the

Amani start
water. Her dr
she'll take wha
the beverage
autograph.

"I'll sign it
spring water,"

"Sure!" the
you need me
millions?"

"Very soon
starts to cra
falling, then

"Have you
"Sorry abo
"Here..."
"You need
Amani to the

Amani drinks the water with one long pouring. As she gulps the water, the plastic bottle crushes with every swallow.

"Wow!" the young lady says. "You were really thirsty!"

Amani replies, "**Dang** I feel so much better! Thank you so much."

"Need another one? Another two?"

"Yes, please! I'll pay you back when the money comes through."

"You don't owe me a penny. Don't sweat it. With all that you do?" She gasps. "This is on me." She hands over the pencil and paper for Amani to make out to her.

Amani signs her autograph. "What's your name?"

"Gwen Zorn at your service."

Amani just now realizes that Gwen is a nurse. "Oh... you work here. I must have been out of it!"

"Yes you were. I understand that you want to help people, and that is totally spectacular as ever! But, you got to take care of yourself. You're too important to us, Amani."

"True. I let stress get the best of me."

"What are you doing in Springfield?"

"Checking on a friend." She pauses. "Can you tell me what's going on with a woman by the name of Joan Jacoby? She was brought to Emergency a couple of hours ago with a gunshot head wound."

"Yes! She is a fighter. They're saying she may make it through this, but the damage is... it's really bad."

Amani ducks her head and cries. Gwen is shocked that a woman of Amani's stature is susceptible to tears! She hugs Amani and gives her encouragement.

"Let me get more of that water for you," Gwen says.

Amani feels regretful and blames herself for her actions leading to this outcome. She asks herself if it was worth stepping in, but only time will tell.

When Gwen returns with water, Amani asks her to keep the relationship she has with Joanie confidential, if possible, and Gwen agrees.

Joanie is in a coma. The doctor tells her sister-in-law everything that she needs to know; where the bullet hit, the potential brain damage she may have, the estimated time of recovery, and the medication she will need. Rebbecca relays the message to Amani before she takes off.

ԐⵗԐ

At the Turner residence, Amani's family waits for her. They are curious about the details of Joanie's condition. Mr. Turner has not heard from his longtime neighbors, the Hutton's, but they were never that close. He still wonders if they heard the news about their daughter.

When Amani makes it in, everyone gives her a tight embrace. After everyone is seated, Amani gives them all the details of the night, then afterward, they eat.

Ivy lifts her glass and says, "Attention everybody! Here's to our first day of work as a team." Everyone lift their glasses. "The most ghetto superhero team in the world!"

Amani replies, "No we're not ghetto. I'm not claiming that."

"Please, we got Amani flying around with her cellphone!" They all laugh. "Auntie Eva calling in all messed up, saying, 'There's this naked man on TV who wants you!'"

Eva says, "I didn't say it like that, Ivy. Don't tell that lie."

"Auntie, you dialed me first!" She laughs loudly. "I told you to call Amani, then you called me by my real name on the secret line!"

"I admitted to my mistake. Don't start with me."

Amani gently pats her Auntie Eva on the shoulder. "It'll be okay, Auntie. We'll just have to work on a few things. I think all of you, including Lt. Vega, did a good job."

"That's all I'm saying," Ivy replies.

"Soon, we'll be great at what we do. And hopefully, we'll have better equipment soon. I want my own network built from scratch.

"This is going to be quite expensive, so I may have to put my other dreams on hold. And like I said, I will take care of you first."

Mr. Turner asks, "So, what's taking them so long? Are you the last to get paid?"

Amani takes out her mobile phone to check her account. "It seems that way. Then again, I've been so busy that I forgot to check my account." She stops. Her jaw drops.

"What is it, Amani?" Ivy asks. "Are we rich, yet?"

Eva asks, "What's that on your phone?"

Amani faces the touchscreen toward her family. "$97,900,000!!"

Ivy jumps up and screams! Mr. Turner and Eva have delayed reactions. Amani runs around the table to her father. She never really thought about the money at first, but now that the funds are in her account, it hits her.

"I can't believe it!" Amani shouts. "It's real!"

Mr. Turner wipes his tears of joy. He is proud of his family, wishing his late wife was still there for him to touch. He still misses her greatly.

Once they calm down, Amani speaks. "I love you all. We saved lives today. Not just me, all of us. And we will continue.

"The situation with Joanie hurts me deeply. I'm still not over it. No money amount or anything is changing what had happened to her.

"So, I will feel even better when she makes it through her struggle. And until then, I will have her in mind. She shall have a part in this, just as I planned. I believe it!"

❦ ❦

The sun shines brightly the next morning. Amani makes one last stop before heading to her mansion after spending the night with her family. She glides down to a cemetery in Detroit, holding a bouquet of flowers in her hands.

Amani stands before the tombstone of Officer Donnell Price. This is the grave of the man who was accidentally murdered by the swing of Amani's fist. She takes a cloth and wipes over the inscription.

Amani says softly, "I know your soul is not buried in this grave, but I believe you can still hear me. I hope I am redeeming myself with the lives that I saved." She lays the flowers down at the grave. "If only I knew how you feel. Where you are."

"In a better place than this," a voice says.

Amani is completely surprised! Someone has managed to walk right up to her without detection. She wonders how.

She suspiciously looks over her shoulder and sees a tall, handsome man behind her. The look on her face is comparable to her facial reaction after discovering the millions in her bank account. She stands up stiffly.

"I hope I didn't scare you," the man said.

"Why didn't I hear you?" Amani asks.

"I guess you were busy talking to..."

While the gentleman speaks, Amani is thinking to herself, "Damn this man is fine! And his voice... Wait, not here." She barely heard what the man was saying.

The man continues, "You know what I mean, right?" he says with his charming smile.

Amani says, "Uh, you got to excuse me. I've been a little off, as of late," then she walks away. There is something about this man that makes her nervous, other than his attractiveness. It is his aura.

After making it past the cemetery gates, Amani slows her steps. There is something from within that holds her back and prevents her from flying off. She looks over her shoulder, watching the mysterious man as he kneels at the grave site, far from where she stands.

"Who is this man?" Amani thinks to herself. "And why do I feel the sudden need to stick around?"

The man gets up from his knelt position, then looks around for Amani, whose abrupt dismissal left him puzzled. As he drives his car through the entrance gates, he notices Amani standing in the area alone, so he then decides to drive up to her.

"Are you waiting on someone?" he asks Amani.

"I was," she replies.

Confused by the vague response, the gentleman steps out of his vehicle for a full conversation with Amani. "Where have I seen you before, Miss?" he asks. "Or is it Misses?"

"Could have been many places," Amani says. "I don't know. And it is Miss, far from Misses."

"Oh really? So, you knew my dad?"

"Who?"

The man chuckles. "You were standing at his grave a moment ago. Mr. Donnell Price?"

Amani is shocked! "Oh! I mean... yeah."

The man tilts his head and asks, "We're not family, are we?"

"Absolutely not! Not even cousins."

The man lets out a sigh of relief. "Good. That would have been embarrassing, flirting with my cousin's cousin outside the cemetery."

Amani laughs it off. "Well, it's a good thing we're not family. Can you give me a ride to the airport? The one right up the street, of course."

"Sure! But, I do know you from somewhere. Just can't put my finger on it."

"Come on. When guys say that, they know."

"Really, I don't know where I've seen you before."

Amani hears no sudden changes in the man's pulse. But, it was the same as with Dylan when he lied about not being crazy enough to do what he eventually did to Joanie.

However, Amani still trusts this man who stands before her. His heart is patiently consistent. It plays a beat she can groove to.

"What is your name?" the man asks.

"Amani."

"Like the super-lady I keep hearing about? That's a pretty name."

"Thanks. Don't you watch television?"

"When I can. I work as a paramedic, and my free time is limited."

"Oh, I get it. So, what is your name?"

"Same as my father's. You heard of him but never heard of me?"

"Donnell Price, Jr? Or the third?"

"The second." He laughs. "And, I hope I didn't interrupt your time with him a few minutes ago."

"No, I'm good. The flowers are in place."

"Great. Thanks."

Donnell opens his car door for Amani and closes it once she is seated. Now, she takes time to think about what is happening right now. Amani has eyes for the son of the man whom she killed by accident. A bizarre predicament, but she chooses to remain in his presence.

Amani doesn't want to leave without assuring that they will meet again. She wants this man's company and there is no question about it. But more importantly, Amani hungers for redemption. A way to make up for the mistake she made.

While riding to the airport, Donnell asks, "So, are you a news lady? What do you do on television?"

"I don't do anything on television." Amani replies.

"Then why did you ask if I watched TV when I asked you your name? It was as if I was supposed to know it already." Amani grins without answering. "How did you know my dad anyway?"

After some hesitation, Amani says, "He came to my aid years ago. I respect him for that."

"Oh..." Donnell says as they make it to the local airport. "You know, I didn't think anyone went to this airport. It always looks desolate. Do you work here?"

Amani loses patience. "Why don't you skip all of this talk and ask me out already?"

Donnell is stunned by her aggression. "Um, can I take you out some time?"

"Hold on. Let me think about it." She looks up, finger on the chin. Donnell laughs at her playful display. "You seem like a nice guy, Mr. Donnell the Second. I guess I can be safe with you."

"Sure you can. I won't let any harm come to you." Amani giggles. "What's so funny?" he asks.

"Nothing."

They exchange numbers and set up a date, which will be on the night just before Amani's public conference. Donnell lets Amani off at the front gate of the airport. She waves goodbye to him once he pulls off.

When Donnell makes it far away, Amani flies up as high as the clouds. She celebrates by flying in loops and shouts out loud, with the sunlight illuminating behind her. There is a feeling of great relief in Amani's heart. She credits all of this to Divine Order.

PLOTTING

Two suited men meet at the subway in NYC. They are members of the secret group linked to the CIA; Agent Red and Agent Gray.

"We must act now," says Agent Gray.

"Is everything in place?" Agent Red asks.

"Yes. I have all the codes to the machines. If we're going to time this right, then we got to put a move on it."

"Then, I'll book a flight to Iraq." He shakes his head. "Ten years wasted."

"Not for us."

"But, for the others," he smirks, then says, "very unfortunate."

"Indeed."

"Can you believe that jackass Director? He doesn't know how to properly start a war."

"Then, we will have to educate him."

Amani arrives back at her mansion, feeling good about her short time with Donnell. She surprised herself when she put pressure on him, earlier. It was out of character for Amani, but she's glad that something came over her.

Then again, this is still an awkward situation. Donnell doesn't know exactly who she is. If he only knew how his father really died. Amani feels that this will have to be kept a secret.

Amani feels that, in some way, she could bring more happiness into his life. If nothing less, she can be a close friend when in need. She owes it to him.

Amani notices the many voice messages left on her home phone. Everyone is trying to get her on their talk show. She would like to make the big money, but she has a job to do.

Her new plan is to let her sister handle the phone calls and mail. Ivy will never have to work a regular job again.

Had Joanie not been hospitalized, she could have had information on the most sophisticated means of communication. The mobile phone strategy is not going to cut it.

After listening to the many messages on her answering machine, Amani learned that her flight suits were ready as early as two days ago. She has to go to the parcel service branch location in order to pick them up.

Amani calls Ivy. "Sis, do you want to make a little more money?"

"You already know the answer to that," Ivy says.

"I need you to be my secretary. I will get a special telephone system installed whenever you get your new home."

"Then, you're talking about a week from now. I'm trying to decide between Florida and Arizona."

"Arizona!"

"Dang! Can I pick where I want to live?"

"You can do your job more effectively in the mountains. That's a good idea!"

"What about what I want? Let me check with Jermaine, first."

"Why? He's trying to be your husband now?"

"He has always been loyal!"

"Yeah, after the DNA test. But anyway, think about how you're getting paid and why. Be smart about this."

"I will. How are you holding up, Amani? I know you have Joanie on your mind, still."

"I do, but I'm optimistic. Everything else is going so well. I even have a date tomorrow night."

Ivy screams away from the phone. "I can't believe it! You finally found a date! You?"

"Whatever, Ivy."

"It's been years! Who has enough courage and confidence to ask <u>you</u> out on a date?"

"He doesn't know who I am."

"Uh oh... This is not good."

"I think it is, but I can't explain it. There is something about him."

"What's his name?"

"I'm not ready to tell you that."

"Amani, you are hiding something. That means this is **really** bad news. What is he lookin' like?"

"Lookin' like a smooth, chocolate, debonair man!"

"Alright now! Did you scan him?" Amani blushes quietly. "Giiiiiirl, I can hear you blushing! I got powers, too!"

Amani laughs. "He moved a little, so... I peeked."

"Freak!"

"Shut up, Ivy. I shouldn't have told you a thing."

"There's nothing wrong with having some freak in you! It's about time! So, where did you meet this man?"

Amani wisely cuts off the conversation. "I am glad you are taking the secretary position within the next week. It is paramount."

"Oh, so you're just going to change the subject on me, huh?"

"Talk to you later. Love you!" She hangs up on Ivy.

Amani uses the rest of the day trying to decide how she will budget her fortune. There are so many things that she wants to do for poor communities, but she's not sure what her expenses will be once her operation is on full blast.

Building cell sites is going to be costly. Then, she must find the personnel to operate them. They won't do it for free.

The lump sum Amani received from the interview and endorsements will not suffice for the remainder of her life. She needs to invest in something that she can count on.

Amani has no accountant and no lawyers, because she has a hard time trusting anyone. Her mind is scattered with so much to do, thinking that she can do everything with the help of only her family and Lt. Vega. Amani must learn to trust.

She accepts the fact that in order for her to have a big operation, she must trust new faces. Amani makes a document of the new names she came across. Lucy and George Stallworth, Sgt. Paul Orton, and Gwen Zorn are listed as "potentials".

She also accepts that in order to have more money coming in, she must endorse products that she doesn't know much about. If the money is right and there seems to be no harm done, Amani would probably endorse it.

Amani still wants to open a school and fix up houses, but she has to think about what her dad and aunt said, and they were right. She needs more time and help to be successful.

Her specially-made suits will inevitably take damage in battle. That will be a growing expense for her. It is going to take over a year to see what Amani can actually afford.

There is an incoming call from Eva on the private line. "What is it, Dispatch?" Amani responds.

Eva says, "We have another crazy person who demands to see you."

"Not again. I see a trend going on here. People like this will ruin our reputation."

"She's sitting on a ledge, preparing to jump if you don't come by and spend time with her. Her location is in Dallas, TX."

"I'm not buying it. There's no way I'm going to let her waste my time for her minutes of fame. She's just going to have to jump."

"I know that's right. These people think they can make you show up when they say."

"Right, and I'm not having it. That is why I couldn't be there for Joanie. The police are going to have to handle it."

After the call ends, Lt. Vega calls in. "Don't even bother, Amani," he says.

"I don't intend to. We saw this coming, didn't we?"

"Sure did. And this woman, April Haynes, has a record of fraud. She is one of those people who are always trying to get a lawsuit for any situation."

"A crook. She'd probably even find a way to sue me."

"Yep. Don't trust her."

"Thanks, Vega."

Hours later, a mother is tending to her child in a Detroit home. She is interrupted by the ringing of the doorbell. She answers the door with her baby in arms. Standing at the doorstep is Amani.

"It really is you!" the excited mother says. "It's so good to finally meet you! My name's Jewel."

"Pleased to meet you," Amani says.

"Come on in and have a seat."

Amani sits on the sofa. She can't take her eyes off of the baby. He looks a lot like his father.

Jewel introduces her child. "This is Tariq. Say hi, Tariq!" Tariq stares at Amani silently. "He acting all shy. He ain't shy."

"Hi, little cutie!" Amani sings to Tariq.

"He looks just like his daddy, doesn't he?" Amani agrees. "I'll go tell him you're here. He's in the basement, where he does his writing."

A minute later, Eric James enters the room. He is very happy to see Amani. He has been out of jail for two years. They hug, then sit together with Jewel and baby Tariq.

"Amani Jett," Eric says. "Wow. You really made a name for yourself, homegirl."

"Look who's talking," Amani replies with a smile. "Mr. Motivational Speaker."

"I have you to thank for that. I was on the wrong path, you were on the right one. But, you freed me when you shot that gun out of my hand."

Jewel says, "That is just amazing! I'm glad you did it. So is Tariq."

"Yeah, and sending those letters to me when I was locked up. You were the only cop I knew that locked people up, and then wrote to them while they were in jail."

"I didn't write to everybody," Amani says. "Some of you, but not all of you. What about that lawyer of yours?"

"Still up to no good. You're going to have to bend the law to get that dude. I stopped dealing with him."

"Good."

Eric asks Jewel, "Did I tell you how she was about to break my bones? I was the first one to see what she could do. Nobody would believe me."

"Oh my god," says Jewel, "you must have been terrible!"

"I did one of the dumbest things a man could ever do. It took her some years, but she moved on from it."

Amani asks, "Where have you spoken, so far?"

"I spoke at the boys' home and our old high school. I saw many old faces. Mrs. Gilbourn is still teaching there and she hasn't changed a bit."

"Well, that's unfortunate."

"Coach Sanders is still there. Coach Pratt was fired not too long after we graduated. It was for indecent exposure." Amani chuckles. "It threw me off when I heard about it. Dude was a pervert!"

Jewel says, "One of the coaches at my old high school used to flirt with the girls a lot, with his old freaky self."

"What a shame," Amani says. "So tell me, Eric, how would you like to open up for me at the public conference this Saturday?"

Eric is quite flattered. He did not anticipate this proposition. Jewel is excited as well.

"I would love to!" Eric says. "Of course I would! You're my homegirl!"

"Cool. I know it's short notice, but you can do it. You're a passionate man who's been through a lot."

"I won't disappoint you, Amani. Real talk."

They hug again. Jewel thanks Amani for giving Eric the opportunity to speak at the conference.

Amani smiles at Tariq. "May I hold him?" Jewel allows her to pick him up. By this time, Tariq is warmed up to Amani.

Jewel asks, "Do you have any little ones, Amani?"

"No."

"What are you waiting on?"

Amani smirks. "A husband would be a nice start."

"Oh... sorry."

This was not the first time Amani dealt with that asinine question from someone. Jewel was a little embarrassed for asking.

Amani distracts the shame. "You two have a beautiful child." She hands Tariq back to his smiling mother. "I'll be on my way. See you in a couple of days."

After they escort Amani out, she flies into the sky. The two are very excited about the public conference. Eric has truly turned his life back around.

EXECUTION

Malibu, CA. Luther Cobain, also known as Agent Blue, is having family time with his wife and son in their home near the shore of the Pacific Coast. This spacious room where they gather is surrounded by large glass windows on each side, overlooking the ocean on one side and the landscape on the other side. A wet bar is stationed near the center, closer to the ocean windows.

"Let's do Paris this time," Mrs. Cobain says. "An all-inclusive stay off the beach."

"I'm tired of beaches," her son says. "We live on the beach."

A shadow quickly passes by, like a flicker. Luther is the only one who notices this. He gets up to look out through his window facing the ocean, but he sees nothing.

"What is it, Dear?" Mrs. Cobain asks.

"Uh, nothing," Luther says. "It's clear."

"Maybe you saw a bird?" his son asks.

Luther turns around and says, "Maybe that's what it was-" He briefly sees a glimpse of an aerial object through the window facing the land. "Go upstairs for a minute, please."

"Honey, what is it?" Mrs. Cobain asks.

"Just go upstairs!"

While his wife and son go upstairs as ordered, Luther flips out the painting which hangs above the fireplace. Behind the painting is a hidden twelve-gauge shotgun. He takes it out and pumps it.

Slowly, he walks to the window, but the aerial object lowers behind him beyond the window facing the ocean on the opposite side. This object is a miniature drone, armed with a sub-machine gun. This new model hovers in place with its propellers.

The machine fires through the glass windows. Luther takes cover behind the bar, taking shots in his lower back on the way down. His wife and kid hide in a closet on the second floor after hearing the shooting. When the shots come to a stop, Luther takes a chance to peek around the corner of the bar, though in pain. He can hear the motor, now that the window is blown out. He spots the high-tech drone before it takes off flying again.

"A fucking drone?" Luther says to himself. "Why is it after me?"

Luther wants to get to the telephone, but it is out of his reach. He begins to wonder if this is a way of ending the secret group, but he doesn't believe the Director would order his assassination like this.

The first person that comes to mind is Agent Gray. He was the one agent assigned to monitor all technological advancements.

Luther crawls toward the phone that sits about fifteen feet away from its dock, which is on top of the bar. Suddenly, the drone returns at the other side of the house. Luther fires his shotgun, taking the window section out. Unfortunately, he does not hit his target.

The drone flies away, ascending two hundred yards above, then flies down quickly. Like a kamikaze, it crashes into the house and causes a huge explosion. The house is destroyed, leaving no survivors.

Agent Red is air bound in a passenger plane. He receives a message from Agent Gray: Blue complete. He grins with satisfaction.

Agent Blue is the man who was placed in charge of the secret group, following the former Director's resigning. He prevented the dismemberment of the group by taking over various duties formerly held by the Director(DCI) to keep it in effect.

It was his idea to persuade the new DCI to vouch for the group, so funding will continue from the US Government. Without Luther Cobain, aka Agent Blue, the group could easily collapse.

Agent Red and Agent Gray conspire to eliminate the group and take advantage of their secret technologies and resources; the war machines and the mysterious "Bio-tech" projects.

Amani tries on her new gear. She is very happy with the comfort and designs of all three outfits. She especially likes the suit that was once loaded with logos. It is now a simple costume with a unique reflective material. This material mirrors the atmosphere around her.

The specially-designed under armor is merely a quarter of an inch thick. This is to ensure her "lady parts" won't be exposed if the suit takes damage.

This "Mirror Stealth Flight-Suit" is special to Amani, because she wants her admirers to see their own reflection as they look upon her.

Amani calls up Lt. Vega and asks for him to look up Donnell's background. He is indeed a paramedic and his record is clean. Nothing was wrong with her super-hearing after all.

Now, Amani thinks to herself, "This man's record is cleaner than mine."

She reflects back on the night when she killed Donnell Sr., and then tries to think up realistic alternative actions that could have prevented his death. This is something that still bugs her today, but at the same time, Amani is reminded of why it is imperative that she continues to master her abilities.

"You can have your own reality show!" Ivy shouts. "We could all be in it!" She is freshening up Amani's braids for her date with Donnell later in the evening.

"No way," Amani replies, "I hate reality TV. It's so fake."

"But, it could be like that cop show that's been on TV forever. That sounds like a hit!"

"I already have crazy people trying to make me show up for some nonsense. All I need is more of them who're trying to get themselves on television. Nope!"

"Well, you said you want to keep the money coming in."

"But, not like that. There are too many of those shows, anyway. So, have you made any steps in publishing your book?"

"Naw, I've been too busy with your stuff."

"I just might write a book myself, but I'm not ready to disclose everything."

"Especially the part where you killed that man. Sorry to bring it up, but, you know."

Amani does not know if she will ever tell Donnell about the accident, even if they become very close. Ivy knows nothing about Donnell Price, Sr. Not even his name.

"You know what Lamont's online cult people are saying?" Ivy asks.

"Of course I don't," says Amani. "I'm not even sure if I want to know."

"Well, it's my job to tell you these fools are saying that you're cooning." (Another word for 'selling out'.)

"Cooning? Man, I oughtta..."

"Finish it! You oughtta track them down and kick all of their asses! That's what you oughtta do!"

"This is what pisses me off. How the hell am I cooning?"

"Something about those advertisements you signed up for. They're trying to say you went commercial and stopped reppin' the D."

"Aw, hell naw. Ivy, don't tell me about those jackasses anymore. I swear, somebody is going to wind up hurt."

"That's what I was hoping for!"

"You know the more money we make, the more enemies we'll have, right? Somebody will always find wrong in what we do, no matter what. So with that, I'll choose to keep my cool."

"I guess so, big sis." By now, Amani's hair is combed out to an afro. "You should sport this natural fro, just like this."

"Not today. That's something I can do by myself. French braids, please."

Ivy starts with the conditioning. "We chose to go with Arizona for our new location. Dad won't be too happy with his grandkids being so far away."

Amani shrugs her shoulders. "He's the one too stubborn to move. It's like his ego is stuck to that house. It's not even worth the taxes he's paying, anymore."

"You know how Daddy is, Amani. He is stuck in his ways."

It is 7:00pm, and Donnell reserved a table at an upscale restaurant in Novi, MI. He waits for Amani inside the entrance lobby with a bouquet of flowers. Once he checks the time on his watch, she enters through the glass doors.

Amani is looking her best, dressed formally in a stunning red dress. Ivy did a great job on her hair, once again. Donnell smiles widely when he sees her.

"You look beautiful," Donnell says, then hands her the flowers.

Amani replies, "How sweet! Thank you!"

The hostess identifies Amani right away. She almost lost her breath when she saw her. "Right this way," she says nervously.

The two arrive at their designated table. The area is somewhat isolated for a private, intimate setting. While being seated, there are a few whispers hissing around the spacious restaurant. They, like the hostess, are excited to see Amani in person, especially seeing her with a date.

The waitress comes to the table and introduces herself. Before she hands out the menus, she says to Amani, "We're honored to have you here tonight, Ms. Jett! I am so lucky to be your waitress."

Donnell's eyes light up! He raises his brows to the limits. Amani finds his reaction funny.

"You..." Donnell says, "**you** are Amani Jett? The super flying lady?"

Amani expresses a hopeful smile. "Yes? Is that okay?"

"Absolutely! I cannot believe... it's you!"

"So, you're fine with this?"

"Fine is an understatement! I feel so dumb for not knowing who you were."

"I'm sort of glad you didn't. It makes the date more authentic, even though I had to push you into asking me out."

Donnell blushes. "I would've asked. It was just the circumstances."

Amani confirms that he is telling the truth, then says, "Most guys are intimidated by me. You don't seem to be."

"Why should I be intimidated?"

"Because of the super stuff."

"Amani, it's not like I plan on fighting you, or outrunning you, or... what else do you do again?"

"People can't lie to me. Not unless they know how to trick a lie detector, or are just plain psycho."

Donnell grins. "It's not like I plan on lying to you, either. So no, I'm not intimidated. Let's get to know each other."

The two are having a fun conversation, seeing all that they have in common. Amani and Donnell are both attentive and their eyes do not wonder off.

They share stories of their past works. Amani with her international and local missions, Donnell with his experiences in traumatic episodes. Both of them handle dangerous jobs.

They enjoy their palatable meals. Amani can eat! No carryout doggy bag for her, which is a big plus for Donnell. He likes a woman who can finish.

But, there is something on Amani's mind that will not rest. This is a man whose life could have been ruined by her negligence, yet he doesn't even know that he is highly interested in the one person who is mysteriously behind the death of his father. And what's even more strange is that she is equally interested in him.

Amani asks, "What made you choose your line of work?"

"I want to help people," Donnell says. "And I want to be first on the scene. I want to be there fast enough."

"It's your father, isn't it? If only someone was fast enough and efficient enough to rescue him, then he might still be in your life."

Donnell nods. "Yes. But, I'm not upset at the medics who made it to the scene. They did a good job by saving the lady and her little girl."

There is still that bugging question Amani has. "How do you feel, knowing that the person responsible for your father's death was never convicted, or had to answer for their recklessness?"

Donnell ducks his head and sighs. "There is nothing left to feel. That's where you learn to forgive."

"But, certainly there's some anger. Right?"

"Amani, do you have grievances against the pilots that flew the plane your mother was in? The airline?" Amani can't answer. "Did you choose your last name to redeem her fate? Replacing the instrument which failed your mother's safety?"

Amani never thought about any of these things. She is starting to understand Donnell Price, II. He gains her respect.

Amani says, "But, the pilots' fates were the same as my mother's. And the airline had held itself accountable."

Donnell replies, "Whoever the hit-and-run driver was that night, I believe they were too afraid. Probably driving illegally, drunk, I don't know. But whatever they did, it will come back to them."

"And you wouldn't feel any better if you were there when the payback happened?"

"I don't think so. Like, I wouldn't be one of those people who would sit and witness an electric chair execution. It's not for me. Might even be against it."

Amani grins. "Donnell, you make me feel guilty."

"How so?"

"I'm just waiting on a red flag, assuming you had a few stored in your pocket. I was so wrong. You're one heck of a guy."

Soon after they leave the restaurant together, Amani invites Donnell for a little "flight time". Donnell rejects the idea of being carried in the sky, but he does promise to attend the public conference tomorrow.

Then, a man wearing an old trench coat crosses paths with Amani and Donnell. Like many others, this man recognizes Amani.

"There you are!" the man says. "All grown up." Amani chooses to ignore him, as he continues, "You survived that accident. I remember!"

Amani now realizes who this man is. He was the lone witness from thirteen years ago who asked her, "What are you?" She does not want this man to bring up that catastrophe. She excuses herself and walks over to the man.

Amani says to the man quietly, "I need you to keep it down. I'm spending time with my friend."

The man says, "You have skeletons in your closet. I can get rid of them for the right price."

"Are you blackmailing me?"

Donnell steps in. "Is everything okay?"

"Yes," Amani says. "Everything is okay."

The peculiar man just stands there smiling. As they leave, Amani has an eerie feeling that they will meet again.

Overall, this was a great night for both Amani and Donnell. This is bound to become a close, romantic relationship. They are attracted to each other on many levels.

OPEN TO THE PUBLIC

owntown Detroit, MI. People are gathered at the plaza near the riverfront, where a stage is assembled with colorful spot lights and big speakers. The news media surround every corner of the stage for this highly-anticipated meeting with the public. This will be Amani's first stop, with an estimated one million people present in all of the downtown area.

It all begins with a performance from Amani's high school's marching band from Eastpointe. It is a festive atmosphere. Amani intended for this to be a simple meet with the public, but doesn't mind the added presentations. So much for her not "reppin' the D".

Amani awaits inside a nearby hotel, where there was a breakfast party thrown in her honor by one of the companies that sponsors her. She makes a phone call. "Good morning, Donnie. How soon do you think you can make it?"

Donnell replies, "I really can't say. It's a bit of a stretch, but I might be able to drive the work van to the conference. That will save some time."

"You're still talking about driving an emergency van down here? You know they got streets blocked off and it's crowded as heck."

"Yeah, but that won't stop me. I'll turn on my emergency lights and get through that way."

"You have no shame, fooling the people like that. Then, look, give me your truck number so I can let the police know to look out for you."

"Sounds like a deal."

"See you there, handsome."

Amani is so excited about Donnell being there! It shows with the big smile on her face.

Local celebrities introduce themselves to Amani. They come to her with collaborative ideas that she could really use. Who knew she would come across this much valuable information?

The future is looking brighter for Amani, now. She is establishing relationships with local leaders who actually have thorough plans and know-how. These are the people who she can learn from.

One of Amani's assistants says to her, "Ms. Jett, Eric James will be on stage in thirty minutes."

"Thank you, Cathy," Amani says.

Twenty minutes later, Amani flies toward the stage area in one of her new suits. The people cheer and take pictures of her in flight. She waves back at them. Some young people are actually crying. This doesn't fit well with Amani, but she's not disgusted.

Her family members are together at a nearby location. Even the cousins from her mother's side of the family are there with them. They came from out of state to spend time with their Detroit family on this special day.

Amani looks around for the emergency vehicle that Donnell is supposed to drive. He has yet to arrive.

It is now time for Eric James to speak in front of millions. He gives his testimony of how his life was turned around. He is indeed a good speaker and he was the perfect choice to set the tone for this conference.

Eric speaks with great passion. Talking about his son leads to tears. And overall, he encourages his listeners to get the most out of life and never settle for the lesser them. He repeats, "Never settle for the lesser you!"

He introduces to the stage, the woman of the hour, Amani Jett. There is an enormous ovation at the mention of her name. She takes a minute to speak.

"Hello Detroit!" Amani shouts into the mic. "Whaddup doe!" She smiles following the famous local greeting. "Okay y'all, let's get to the business. Some of you are familiar with me, some of you aren't. Those who are, know me as an everyday woman with a little something extra."

Someone screams, "We love you, Amani!" and the cheers elevate again.

"And I love you, too." Amani says. She sees the emergency truck driven by Donnell with its flashing lights activated. He finds a nice spot to park, where he can get a good view of the stage, while Amani begins her speech:

"I am so grateful for the love that you show me. I really am. But, you will see very soon that I'm no more super than you are.

"Who you see on this stage is someone who pushed to get where she is. I'm not an overnight miracle. It took a lot of work, and it took making some mistakes.

"I'm still learning how to be your shero. I can learn a lot from **you**. So, you might see greatness in me, but I am sure that you can find greatness in yourselves.

"No need to cry at the presence of me, I'm just me. Flying is only my means of getting around. The most significant work happens where you stand.

"Mr. Eric James delivered a superb speech, didn't he?" Everyone claps for him. "If he can turn his life around, anyone can. That's why I hate to look at people at their worst and make an overall judgment of them just by that.

"People can change. So, that's what makes war so despicable. I've seen a lot and I've learned a lot.

"And as you may have been aware, since my interview with Susan Dunn, I will be calling my own shots. I will take on the most overwhelming jobs to reduce casualties. Jobs that may be too critical for some, too risky for others.

"I will also pay more attention to what you all have to say, which is why I'm having these public conferences; to answer your many questions and revealing my mission to you directly." She points to the seated rows in front of the stage. "These first two rows consist of people who were here first. They will be the ones who will come with their questions for me to address. I understand you were camped out here for a long time."

The family of Amani Jett have a clear view of the stage from the building they're in, but they watch the coverage from the news station on a television. This way, they can clearly hear what is being said.

Elsewhere, the new Director of the Central Intelligence Agency is watching the news coverage from his office alone. He is nervous after recently being informed that Luther Cobain and his family died in a house fire, yesterday. The cause of the explosion has yet to be discovered.

The DCI doesn't know what to make of the group anymore, now that Agent Blue is gone. He hopes that Amani is careful with her words at this public conference. All major networks are airing this event in a live broadcast.

Amani is now taking questions from those in the audience. The first question: "Hi Amani! You told Susan Dunn that you regretted not being there during hurricane Katrina. If you were there, what difference would you have made, being that it was more chaotic than hurricane Sandi?"

Amani says, "The big deal about Katrina, besides the obvious winds, was the breaking of the levees. That was already anticipated and I truly believe that I could've helped with the evacuation process beforehand."

The next question: "There are emergencies every day all around the world. How do you decide which problem to attend to?"

"I go by the number of lives at stake, the most time-sensitive, and the distance. By those factors, I make my judgment call. And I also try to determine if this is something that no person other than I can handle."

The next question: "You recently earned a lot of money through your record-setting interview and numerous endorsements. How much would you contribute to your birth city, which so happens to be one of the poorest in the country?"

"It's funny how everyone knows how much I make, but I have no idea how much you all make. While I'm just now bringing in big bucks, it might look like I have unlimited cash flow, but I learned that a lump sum of money can go quickly.

"There are about one million people here at this event. If I gave each of you one hundred dollars, then what? I'd be broke and all you got is less than enough to pay a winter heat bill.

"Money alone is not the issue, it is the system. A constant flow of capital working for you. That is a political issue, not something that I specialize in because of endorsements and interview money.

"My answer to your question is, I can't say how much, but I've **been** contributing. Done a lot for this city, including some things money can't buy."

The next question: "You've recently flown from Illinois to Minnesota, which is so cool! My question is, how does the high altitude affect you? Do you also have super-breathing for aerial travel?"

Amani laughs to herself. "Thank you for asking. I appreciate everyone's questions, but I must say, that's the best question I've heard.

"Flying long distances has been a problem for me, and the thin air may have been the biggest detriment. That's why I get so dizzy after long trips! Oh my God, this is so embarrassing.

"Of all the things to calculate, I failed to measure my altitudinal limits. Once I get that information, I'll acquire the proper equipment to fly higher. I think that may be my solution to go international."

The next question: "We have the most powerful being on the face of this earth in this city, but the crime rate hasn't changed much in your absence, and in some cases, it's gone up. How often will you be around, now that you claim your independence, and why should we be excited about it?"

"If you're excited, then I'm excited. Your positive energies will go a long way with me, but please keep in mind, I am only one person. One human being should not be the answer to all of our problems.

"I need you to realize that one woman with my abilities cannot match a powerful force of one. The police and the community can work together to stop crime. Too bad it hasn't been done here.

"I understand that the threat of my presence can reduce crime, so I'll be just a call away.

"However independent, I work within the laws. I can shut a drug operation down, but not in my own way. I did it before and another one popped right up- New and improved.

"When I was gone away in the past, oftentimes, it was from doing long missions overseas. I had no way of returning on my own. That will change."

The next question: "What was the final straw that led to your decision to serve without the backing of the federal government? By working with various government agencies for so many years, have you lost your faith and trust in the leadership?"

On the fortieth floor of a tall office building across the street from where the public conference is taking place, a window is partially open. Kneeling behind that window is a man holding a fifty-caliber sniper rifle. He has Amani in his cross hairs, preparing to fire.

Amani tries to find the best way to answer the question without being too overt. As soon as she opens her mouth, a gunshot fires. The deadly bullet hits Amani right in her head. She places her hand on her temple and looks up directly at the shooter.

The sniper is so afraid that he wets his pants. Filled with rage, Amani slams the microphone down, picks up a stage speaker, then throws it accurately through the window where the gunman posed.

The shooter leaps out of the way, successfully avoiding the tossed object. Amani flies from the stage like a cannonball.

Donnell looks on in disbelief. He can't imagine who would try to assassinate this woman. Eric stands in his seat. Mr. Turner, Ivy, Eva, Lamont, and the rest of the family can't believe it either.

Ivy screams, "Get'em sis!"

The shooter rises up slowly after diving to the floor. Once he gets up to his knee, he feels someone's hand on his shoulder. He turns his head and sees Amani's fierce eyes glaring at him.

Amani tosses him against the wall and rams him with super speed before he could touch the floor, making him cough up blood. She pulls him up by his hair, leaving his feet dangling.

"What **idiot** do you work for?" Amani yells.

The shooter says, "I don't-" Amani smashes his entire hand with one squeeze. He screams at the top of his lungs.

"You better tell me," Amani says, "or I'll rip your-"

"Pssst..." is the sound coming from the shadowy corner of the room. There stands the figure of Agent Red, wearing a black suit, red tie, and sunglasses. Amani drops the shooter and speeds over to Agent Red in less than a second. She grabs him by the collar.

"Who are you, and how did you sneak up behind me?" Amani asks.

There is something strange about his heart rate. It doesn't seem natural. He arrogantly smirks when questioned who he is. Just as Amani did with the shooter, she squeezes his hand to a mush, but he has no reaction, feeling no pain.

"What the hell are you?" Amani asks.

Suddenly, there is a weirdly-pitched sound that causes Amani to lose all concentration. It affects her nervous system, making her lose balance. She screams out of frustration as her equilibrium has gone haywire!

Everyone in attendance of the public conference is looking upward to the building, expecting to see Amani fly out victorious. Ivy wonders what is taking her so long. Amani's potential beau, Donnell, is standing on the hood of the emergency vehicle.

Unexpectedly, that entire section of the building explodes extensively! Viewers are horrified. Civilians in the area take cover from the falling debris.

As Donnell Price II watches on, he notices a unique flame falling from the explosion. He gets in the vehicle to rush to the point of its fall, but people are scattering everywhere. He then decides to fight his way through the crowd on foot.

After many bumps, dodges, and pushes, Donnell makes it to the area. There he sees Amani lying unconscious with her new suit burning with the fire from the blast.

Donnell removes his outer shirt and covers Amani with it in attempt to smother the remaining flames. He proceeds to roll her on the ground. Fortunately, the suit is fire resistant, but her skin appears to be damaged.

Amani is not breathing regularly, so Donnell performs CPR on her fallen body. He must use extra force when doing chest compressions on Amani's strong frame, which catches the attention of bystanders. They take out their phones and snap pictures of the rescue, instead of assisting.

After a strenuous effort, Amani starts coughing. Donnell picks her up immediately and carries her to the emergency van. The crowd breaks apart when seeing Amani being helped. They chant her name all the way to the van.

👀

"Vulnerability. A word that's never been associated with the Eighth Wonder of the World, Amani Jett." Video footage is being shown on the news station. "She lies there helpless, being rescued by a regular human being.

"Some are praising her strength and her survival, while others are disappointed by the fact that she fell unconscious from an explosion.

"The questions being asked are, 'Who took the shot?', 'What caused the explosion?', and 'Did they survive?'

"It is a sad sight, here in downtown. Nine dead, four injured, as firefighters continue their search through the rubble for more remains. That number is expected to increase. There is no word, yet, from the floor where the shooting took place, but we will have that information within the next few hours.

"The search is expected to go on for another twenty four hours. We will have an accurate count.

"So again, Amani Jett; hospitalized. Many thought it could never happen, but it is a reality. Scott Williams, Click2 Action News, Detroit."

Radio Talk Show Host, Billy J. Marshall

"America! Do not be blinded! This was staged! I repeat... Do not be blinded! This was staged!

"I've been saying it time and time again! They called me crazy. A wild man! And yet, they are the ones who are deluded!

"And I will prove what I've been saying all along! I told America on this very show, that Amani Jett is a hoax! She is an experiment conducted by the US government!

"Everyone is afraid to talk about her. For one reason, she has all of these super powers. I can understand that, being that she's a proven bully!

"You're not supposed to use free speech against her, because she's a minority and that is just too offensive to Blacks. So, any word against her isn't politically correct!

"Oh, and don't speak ill of a poor lady! News flash! This is no lady at all!

"Amani Jett is a killer! She was and still is a mercenary! A mercenary now with celebrity status!

"She was strategically put where she is. The unlikely 'shero' who everyone trusts. My god, if it was a grisly-looking man with those super abilities instead of her, **then** people would get smart and start to ask questions!

"The CIA and the military are smart. They knew exactly who the people would love. They used the least-threatening figure in today's society!

"She comes in flying to the stage at this phony conference. At least the President shakes hands. If someone as low as him can shake hands, why can't she? How can she say she wants a more personal relationship with the public, but refuses to shake hands?

"And look at this; for the first time, she is wearing her special, tailor-made, uniform which is flame resistant! How convenient of her to wear clothing made for combat! At a public conference!

"Are we stupid? Are we to think she wore it just to show it off?

"America! Do not be blinded! This was staged! These conniving people are blatantly insulting your intelligence!

"She poses as a rebel, all of a sudden. Ten years of killing for the US Government and now she's 'independent'? Their strategy is so clear, and if you don't see it, shame on you!

"They're trying to get everyone on her side! One thing that's been proven throughout history is that people follow those who are victims of assassination attempts!

"They want us all to mourn for Amani Jett, this **killer**, and pray for her like good ol' Christians. But, we don't even know who or what this woman worships!

"So, here is this gunshot. Who didn't know that a sniper shot would have no effect on her? Come on! She fought wars by herself, believe it or not!

"How would anyone be so stupid enough to make an attempt on her life with a gunshot? I'm not buying it and neither should you!

"The shooter fired his weapon at the perfect opportunity! Just when she was asked a question about her employer and was hesitant to answer it!

"The government wants us to be too afraid to ask about their hidden agendas! They sent the message that this is what happens when you inquire! That was the purpose of the fake conference!

"One more piece of factual evidence that this was staged. The man who 'rescued' Amani Jett after the explosion... was seen at a restaurant with her on the night before! Can someone say setup?

"Apparently, they met with each other to work out the plan! And now, they're making it look like a love story between these two. Where was this man of mystery just one week ago?

"People, if you are still believing this facade of a story, then you are seriously lost. I have given you enough evidence to help you see clearly that I told you so!

"With this charade, Amani Jett, and the devious US Government, and the UN is going to come back with great vengeance!"

HardcoreUnapologeticTruth.com

Hardcore Brother X:

"The devil and his wench got niggas fooled. She imitates a Black leader and makes y'all feel sorry for her. Down with Amani Jett, the unnatural whore, and her marriage to the evil that enslaved us for centuries!

"People of Black knowledge won't fall for her trickery and she will burn for real when the fire of Truth rages on her! No mercy will ever be shown for her!

"Her desire to invade the Congo is obvious. She wants to rape the Motherland of its pure resources, just as her master does. She-devil, you better not try! A coon in the Congo is like a bullet in place of a seed of the most precious fruit. Shalom."

Reply by MarcusRealjusticeaintcolorblindW

"Deep! I knew from the start, that witch was a sellout. I pulled her Black Card a long time ago. And when she started endorsing bullshit products, I was like damn! A nigga can't have power without selling her soul.

"She's quick to slap a jiggaboo in a club, but ain't going around slapping these White people. Not when they're paying her so well. She's up in Minneapolis saving these White kids, when you got all the troubled Black kids in her own city."

Reply by Shaana

"@ MarcusRealjusticeaintcolorblindW...

"I feel you. You can't make it that big in the White man's world without a little hoeing. That's been proven a million times over. And Amani is the biggest one thus far!"

"A coon in the Congo is like a bullet in place of a seed of the most precious fruit."

"Preach, HBX!!"

Reply by Hardcore Brother X

"And watch all these coons still follow her and praise her like she's a goddess. In the end, they're going to get it just as bad as the she-devil herself!

"Look who she did her interview for; the whitest face in America. SMH! I know a lot of African conscious hosts that could've done that interview. She's lost in the white smoke."

Reply by LamontmanwithaplanAdams313

"She survived and is in a coma, just like her White best friend. When you want to be like them, you end up like them."

WHILE YOU WERE SLEEPING...

The Director of the Central Intelligence Agency invited a guest to his office, flown in from Georgia. His name is Agent Arnold Blunt. He specializes in "getting answers" and he may be the best at what he does.

"I want you to track down Agent Bryant Burns, who is called Agent Black of the covert alternate group," The DCI says. "He is one of three faces I recognized." He hands Agent Blunt a copy of Burns' file. "One of the other familiar face's house was blown to bits with him and his family inside."

"The house in Malibu County," Agent Blunt says. "You're talking about Luther Cobain. He was a part of this group?"

"Yes, along with seven others. The other face I recognized was Margaret Zalewski." He hands over a copy of her file. "I need your crew to track her down as well. You should approach Agent Black first. He's a crafty military expert in Boston."

Blunt skims through the file. "Crafty indeed."

"One last file," the DCI says while opening the folder. There is nothing in it but hazy pictures.

"This is Agent Red. The picture was retrieved from the security camera of the building before the explosion. This is him making his way to the fortieth floor on the day before the conference."

"Is he the suspected shooter?" asks Agent Blunt.

"That's the strange part. There were two bodies found in the area where the explosion originated." He types on his computer to retrieve the report that was sent to him. "One of them, we believe to be Agent Red. We're waiting on the DNA test results. Not much remains of him."

"And the other body?"

"Hasn't been identified, yet. And there is no video footage of him entering the building."

Agent Blunt ponders. "So, we don't have Agent Red on file?"

"We believe there has been a security breach. I can't make a match of him in our database. Agent Cobain may have known who he was."

"And the former Director?"

"Possibly. I will talk with him personally. As of now, I need you to get your team together and apprehend Agent Black."

In the Trauma Center of the hospital where Amani was taken, she is still laying comatose. She was never transported to her own room. The doctors and nurses do as they were instructed by cutting off Amani's hair at the pigtails, taking a swab of her mouth, and they even check her feet for dead skin.

Their duty is to collect whatever they can from Amani's body as she lies dormant. This order came directly from the DCI. They open Amani's combat suit in an attempt to take blood and bone marrow samples.

While inspecting her skin, they discover what appears to be a breakout of hives and blisters. This discovery does not match with her earlier report.

"What is she infected with?" a nurse asks. "I hope it's not contagious!"

One of the doctors checks her file, which hangs at the foot of the bed. "This is not right. Or, maybe she's breaking out due to something in this room."

A second doctor says, "Keeping her here was a terrible mistake!"

"But, we had our orders. How do we argue with National Security?"

"They don't specialize in what we do!" He snatches off his rubber gloves. "She needs to go elsewhere. We can't hold her here. We don't even have the right tools to pierce her exterior."

The nurse asks, "Does such a tool exist?"

The first doctor says, "I'm not sure that I want to go against direct orders from a government official. That's like putting us all in danger."

The surgeon says, "I agree with Dr. Sada. This is what we specialize in and we know what we can and cannot do." Now, he also removes his gloves and mask. "It's obvious they are using us to collect samples from her for their own selfish schemes. Opportunists! This is not why I became a surgeon!"

The surgeon leaves the area, followed by the second doctor, Sada. The remaining doctor is lost without a solution and is left there with only one nurse. This results in the lone doctor opting to send Amani to another room. In their travels, they run into Mr. Turner and his sister, Eva.

"Wait!" Mr. Turner shouts. "That's my little girl!"

The doctor asks, "You are Amani's father? You're really her father?"

"Yes! Now, let me talk to her! You've kept her from us in that room for too long!"

"I can't let you come too close to her. She's infected."

"Infected? With what?"

"We are not sure, yet. We can't test her."

Mr. Turner takes a closer look at Amani. "What did you do to her hair?"

"Sir, we understand your concern, but we must take her to her room."

"You better not try anything on my daughter!" He and Eva follow the doctor to the room. They are not let in.

Eric James and his family are spending time together. His fiancée, Jewel, has a daughter who is home from school. Eric helps with her homework.

"You got it, Toya!" Eric says to encourage her.

Jewel yells out from inside the kitchen, "Eric, can you take this garbage out when you get a chance? It's starting to stink."

"In a minute."

Soon afterward, Eric takes out the garbage to the dumpster in the back of the house. As he walks back toward the front, he sees a car pulling up in the driveway.

Eric is leery of who this visitor may be. When he investigates, he sees the passenger is his former lawyer, Richard Twain. Eric is not familiar with the men who accompany him.

Richard steps out of the vehicle. "Eric! Long time no see. In person, that is."

Eric is not happy to see him. "Aye, man. What do you want?"

"I'm here to congratulate you, bro! Aren't you happy to see an old friend? The one who was by your side when you were in trouble?"

"You talkin' ten years ago? Man, what's up with you showing up at my house?"

Richard steps in closer. "Just business."

"Well, I don't want to do business with you. We ain't cool no more."

"You have a debt that you owe me, Eric. I hope you haven't forgotten."

Eric shows regret. "What do you want from me, guy?"

Richard puts his arm around Eric and walks him away. "You've gained national attention with your speech, the other day. People know who you are. I want you to campaign for me as a repayment for all the money that is owed to me from years ago."

"So, you want me to endorse you as a judge? So you can protect your partners from doing jail time like I did?"

Richard chuckles, then removes his arm from around Eric. "Judge? That is old news. Did you not know that I put in my bid for mayor?"

Eric laughs. "After all the political drama in this city, you think people are going to trust you?"

"After they hear you speak about how good of a man I am, and how deserving I am, and how much this city needs a man like me, the people are going to trust me."

"You gotta be joking."

Richard has a serious expression. "I didn't come all this way to tell a joke. This is how you'll pay me back." As Eric turns his head, Richard demands attention. "Listen to me! Your flying friend can't help you anymore. And don't think I forgot about you ratting us out back then."

"Man, I don't know what you're talking about," Eric says.

"I don't believe in coincidences. That chick scared you into ratting everyone out, but... I see you as an asset, not a liability. Do not ruin my perception of you."

Jewel opens the front door to see what is taking Eric so long. "Eric! What's going on?"

"Give me a minute," says Eric.

Richard says to Eric, "Get yourself ready. I'll keep in touch." He pats Eric on the shoulder, then leaves the premises.

~~

Mr. Turner and Eva are still waiting outside of Amani's hospital room. The doctor comes out with a confused look on his face.

The Hospital Director shows up along with his assistants, the doctors who earlier declined on the operation, and the nurse who also left the Trauma Center. They are discussing what to do with Amani. She cannot be tested for certain diseases, because there are no needles that will penetrate her skin.

Mr. Turner jumps into the debate and demands that they allow him to finally see his daughter. The family was never allowed inside of the Trauma Center, because it is against policy. The DCI knew this and ordered for Amani to be kept there to avoid any interference.

The Hospital Director says, "It is an honor having you here with us, Mr. Turner, though under these unfortunate circumstances. We have been ordered to prohibit visitations to Ms. Jett, but as you see, that order had to be compromised. With that, you are allowed to spend time with your daughter, but you must wear the proper clothing."

"Did you find what she is infected with?" asks Mr. Turner.

"Not yet, being that we were unable to take any samples to test it out. Whatever it is, it's not common."

Mr. Turner is let into the room, wearing the appropriate gear. "Oh, my baby!" He shouts. "What did they do to you?"

A nurse also joins Mr. Turner. Amani's blisters have enlarged since they were first exposed. Mr. Turner cries as he rubs his oldest daughter's head with his gloved hand.

"Be strong, Amani," Mr. Turner says.

The nurse asks, "Do you have any idea why the authorities wanted her hair samples?"

"Authorities? Who are these authorities?"

"It's rumored to be the CIA. They wanted samples of everything. They even requested a urine sample from her."

Mr. Turner becomes very angry. "The only authority over this woman is her daddy! And that is me! Y'all better not touch another hair on her head!"

Suddenly, a group of three men wearing rubber suits step in. "You are not authorized to be in this room!" one of the suited men says. "I order you to leave at once, under the-"

"Hell no!" Mr. Turner hollers. "This is my daughter!" He takes a scalpel from the tray of surgical instruments left behind by the doctor. "Step closer, and I won't hesitate to cut you deep! You take her over my dead body!"

"D-Daddy..." Everyone looks and sees Amani awakening from her coma! She is still weak from the illness. This is her first time conscious since the explosion.

Mr. Turner says to Amani, "Sweetheart... I'm so glad you're up, now." Again, he faces the men. "But, your dad is about to cut somebody!"

Amani tries to sit up, although she's woozy, and says to the three men, "Back away from my father."

The men leave the room immediately. One of them removes his head cover and says, "Now we know where she gets it from." He takes out his phone and makes a call. "She's awake." Eva hears this and smiles.

CLONES AND DRONES

Waterboarding; an interrogation method that was banned back in 2009. This is the method currently used by Agent Blunt to get the information he wants.

A man is held down on his back by two men with a towel covering his face. Agent Blunt slowly pours water from a hose onto the subdued man's face, as he gasps for air and fights against the men who have him pinned down. Agent Blunt snatches the towel off the man's face, revealing it to be Agent Bryant Burns aka Agent Black.

"I will do this until you drown," Agent Blunt says. "So, let me ask you again... who's Agent Red?"

Agent Black is short of breath. "We only... go by... code names. They're agents like us."

"Us? You don't know the type of agent I am."

"Who knows anything? I'm just finding out who Luther Cobain is! I only knew him as Agent Blue!"

"What do you know about the security breach of the agency's database?"

"Less than you do! Please don't make me suffer. I swear to you I'm telling the truth!

"Protecting him does not benefit me. I only do what I'm told, and the men who were in charge are out of the picture. I don't even know if we have a group anymore!

"I don't know what Red was doing in that building. It could have been his assignment. The DCI sent you, correct?"

Agent Blunt says, "The Director did not order the hit on Amani Jett. Maybe you or another member of your group."

"I promise you, I had nothing to do with it, sir. I promise!"

Agent Blunt orders the men to let Agent Black up. They pull him to his feet without releasing his arms. He catches his breath.

"I am also looking for another member of your group," Agent Blunt says. "I guess you would only know her by Agent Violet."

"Yes," Agent Black says, "but I have no idea where she would be, either. It's designed that way. That's how covert alternates work."

"Very well. I'll tell you how my position works. Then, you will know the type of agent I am." He turns to his medical bag placed on a table in this torture chamber, then he opens it. He takes out a mechanical syringe. "You are about to be bugged. If you try to remove this mechanism from your body, there will be consequences."

Agent Black is frantic. "No... Don't put that thing in me! Please, no!"

Agent Blunt proceeds with the injection. "It will only sting for a minute."

Two men armed with AK-47 assault rifles in an armored truck are escorting a restrained visitor in Baghdad. This visitor is bound by the rope on his wrists, and his head is covered in a black cloth while being led to a secret location.

At this location, the visitor is sat down before a man of importance, guarded by two more of his soldiers. One of the armed men who brought the visitor removes the black cloth, revealing the visitor as Agent Red!

"Can you free my wrists, as well?" Agent Red asks.

"No," says the apparent leader. "We do not trust you Americans."

"That explains the warm welcome. But, I can understand you being paranoid."

"Paranoia is a sign of fear. We do not fear you. And you, we do not trust."

Agent Red smiles. "I come to you with a business proposition." The leader doesn't respond, but waits for the conclusion. "Well... you have gotten your asses kicked by my country. Your numbers dwindle from month to month. You try to sound as if you have an enormous army, but you really don't.

"You barely have any technology, and yet, you think you're going to rise again in this very country. A country in which the leader was taken down in a matter of months.

"You Taliban guys are humorous! Terrorizing, blowing yourselves up for a truckload of virgins. I'm guessing you're expecting heavenly stamina, so you can please them all with a godly penis above the clouds, huh?" The guards who stand behind him point their rifles at him out of resentment.

"You Americans are so arrogant," the Taliban leader says. "You have your technology and your flying woman, but-"

"Wait! Let me stop you right there. This flying woman you speak of is no longer a threat to you. She's been compromised."

"Nonsense! What army defeated your witch?"

"No army. I did." The rest of the guards point their rifles at him.

"If this is true, then tell me what are your extraordinary abilities."

"I have none." The Taliban leader and his guards laugh. "What I do have is smarts. I plan things out, they get done. That's why it would be wise to accept my offer."

"Then, tell me. What business proposition do you offer to us?"

"Cloning technology. I would like to start here in this country. This would be the perfect place to manufacture the organisms."

The Taliban leader stands to his feet. "You are of pure evil!"

"I've heard."

"We will not allow you to use our holy lands for your demonic plan, you evil beast!"

"You speak as if this is really your land."

The leader pounds his fist on the table. "You come here and insult my army... You make fun of our beliefs... You tell us lies of defeating Amani Jett... And, you want us to do the work of evil?"

"It's for a greater cause."

"You insane American!" He draws out his dagger. "I should make you a dead American!"

"Ironically, Americans think I am dead."

"Then, no one will miss you."

"You're missing my point. I successfully created a clone of my own. It was destroyed in the process of defeating Amani Jett."

"So, you're saying this technology is more than just a theory. You deceptive devil."

"Look, before you start throwing shoes at me, remember who it was that helped the Taliban become what it is today. Besides, your former president had lookalikes, didn't he? This could benefit you the same, but without real casualties."

The leader sits back down. "You took a big risk by coming to this territory. You came with no weapons, and no explosives. You must be working alone."

"You know this is an excellent opportunity that you'll never have again. Definitely a true benefit for the both of us."

"I will have to see this technology with my own eyes before I commit to your business proposition."

"Very well. But, you must agree that after I prove myself, I can start shipping parts of my new lab, piece by piece."

"Your new lab?"

"Yes, **my** new lab. Is there a problem with that?"

The leader hesitates, then says, "You will own nothing in this country!"

"Okay, fine. But, you should really leave your emotions out of business dealings. You can be quite irrational at times, so..." He opens his mouth, then removes his tooth cap. "This special incisor, right here, serves three purposes. It's a tracking device, for one. It's also a detonator, and... it's useful when I get a little hungry."

The leader and his guards go into a panic! They grab him and put their guns to his head. Three small drones hover above ground, outside of the once secret location, having the same design as the one which destroyed the home of Agent Blue.

"Where are your people?" yells the Taliban leader.

"People?" Agent Red replies with a smirk. "I can't promise you people, but those mechanical friends of mine can guarantee my safety."

The Taliban leader commands two of his guards to check outside, speaking in his native language when giving orders. The guards carefully make their way outside, while Agent Red is restrained by the leader and his men.

Two guards on the outside look around and see nothing at eye level and below. All is quiet, until the men are shot up by the aerial robots. They fall dead not knowing what hit them.

After noticing this, the Taliban leader steps in front of Agent Red and places his gun barrel right between the eyes of his captive.

Agent Red says, "You're pointing the gun, but you are my prisoner. That is, unless you agree to the deal. The deal where I ship the components for **my** fucking lab!"

Though a hard man, the Taliban leader gives in for the moment, agreeing to take the deal, but he is very watchful of Agent Red. He orders his men to let him go.

Agent Red straightens his suit, fixes his neck tie, then says the cliché, "Nice doing business with you." He takes his replacement tooth and puts it back inside of his mouth.

There is a vehicle waiting outside for the rogue agent, and he gets in. The two drones follow the armored vehicle to protect Agent Red. Apparently, these machines are being controlled by Agent Gray in a remote area.

WILLPOWER

Cameramen, reporters, fans, and admirers alike are camped outside of the hospital, where they just learned that Amani had awakened from her short-term coma. They are waiting to hear a word from her.

A woman in a dress suit and pumps boldly walks through the crowd and into the front entrance. She is a professional lady in her fifties who knows just where she is going; to the room which holds Amani Jett. Two volunteering police officers stand outside of Amani's room to prevent unwanted visits.

The lady of mystery steps up to them and shows her badge. "Margaret Zalewski; CIA. I am here to see Ms. Jett." This is Agent Violet.

One of the officers asks, "Under whose orders?"

"The President of the United States." The officers look at each other with uncertainty. "So, let me in."

The other officer tells her, "You can't go in there without the proper clothing to protect you."

Agent Violet sighs. "That won't be needed. Excuse me." She brushes past the officers, goes into the room, then closes the door behind her.

Immediately, Amani asks, "The President sent you with no one accompanying you?"

"I said what I said for them to let me in," says Agent Violet.

"Why couldn't I tell you were lying? Are you psycho?"

Agent Violet chuckles. "No, dear. I've been trained to trick lie detectors. It's part of my job."

"What are you here for, Marge?"

Agent Violet walks up to her and checks the blisters on Amani's skin. "That looks familiar. Poor girl. You must barely have any feeling right now."

"The doctors said they never saw anything like this before. So, Margaret, what do you know about this infection?" Amani asks suspiciously.

"That it's not a typical infection at all. What you have are genetically modified parasites."

"You're saying this is man-made?"

"Use your hearing. Listen closely to your own body. They are constantly working their way through the layers of your strong skin."

Amani is furious! She wants to get up and grab Agent Violet, but she is too weak. Agent Violet's knowledge of this evil barnacle shows her affiliation to whoever caused this.

"Rest yourself, Amani," Agent Violet says. "The parasites are programmed to attack your nervous system. They are strategically placed at pressure points on your body. You need them removed."

"Tell me how to get rid of them!"

"I will, but you must promise to stay quiet about our nation's affairs. The people are not to be aware of everything, or it would cause utter chaos."

"So, this was all done to keep me quiet?"

"No. That agent, Agent Red as we called him, worked on his own. That is as far as I can tell." She sits next to Amani. "He was an expert of bio-technology. This condition you have has his name all over it."

Amani asks, "And why do you know so much about him?"

"I am not allowed to tell you that, Ms. Jett. You understand how that goes. So, do we have a deal?"

"First, I want to know why was this bio-weaponry developed. This is a lot of trouble to go through just for your average human being. It looks like it's designed just for me."

"Some people are afraid of you, Amani. I hope there is no reason for them to be."

"I never had any plans to leak government secrets. Not all of them. You are a paranoid bunch of people!"

"If not all secrets, then which ones?"

"Where do I start? The many war crimes of the last ten years? How the rich get richer and the poor get poorer?

"What about those who really run this country? Where the money is really going?"

Agent Violet gasps in disgust. "Don't you think to some degree that even though the tough decisions look bad on the outside, they are still necessary?"

"Necessary. You people love to use that word. It doesn't justify anything."

"If you believe in preserving the American way of life and keeping the American dream alive, then you would respect the hard decisions made by our chosen leaders."

"The only people who preach about the American dream are the ones who got it like that! Everybody living here is not living the American dream! Look around you!

"There are people suffering like it's a third world country! When you talk about the American way of life, what percentage of the people are **you** talking about?

"I've seen people get blown up by million dollar missiles dropped by million dollar aircraft! More money was spent on wars than <u>necessary</u>."

"Amani, I've had this discussion with you a while back," Agent Violet says. "I know where you stand. But, I don't want you to use your power as a way to do whatever you want."

"Isn't that what **you** all do?"

Agent Violet stands up. "I can't help you with

that problem of yours. You're killing yourself over pride. I hope you reconsider."

"I'll fight with or without you."

Agent Violet leaves with no reply. One of Amani's volunteering cop friends, who was standing guard, comes in afterward and asks what went on.

"That was no regular explosion," Amani says. "It's hard to explain, because I don't totally remember."

Minutes later, Amani lies silently in her hospital bed, trying her best to come up with a solution for her current predicament. Even though Agent Violet would not inform Amani on how to remedy her sickness, she did confirm that there was indeed a way to eliminate the parasites.

The blisters on Amani's body are nests for these mutated parasites. As Amani meditates, she can hear them feeding through her skin.

Amani thinks to herself. "I do recall poisonous bombs used in Iraq, but nothing that embedded parasites! This is creepy! These things must be immune to extremely hot temperatures, being that they survived the explosion.

"But, if they were strategically placed, as Marge put it, then it would mean that this Agent Red used some sort of weapon, perhaps while I was dazed."

"Desperation" is a good word to describe what Amani is going through at this point. She looks for the tray of scalpels that was incidentally left earlier by the surgeon, but since guests were allowed to enter the room, the nurse was sure to remove it.

There is one thing that catches Amani's eye while surveying the room; her food tray containing empty plates, plastic utensils, and a small bottle of apple cider with a straw. Amani takes the straw out of the bottle, then puts it to her lips. She blows through it to discover the fine current of her arctic blast.

"This just might work!" Amani thinks with a glow in her eyes. This is a dangerous idea that can lead to frostbite, which could damage her permanently, but it is a risk she is willing to take. She aligns the tip of the straw at the center of the blister on her forearm and blows through it with her deep freezing power. She continues to the point where she can no longer withstand the discomfort of the cold.

The blister is hardened and rigid, as Amani takes her sharp-edged fingernail and carves through the outer layers of her frozen dead skin. She carefully removes the cyst-coated organism, inspecting the properties of this bio-weapon with her keen sight, but it is not enough. A microscope will be needed.

Amani summons the nurse, along with one of the guards from outside of her room. "I need you to store this in freezing temperatures," Amani says to them with the parasite in her palm. "Then, you need to take this to a man named, Professor Scott Borek. He teaches at U of M. Do not let this thaw!"

Prof. Borek was Joanie's closest instructor when she attended the university. He is the first person that comes to Amani's mind, though she only met him once. With the mention of Joanie, the professor will be sure to help.

The nurse asks, "How on earth did you remove it, Ms. Jett?" She checks Amani's arm.

Amani says, "Where there's a will, there's a way."

The frozen, dislodged parasite is put into a metal container to be transported to the professor. Amani was able to determine that this parasite had no metallic properties, so an MRI is suggested for the remaining organisms by the doctor.

The purpose for this is to see how far advanced the other parasites have made it through Amani's once-believed impenetrable skin. This will show her how much time she has left.

Amani doesn't like the idea of being scanned by any machine. For one, she doesn't want records of her anatomy available to anyone. Also, she has a fear of what the scan may reveal to her. Amani is afraid that it would show hideous abnormalities, questioning her humanity. This is a fear that she keeps to herself.

For a thorough recovery, Amani seeks the help of a famous holistic doctor that she once met in South America. She spends one million dollars to expedite his special travel to the United States.

This bold decision to contact the holistic doctor could certainly become a controversy if discovered by the media. Amani makes this particular request despite being in a hospital full of doctors.

Amani has always been into holistic health and therapy. It is what helped her become the physical specimen that she is. She has no personal doctor, nor does she have health insurance. Amani always listens to her body for anything out of the norm.

Donnell Price drives up to the hospital entrance. Neither he nor any visitors for Amani are allowed on the hospital floor at this time. This is by Amani's request. She wants to avoid letting anyone see her scan results, in case of an anomalistic finding.

It is a festive atmosphere in some areas outside, where loyal followers cheer for Amani's recovery. However, there is a protest across the street from the hospital. A group of men and women dressed in black suits, red ties, and sunglasses are defying Amani's movement. They imitate Agent Red after seeing the video of him entering the building on the night before the explosion.

The video shot of Agent Red's clone has been on the news channels, magazines, and newspapers. There is a lot of hype surrounding Agent Red.

Thanks to constant media coverage, Agent Red's profile has become famous overnight, as if he is a celebrity himself. He has become the face of many anti-Amani Jett hate groups. "The Man With the Red Tie". The running question about him is... why did he do it?

A reporter interviews a red tie advocate. "I think it's obvious why he did it," the advocate says. "He did it for our country! Amani is anti-American, which we should all know by now."

The reporter asks the over-confident woman, "Why do you call her that? Anti-American."

"Well, because she clearly chooses fame over loyalty. And she is defiant to the leaders we have chosen. She was never chosen by the people."

"So, she should have an attempt on her life? And what about the people who were in the building?"

"We don't know if he caused the explosion."

"Now, come on, there's been evidence of a bomb recovered this morning!"

The advocate looks dumbfounded, however she refuses to hang up her tie and lose the argument. She and her associates were out protesting before the bomb discovery was reported. They didn't wait to find out more about what went on and why, and they were too eager to criticize Amani. These people couldn't wait for the opportunity to feel important.

"Please, don't get me wrong," the advocate says. "We have sympathy for the casualties who were caught in the fire. But, I'm not sure he tried to kill or injure any of them."

"What if he did?" asks the reporter.

"I'm not going to entertain that question, because I don't believe he did. That's my belief. He sacrificed his life, too."

Those who support Amani are now avoiding similar dress as those who oppose. People have gone crazy. Again.

Amani is set to take her MRI scan. She tries to calm herself from the fears of scary results. Once inside of the contraption, she thinks about the incident that led to her being in this predicament.

After crushing the clone of Agent Red's hand, she recalls hearing a weird sound that even the shooter was suffering from. Then, Amani thinks to herself, "Infrasound. Clever."

Amani now believes she was hearing a frequency unheard by the common ear, and it had the same effect on her as anyone else. Discombobulation. She has to come up with a preventative solution, so it won't happen again. Infrasound is also deadly.

The result of the scan is good to Amani's eyes. She was more concerned about her inner structure than the advancement of the parasites. Her inner body is visibly normal and not out of the ordinary.

The hospital floor is now open for visitors. Donnell rushes to see Amani, who is content, but needs to heal. Her father, Mr. Turner, was also waiting. The two men cater to her needs, building a bond between Donnell and Mr. Turner. Donnell spent many years without a father figure and Mr. Turner never had a son. These are special moments that Amani takes notice of. This brings a smile to her face.

~~

Two days have passed since Amani was paid a visit by Agent Zalewski/Agent Violet. All parasites have been successfully removed and the healing process is going steady.

Amani has regained all of her feelings. She is mobile and ready to face the world again. Thanks to the help of the holistic doctor, who made his visit in secret, Amani feels she is rejuvenated. Her skin still has blemishes, but they will heal in good time.

After gaining her senses back at full peak, Amani hears a faint sound once the room goes silent. The television is off and the air conditioner has stopped for the moment. With both Mr. Turner and Donnell gone at the time, Amani can trace this sound.

Amani then reaches beneath the bed and finds a tiny electronic device hidden beneath the mattress. "Margaret..." she says to herself.

So, the room has been bugged for the last three days. Fortunately, Amani hadn't revealed anything that would lead to a compromise of her mission. She was leery of discussing her ulterior plans in the hospital, regardless.

Donnell returns as Amani smashes the tiny spying device into dust with her fingers. "What's the matter?" Donnell asks.

Amani answers, "Snoopers. Not you."

"Don't let those nosy people affect your mood." He removes his hand from behind his back, pulling out the bouquet of flowers that he was attempting to hide.

Amani pretends to be surprised. "Oh my! You are such a sweetheart. And a lifesaver."

"So are you."

Then, there is the look. They lock eyes in a way that could only mean one thing; Love is in the air. Donnell walks over to the bed and kisses Amani passionately on her lips, while she caresses him tightly, pulling him in closer.

"I can't wait to take you home," Donnell says, following the long kiss.

Amani is excited! She is aroused like never before, but she is not completely ready. This would be her first time and she wants things to be perfect. They are not quite there, yet. Even though Donnell saved her life, she still wants more time with him. One other thing that continues to haunt her is her big secret. The reason Amani fears a deep, open, and honest relationship with Donnell. The mystery of his father's death.

AGENTS' AGENDAS

Lamont is disgruntled by the amount of money that Amani funded him out of her big payday. She gave him five thousand dollars out of her near one hundred million.

He watches on as Ivy's older children pack away their belongings for their move to the mountainous state of Arizona. Ivy wanted to move sooner, but Amani's incident delayed her relocating. She also wanted to have her wedding before leaving.

Lamont complains to Ivy, "How is this little bit of money going to last me?"

Ivy responds, "Lamont, please, I know you aren't complaining. I wouldn't have given you a dime if I was her! Not with you chatting on the computer with those people who hate all day!" She begins to empty her closet.

"But, she's supposed to be family! That's alright, I'll get mine."

"Get what? A job? Finally, after staying with me and my family rent free?"

"Why are you still complaining about that? You get to move out west in a big ol' house!"

"My concern for you finding work was for you, not for me. Boy, you just don't know how many arguments I had with Jermaine over you. Amani was right."

"Amani ain't right. You only say that, because she's paying you off. I should've told her to keep that five grand."

"It ain't too late. Tell her! You grown!"

"I know what I'll do with it. Put it towards my people! That's the total opposite of what Amani does with money; helping out others instead of her own."

Ivy stops momentarily. "That money can get you into a house. Houses are super cheap in this city. You need to help yourself, Lamont, instead of being impressionable to those web freaks." She proceeds with packing.

"Those cheap houses need a lot of work."

"Then, do it yourself. Be a man! You're sounding like you want your own place, but don't want any responsibilities."

Lamont leaves the room without replying. He doesn't want to face what he must do. His first decision was to take over the rent, which would drain his money in a matter of months. He is upset with his situation and angry with Amani.

He logs on to the internet and goes to his favorite blog, ready to spew anger toward his cousin. He also logs onto the social network that he frequents, looking for a particular avatar and finds her; a very pretty lady with the screen name, Queen Nubia.

"Queen Nubia" is the name that the online friend goes by, because she says it is too dangerous to put your real name on the internet. Just another way the government tracks people down, as if they don't already have everyone's info. The name she gave Lamont over the telephone is Angie Jenkins.

Lamont is attracted to this woman in every way she presents herself. He likes her online photos and the picture messages she sent to his mobile phone. And with the many late night phone conversations with her, Lamont thinks he is in love. She claims to feel the same way about him.

Angie resides in a different state. They promise to meet someday soon, but Lamont has financial limitations. He talks about not wanting a woman who is all about money, but at the same time, he wants to impress her with finances and is too ashamed of not having his own home or income.

Lamont feels close to Angie, enough to tell her about his relationship to Amani. He asked her not to tell anyone. Angie agreed, but keeps her stance on Amani, though she does not know her. With Angie's influence, Lamont continues to badmouth his cousin online.

Lamont sends the text message, "Thinking about you, my Nubian Queen, my African flower."

Angie replies, "That's so sweet. Love you!"

"Love you more. I'll call you tonight. Is that fine with you?"

"Always, as long as I'm not too busy."

Lamont logs off of the computer, feeling better about himself. His online love interest, Angie, also logs off. Problem is, "Angie" is not who Lamont thinks she is. Sitting behind a laptop computer in Delaware is a lame, slouchy, overweight Caucasian woman eating fries, a cheeseburger, and drinking a chocolate milkshake.

The imposter's name is Deborah O'Toole. She has been on this site for over a year under different names, having a total of ten profiles, with none of them being her true identity.

Her online persona talks about Black knowledge, but can't do much other than criticize the powers that be. She may find and post an article pertaining to African awareness, but has no true knowledge of her own. She has a query of such articles and will copy and paste the literature from time to time.

Deborah's whole shtick is propaganda, and she works with someone close to aid her into riling up specific demographics. She has no shame in fooling people like Lamont and feels that she is doing them a kind service by giving them someone to talk to. Deborah is hardly concerned about the eventual heartbreak, because it's something that happens in real relationships, anyway. They will get over it.

A man sits alone at a park bench, until he is joined by Margaret Zalewski, aka Agent Violet.

"Hi, Green," Agent Violet says as she sits next to Agent Green.

"Afternoon, Violet," says Agent Green. "How was Detroit?"

"Boring. As I stated in the message, she didn't give in. And after a couple of days, she detected the bug."

"What? The device virtually had no sound! Where did you place it?"

"Where I said I would."

"I don't understand. Do you think she's getting more powerful?"

"Let's hope not. This is why the group decided never to make an attempt on her life without being completely sure of the results."

Agent Green pounds his fist. "Agent Red screwed us all!"

"He saw that the group was falling apart. I guess the explosion was his goodbye present. A waste."

"Then, why do we continue with our part of the directives?"

"Just because the group is in disarray, we still must consider the potential threat. She is still upset. About everything."

"Damn it. I was able to get a translation from the recording you sent yesterday. The man speaking was a holistic doctor, from South America."

"She sent out for a foreign doctor while in the hospital?" She thinks for a brief moment. "We must publicize this right away."

"I bet the hospital staff had no idea who he was. We should track down this doctor to see what he knows about her power. He may have something to do with it."

"Good idea. You still have ties with Agent Black, don't you? You two have done a lot of work together in the past."

"I haven't heard from him at all."

"We have to find a way to reach him."

Agent Green is a communications expert who helped Agent Black hunt and spy on different targets during the last ten years.

"I have some good news," Agent Green says. "My associate in Delaware said exactly what you told her to say. This guy, Lamont, is opening up to her."

"Oh, Ms. O'Toole," Agent Violet says. "That is good."

"What's even better, I've done research on a lot of the people in that online forum. You'll want to check them out. I believe that with your psychiatric expertise, you'll get a load out of them."

"What is it about them?"

"Many of them are phonies. They preach Afro-Klan stuff, but the guy who moderates the site has a history of dabbling with White women. Some never had passports and never been to Africa."

"Very entertaining. Ms. O'toole fits right in. I just might have a way to get more out of Lamont than what I planned initially."

"What will you do with him?"

"Make a public figure out of him. He's the perfect candidate for those people. And Ms. O'toole will really come in handy."

"Excellent. But, who do we report to?"

"No one. We're on our own, for now. And since the Director opened the idea to bring her family into this, I'd rather not be a part of the group anyway."

Elsewhere, the Director is met in his office by Agent Blunt. "Your 'Espionage Expert' is a dud," Agent Blunt says. "He knows nothing. I do think we have a lead on Agent Green, however. This group truly was top secret."

"Had to be, if I knew nothing about it," the DCI says. "Rumor has it, Agent Violet was in Detroit not long ago. She's quick, so we'll have to be quicker."

"Did you meet with the former director?"

"He's... out of the loop. If you can make contact with Agent Green, that may be a good advantage."

"Yes, sir. Will do."

The truth is, the former Director wants nothing to do with the group, anymore. He is not open to speaking on it or his former position with the CIA.

When Agent Blunt leaves the office, the DCI looks over his short list of agents who belonged to the dismantled covert alternate group.

Agent Blue
Luther Cobain: Orchestrator and keeper of records; Deceased.

Agent Black
Bryant Burns: Espionage and military. Bugged.

Agent Violet
Margaret Zalewski: Psychiatric strategist; AWOL.

Agent Green
Unknown: Communications and master of decryption. AWOL

Agent Red
Unknown: Bio-weaponry and biological sciences; Deceased.

Agent Gray
Unknown: Robot technology. Mechanical warfare; AWOL.

Agent White
Unknown.

Agent Brown
Unknown.

Istanbul, Turkey. It is nighttime in an old, raggedy bar. The place is preparing to close down at this hour. No customers are left, but agents Gray and Red.

The non-English-speaking owner and bartender of the bar waits patiently for the men to finish their last drinks. They pay well.

"She may be alive," Agent Red says, "but we can stay the course. As long as some lost faith in her."

Agent Gray replies, "It would be much easier had she not recovered so quickly. Or not recovered at all."

"This is not about her anymore. It's about a stronger weapon. The collective minds of the American people."

Agent Gray lifts his shot glass of whiskey to give a toast. "To the future leaders of the free world. Forever challenging one another."

Agent Red raises his glass. "Making each other stronger. Forces to be reckoned with."

The two men drink from their glasses. They celebrate as if they had already carried out their plans. These are arrogant men.

"Tell me, dead man," Agent Gray says, "did you expect to have a following so soon? You have kids wearing red ties and sunglasses in your memory."

"It's a complete surprise," says Agent Red. "That's the power of a dead man. And the more Amani Jett is defamed, the better my efforts will look. I'm already a hero."

"The respect of the dead. That's a big head start you got on me, Red. But, they need a real leader. The sheep will gather quickly when it's my turn."

"Too bad we couldn't bring Violet in on this. She's too damn close to Subject A(who is Amani) to ride along with us."

"Agent Violet had to get closer to her. It was part of her assignment."

"She did profess her 'love' of Subject A, but maybe that was just to persuade the new DCI. I can never tell with Violet. She's good at what she does."

"Which is why we can do without her. She would psyche us out like anyone else. There's only room for one persuader of the people, and that is me."

"On the contrary, Agent Gray. My following has already started and is destined to multiply rapidly."

Agent Gray leans back with a smirk. "Americans are loyal to their country, not because of its dead leaders, but its hope for protection. My leadership will be equipped with the mightiest robot army."

"And while you give them protection, I will give them hope. I will manufacture heroes. I will touch their hearts and break them, only to bring in the next savior."

"They will surely take my consistencies over the sentimental hopes of heaven on Earth that you'll give them. And let's not forget the effectiveness of convenience. Winning over the American people will be effortless, once my corporations present this new robot technology."

"There's nothing new about it, actually."

"But, to them... it is. And just like you, I will start in the foreign market. And, I'll develop my weapons of war with the bold promise of no more human fatalities."

"You promise a war with no domestic bloodshed. You can't touch hearts without casualties."

"We will see..."

"Well then, Gray, I hope you've picked up enough pointers from Violet." He requests another drink from the bartender. "I thought you would have had your surgery by now. Don't tell me you're getting cold feet. Can't let the old look go just yet?"

Agent Gray also orders another drink. "I'm scheduled for later. There's no rush for me to change my face. I will in due time."

"Make sure they make you handsome."

"You mean handsomer."

"Okay, sure. A shade lighter, since you already have that bi-racial thing going for you. Those minority groups are becoming more important each election year."

"I'm fully aware."

"This will be a fun game," Agent Red says, as their drinks are served. "Two opposing forces with the same agenda."

Agent Gray replies, "Our rebellions should kick things off within the next year. Your clones, my machines. One hell of a ride."

"Remember, we must **never** agree on shit. Keep the people divided, giving them their power to choose."

"Yes. When you let them believe they have true power, they will find no reason to fight for it."

"But, we must come together occasionally. There has to be moments of peace."

"Most definitely. It can't be all bad news. We'll work together in disastrous moments."

"While at the same time, we'll be celebrating our diversity."

"Our influence on the news media must be made powerful. I will cover mainstream, you can cover other syndicates."

"I'd like to deal with that one radio guy. Can't think of his name, but he's a dumb ass. I want him to keep up the good work."

Agent Gray laughs. "You're talking about Billy J. Marshall?"

"Yeah, him. I could really use a fool like him. Especially with his faithful listeners."

"Good idea."

"There's White, colored; religious, atheist; liberal, conservative; straight, homo; rich, poor; good, evil... We have a lot going for us, Gray. With so many divisions already in place, we can't fail."

"I'll drink to that," Agent Gray says as he gulps his final shot of whiskey. "History is on our side."

Agent Red takes a look at the bartender, then asks Agent Gray, "What do you think?"

Agent Gray shrugs his shoulders, then says, "Yeah, I guess."

"Whose turn is it?"

"I think it's yours."

Agent Red hides his pistol under the table, twisting a silencer onto the barrel. "Not that it really matters, but I didn't want to be rude."

"Be my guest..."

Agent Red lifts his gun and shoots the bartender three times. The two former agents get up to make sure he is dead. The shots were right on target. Agent Gray leaves a tip.

WHAT DOESN'T KILL HER

"Mark my words," Amani says. "I'm coming back stronger than ever. All they did was give me callus. I will not allow myself to be distracted again."

Amani stands firmly in front of her family before leaving out of the hospital. The news reporters are waiting outside to bombard her with questions.

Instead of exiting through the hospital's main entrance, Amani finds her own exit; an opened window on the floor where she stayed throughout her recovery. She flies out of the hospital with a wave to the crowd. The people cheer for her as she zips through the sky.

Amani's first destinations are the residences of victims of the explosion. She offers to cover any outstanding expenses as a result of the incident. Some are open to her offer and some refuse out of hatred. The ones filled with hate blame Amani for everything. They are unforgiving and spiteful.

Amani can't understand why they put the blame on her, as if she set the bomb. Perhaps they never liked her to begin with.

Afterward, Amani goes to the hospital where her friend, Joanie, is being cared for. Preceding Amani's hospital exit for her own injuries, Ivy informed her of Joanie's awakening. Joanie is expected to make a good recovery, but it may take years of therapy. She is very fortunate to be alive.

Amani spends hours with Joanie's Illinois family, Joanie's daughter, Justine, in particular. She wants to keep her encouraged through the heartache.

Justine tells Amani, "I prayed, just like you said I should."

"That's good, Justine!" Amani says.

Joanie's sister-in-law, Rebbecca, hears this and disapproves. She knows how her brother, Dylan, and Joanie were about religion. They were opposed to it, more Dylan than Joanie.

Before Amani leaves the area, Rebbecca asks to speak with her in private. "I heard what you said to Justine," Rebbecca says. "Can you not discuss religion or praying with my niece? That's not how she was raised, so in honor of that, please don't mention it to her again."

Amani is bewildered. "I only asked if she prayed, because I always thought Joanie was cool with it. I wasn't trying to interfere."

"Then, I'm glad to let you know. Not trying to get myself in trouble with you, but she may be the only thing left between Dylan and Joanie."

"She's not a thing. Joanie will pull through this. She will be back at one hundred and ten percent."

"I'm not sure exactly how that is possible, but I won't argue with a super-being. I just hope that you remember she is not like you."

Amani is annoyed by Rebbecca's unbelief. She also feels partly responsible for not promoting her religious beliefs on television, but the scientists would deny her anyway.

Later, Amani searches the facility for Gwen Zorn, the nurse who helped her the last time she was there. Gwen is overjoyed to see Amani and proud that she had remembered her name.

After reconnecting, Amani goes back to speak with Rebbecca. She inquires about the hospital costs and what was left of Dylan's insurance coverage, now that he is deceased. It's probable that they will need financial help from Amani. She will gladly assist.

Following her leave from the hospital, Amani goes directly to her mansion in Michigan. She calls up Geoffrey Charleston, who is the designer of her recently destroyed battle suit.

Amani greets, "Hello, Geoffrey."

"Hello, Ms. Jett!" Geoffrey says. "I'm very excited that you recovered so soon!"

"Thanks! Your suit was a helping factor. I could use another one like it."

"Excellent! You do remember the deal we made last time, don't you? You agreed to pay off the sponsors for the one suit, so they would remove the logos."

Amani taps her forehead. "Shoot! I forgot about that. Looks like I'll have to bypass those companies and work a deal directly with NASA."

"I'm so sorry, Ms. Jett, but the companies share the patent to the interior design of the suit. You can't legally bypass them."

"It figures. This is why I need a few personal assistants. I can't keep track of all this crap."

"Your best bet is to try talking them into selling the patent to you. That way, you can apply that technology to your other suits, as well. It will be a big purchase, but definitely worth the money."

"Damn! My money is dwindling like crazy. It was a million for the one suit alone!"

"I know, Ms. Jett, but this is your life we're talking about."

"No, I'm not that fragile. That will not happen too often. They are not going to get richer off of me."

"Understood. So, where do we go from here?"

Amani thinks about it. "That interior armor can use some improvements. It could be a little more comfortable in the bust area. I will work with them on the structure, but they'll have to work with me on the cost."

"Then, I'll link you with the companies, so you can work a deal. From there, I can help you with your next suit."

"Make it three suits this time. I should stock up."

The expenses are piling up. Amani doesn't want to make the same mistakes she made with her high-taxing mansion. This mission of hers is very expensive. The multi-state communication hub properties are already purchased. Now, she must buy the hardware and equipment before hiring engineers to run the cell sites. This is Amani's most challenging investment.

There's no doubt she must continue to endorse commercial products in order for her goals to be met. Some will like it, some won't. Amani has made enough to cover her independent company, but desires more to help rebuild communities and help those in need, financially.

There is much sideline criticism about how much Amani makes and what she fails to do for her withering hometown. In spite of it all, she continues her path by her own way of getting there. No one dictates what Amani does with her money, but her.

Amani receives a call from Prof. Borek, with his report concerning the parasite that was first removed from her body.

"What was done with the other parasites?" Prof. Borek asks.

"They're in deep freeze," Amani answers.

"Good! Keep them there for a week. They must die."

"What did you find, professor?"

"It was definitely designed to kill you. That thing ate through stacks of metal! I had to contain it after it thawed by refreezing it."

Amani gasps. "The measures some people will go for murder. I need to find out who created this."

"Ms. Jett, your skin must be very strong. Was it always this way? Or was that simply willpower?"

"It seems as if I evolved. Tough situations like that usually bring something out of me."

"Then, you might want to keep that in mind next time you're facing death. Always believe. So, how is Joanie?"

"You should be proud of your student. She is awake now! Can't remember much, yet."

"Great news! I knew she could make it! And she'll be back to normal."

"Hopefully, sooner than anticipated."

⁂

The telephone rings the next morning. This time, it is Lucy from Tennessee. She and George were the couple who once worked for the Church of Amani, before Amani ruined it. They keep in touch and are planning to testify against the false prophet who they worked for.

"We need a little help," Lucy says to Amani. "I hope it won't be any trouble."

"What do you need help for?" Amani asks.

"When the church shut down for the time being, George and I lost our main source of income. We've been looking for work ever since and haven't found anyone willing to hire us, because we're on your side. Pastor Vance has been spreading lies to the people of this town and they're taking his side."

Amani is thrown off guard. "Then, you weren't volunteers?"

"No, we were on a payroll. We also received tips from our loyal customers. We miss that and we have our mortgage to pay."

This gives Amani an idea that she had totally overlooked! She may have to change the way she's been running her own organization. It hadn't even crossed her mind to run her mission as a Non-profit Organization, because she strongly opposed any governmental help or involvement.

Amani did not want to request approval from anyone. "Legit" was not a word she cared to use when describing her organization. She was simply spiteful.

"I believe I can assist you," Amani tells Lucy, "but the timing must be right and it must be done right. I'd hate to be accused of bribing you into taking my side over the pastor's, or some other nonsense."

"God bless you, Ms. Jett!" Lucy says. "We were so worried, but we had to believe!"

"No problem."

･.･

Later in the afternoon, Amani called for a meeting of her staff. Everyone was able to make it, including Lieutenant Vega. They are meeting at Amani's home for the first time.

"Nice place you got, Jett," Lt. Vega says.

"Thanks, Julio," says Amani.

"So, what did you drag us out here for?"

"Staff, I was thinking. My initial goal was to work independently. To use my personal gain as means to run this system.

"While this seems to be working, I don't know how long it can hold. There are a lot of things I want to do, and by having more time to think about it lately, I decided that I will need more than a reconnaissance team.

"I need you all to become your own Non-profit organization, under the category of Public Safety. I will fund it myself."

"Wait," Lt. Vega says, "You have been doing this all on your own? No government benefits at all?"

"Yeah. I may be a bit over-guarded, but if you were in my shoes, you'd understand. I am hoping you all are okay with running this organization with the objectives I've written down this morning."

Ivy says, "You **know** I'm in." Eva and Mr. Turner both agree.

Amani says to Lt. Vega, "Julio, I need you in on this. I was even hoping that you'd be the head of it."

Lt. Vega replies, "You know I have a job to do with the police force."

"Just do your part in the meetings, that's all. I am adding two more people to the crew. Lucy and George Stallworth from Tennessee will be good assets, but not as reconnaissance team members."

"Give me some time to think about that, Amani."

Amani addresses the entire staff. "With this being nonprofit, I won't be as nervous about my overall spending. Though the tax cuts will soon be over and my lump sum is going to be hit hard, I can benefit by investing into this organization, earning tax deductions. This would allow me to pay you a salary for more than what you're making now."

"Count me in!" says Lt. Vega. Everyone laughs.

"That's what I want to hear. Now, keep in mind, your current duties have little to do with the NPO. The reconnaissance team works for me. The public safety team works independently for the people."

Mr. Turner asks, "So, you're saying there are two different work assignments?"

"Yes. A whole nother job with little time to put in."

"Explain that some more for me."

"Okay, Dad, the communicating we do during missions is one thing, but I will need a company to actually run the new communication hubs.

"I've bought thirty-six pieces of land in twenty-five cities. These areas have high populations and often need assistance. The properties are the future locations of cell sites, consisting of cell towers.

"These cell sites will expand our reach without the dependency of our current network provider. The main hub will be in Arizona with Ivy.

"The lands' ownership will be transferred to the NPO, once it is legitimized. This venture will be very expensive, but it can be done. Real soon."

Mr. Turner says, "So, we're talking about an entire network for public safety."

"Yes, and I am your <u>investor</u>. I have learned of a few open-source, software-based cellular networks that can help make this possible. The NPO will have to be licensed to legally operate the network.

"You can even add callers to this network for two bucks a month, if you wanted to. But, it's for traditional calls without too much of the fancy extras.

"When I invest in this mission from now on, I want it to be through the NPO. Communications are the bulk of my expenses."

Eva asks, "Will you be on the board for this new organization?"

"I'd rather not be," says Amani. "I want you all to officially run it."

"Good. Then, we can hire Lamont."

Ivy abruptly says, "I vote against that!"

Amani says, "Auntie Eva, your son is not stable enough to have anything to do with this operation. You need to check him."

"I'll show her what he's been up to," Ivy says.

"Any questions or concerns? Anyone?"

Mr. Turner says, "Amani, I'm saying this not as a reconnaissance team member, or a non-profit guy, but as your father. Take your time, sweetheart. You're moving a bit fast.

"You're strong, quick, and impenetrable, but no one is impervious to stress. Don't take so much in at once. Let doors open for you, so you won't have to charge into everything.

"I understand you're upset about whatever goes on behind closed doors, but don't let it blind you from the good of this country. You should've done the nonprofit thing from the get-go. What I've learned after my years of being an activist is, too much anger can cripple you and ruin your train of thought.

"Give yourself more time to benefit from your relationships. You never know who has land waiting to donate to our cause. There may be a cellular company ready to liquidate its equipment.

"You don't have to be all super about everything, Amani. And you're not alone. Let the good of the people work for you."

Amani nods and agrees with her father one hundred percent. She's been paying too much attention to the negative statements said about her. It really hurt her when some victims of the bombing partially blamed her and refused to accept her help.

She is highly disappointed and saddened by Lamont's behavior online. He is brainwashed by people he has never met in person.

Amani has to accept the fact that there will be people who will hate her, no matter what she does. Some will dislike her just because of the constant praises and publicity, which is not her fault. The next good deed she does will be followed up with criticism and negative theories from those people. It is merely an obsession for them. An addiction.

Therefore, Amani is no longer affected by those naysayers. They have nothing to do with where she is heading in life. Their harsh words and name-calling will not change a thing. She holds her head up high, secure in her decisions and proud of her promising future.

Amani's father is the last to leave her home after the meeting concluded. He has another question for his daughter that he would rather ask in private.

Mr. Turner states, "I know you said that you will never reveal these secrets the government has. And you're not the type of person who changes your mind over and over again. But, if you can at least let us know what we are to prepare for."

Amani says, "Dad, you raised me to prepare for **anything**, and not everything. I will return that lecture right back to you. It's not about what the government is doing, but what you are doing.

"The officials have plans from A to Z. If you figure out plan X, then they'll just move on to plan Y, without a concern about how informed you are.

"Some folks think they can figure out everything, because they believe they are that brilliant. But in actuality, they're afraid of not knowing, because they lack Faith.

"We were hit with natural disasters, heat waves, and cold fronts, even when unpredicted, and we still made it through. If you think our only defense is to know everything that is about to happen, then you might as well invest in a fortune teller.

"And Dad, I do want you to stay informed as you have always been, but the solution to the threat is to focus on the important things in life and **unite**.

"If we remain scattered, then we are making ourselves easy failures. We can't keep aiming our attention at things that are beyond our control and pretend that we have control.

"Regardless of what the leaders of this country have in store for us, we must bond in spite of our differences. Together, we are more powerful, if we bond in ways that don't compromise our integrity.

"It shouldn't take a natural disaster to bring us together. It shouldn't take a terrorist attack for us to help each other out. It shouldn't take a holiday to inspire us to give.

"There are profitable franchises available in the city for $25,000. A good way to get the experience of running a reputable company. But, even though we have people getting big tax return checks, we can't find them when it's a good time to collaborate.

"People of this country pay too much attention to me and what others are saying about me. They are too fascinated by the stilettos and what Big Rich made off of his last CD. They treat red carpets like holy ground.

"You don't have that problem, Dad. You have nothing to worry about. You always stay alert for the **unthinkable**.

"You did a great job in Mom's absence and you helped me become the woman that I am today. The only ones who can potentially be in danger are the ones who've already been in danger, mentally.

"Things aren't about to happen, they are already happening. There are no upcoming events, these things are ongoing.

"Instead of being frantic or extra concerned about explosives, weapon confiscations, drone attacks, and diseases, I wish we would all check our sanity, first."

THE FINAL SAY

Amani Jett has grown much from her recent experiences and has become wiser by listening to those in her life who are more experienced than she is. She rediscovered humility for the first time in over a decade.

She sits before the computer web cam on her office desk to address the nation. This is to make up for the event which was interrupted by chaos.

Amani begins. "To everyone who is concerned, I am doing well, though my heart still heavy over Saturday's victims. My health is at ninety percent and I am capable of doing my services.

"Thanks to all of you who supported my recovery. Those who never made any idiotic theories about me, but showed me love when I was down. You give me hope for the future of this planet.

"I've read all of your letters. I was so moved by them! I'll post a few on my website.

"Another thing I will do is come back stronger than ever before. My body is healing, but my powers have advanced yet again. I am re-energized by empathy.

"I've flown the fastest I ever had when someone close to me was in danger. This situation was not as dangerous as the previous one, which took place in Minnesota, but because there was an emotional connection with the victim, I really felt charged up, as I was in the rescue of Flight 514.

"By learning this, I find it imperative to use these letters and positive feedback as my 'Jett fuel'. I will hold these words close to me. Thanks to you, I am strengthened.

"To my beautiful Black brothers and sisters, don't be deterred. I haven't forgotten who I am. How could I?

"My emotional ties to our American history pushes me. I cannot forget those who paved the way for me. And if anyone has a problem with me addressing my race of people, then you are out of line.

"I'm proud of my heritage just as you are proud of yours. I don't show my pride in just one month.

"I urge for those who are uncertain of me to only get your information about me from **me** and not from those who assume that they know about me. Don't be fooled by fools.

"Over the last few hours, I have been celebrated, and honored, and praised. That's nice, but more than anything, I want you to look around you and realize the power that you, yourselves, have.

"By working together, you can be greater than any one person. You say I'm super strong, but you can be a super strong force with cooperation. You say I'm blessed with big money, but you can be wealthy if you incorporate.

"Through history, there has always been a superior model of a person whom the people gave reverence, be it a king, queen, pharaoh, dictator, president, or czar. But, I believe the best leader is the one who brings out the best of the people.

"Therefore, I deserve no more praise than those who collectively make this world a better place. I applaud you.

"You do things at a higher risk than I can, by putting your lives on the line. You sacrifice your earnings to get to where you need to get.

"I have benefits that make my job easier. You do great things together even though it is hard. I respect that to the fullest!

"Please do not envy me. Don't wish you had my abilities, because it comes with a price. I have seen horrific sights and learned of awful secrets that were kept for centuries.

"I was never going to expose all the secrets, but I always intended to advise a solution. That solution is to unite. There is power in numbers.

"This country is strategically divided. We're given sides to choose from.

"And then, you have the element of fear. Fear separates us. We are easily rattled when we are separated.

"Why worry so much about what the government is doing if you're truly united? Why would you be so dependent on mayors, governors, and senators if you are organized as a community?

"There is nothing that politicians can do that you can't do as a union. Protection, transportation, food services, can all be achieved by incorporating. But, if you're too concerned about what the next man might do, then nothing will ever change.

"That concern doesn't seem to occur when it comes to politics. You vote these people in, and celebrate their election together.

"Then, they tell you that the tax dollars coming in are not enough to take care of all city services. Complaining about them is not going to change anything. It's our time to stop depending on them!

"If we are the world, then we can change it. If it is power to the people, then let us use it.

"It's not how like-minded we are that makes us great, but the good things we do together in spite of our differences."

Agents Red and Gray are watching this from their respective locations. Neither of them expected Amani to speak on something that was the polar opposite of their evil agenda. Now, they see how detrimental her survival may be to their plans.

Lamont watches this and accuses Amani of not saying that Black people need to work together first, even though Amani thinks that it goes without saying. It is obvious to her, but Lamont and his online friends are accusing Amani of selling out, anyway. They somehow claim that she is telling Blacks to disregard each other in order to unite with other races.

Agent Violet is relieved that Amani didn't spill any secrets just yet. She and Agent Green continue with their plans to defame her character and complicate her morale. They did not find any helpful answers from the doctor in South America.

The Director of the Central Intelligence Agency is also relieved and continues his search for the missing agents of the covert alternate group. He is putting everything in Field Agent Blunt's hands. He no longer depends on the former Director for any help. Scientists are researching Amani's samples.

Ivy is one day away from finishing her move to Arizona with the family. She chooses to return to Michigan for her dream wedding set for a later date.

Eric James reluctantly agreed to endorse Richard Twain in his run for Mayor of Detroit before Amani made her recovery. He has yet to explain this to Amani, because he doesn't want to get her involved.

Amani's aunt, Eva Adams is troubled by what she learned of her son, Lamont. He explains to her that the people on the website are only "venting" and that they have a right to do so. He also tells his mother that what they preach is fair and harmless, compared to the violence that their country has done. He says that he doesn't hate Amani, but will voice his opinion of her. Eva's relationship with her son will never be the same.

Mr. Calvin H. Turner remains in his home, doing what he does. He still refuses to relocate, turning down continuous offers from his daughters. What he hasn't told them is that the house was paid off with the money which he received from the airline company that took responsibility of his wife's death. He is attached to this house by the remembrance of her.

The stage is now set for Amani. She knows what she must do and is more careful, having no doubt that, somewhere, there are people plotting on ways to eliminate her. Those insidious sources have yet to be revealed to her.

Her mind often drifts to Donnell Price, II. She is feeling serious about a relationship with him. But, she still hasn't gotten over the fact that he is the son of the man who she accidentally killed, and never took responsibility for it. Amani doesn't want to hold onto a secret so important. Not forever.

Amani is very sure about her feelings for Donnell, but not so sure about herself. She believes what she is feeling is love, but she questions her feelings. Would it be love if she keeps this secret for the rest of her life? If she tells him, would he leave her? Would he have been there for her to save her life, had he known who she was?

No answer is clear to Amani, but she knows that she wants him as a partner in life. Amani wants no other man and does not want another woman keeping him happy. She doesn't want an accident to ruin what they have, so the secret remains.

Amani concludes her message. "And to those who stand in the way of my purpose... those insidious cowards who are plotting on ways to get rid of me... I'm waiting. Good night, to the rest of you."

The Beginning

THE GOVERNMENT'S PLANS... THE PLOTS OF INSIDIOUS FORCES... SPECULATIONS OF THE PEOPLE... WERE ALL IN VAIN.

ALL ISOLATED AGENDAS LED TO CONFUSION.

DOOMSDAY WILL COME IN THE FORM OF AN UNANTICIPATED ENEMY.

WHAT WAS ONCE INTENDED TO BE THE CALGARY FOR THE COUNTRY'S EVERLASTING BATTLES, HAS OUR NATION'S CAPITAL UNDER SEIGE.

THE CALL HAD TO BE MADE. THE PLEA FOR THE RETURN OF THE ONE WHO WAS EXILED YEARS AGO WAS INEVITABLE.

THE ONLY TRUE SHERO WHO IS POWERFUL ENOUGH TO STOP THIS MADNESS WILL BE SUMMONED.

SHE WILL EMBRACE THE AMERICAN SKIES ONCE AGAIN, IN ALL OF HER AGELESS BEAUTY.

HER COARSE HAIR FLOWING FREELY IN THE THIN AIR. HER SKIN DARKLY TANNED FROM YEARS SPENT LIVING IN HER NATIVE LAND.

SHE SCANS THIS MECHANIZED BEHEMOTH, EQUIPPED WITH SOPHISTICATED WAR TECHNOLOGY. HER ANALYSIS OF ITS INNER SHELL REVEALS VERY FEW FLAWS...

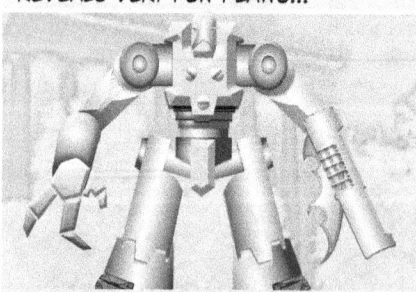

...A NEARLY IMPENETRABLE ARMOR...

...AND AN UNEXPECTED SOURCE OF CONSTRAINED ENERGY.

MR. PRESIDENT??

Next: The Amani Strain